BLACK JACK

JACK RYDER #4

BOOKS BY THE AUTHOR

MYSTERY/HORROR NOVELS:

7TH STREET CREW SERIES

What Hurts the Most

You Can Run

You Can't Hide

JACK RYDER SERIES

Hit the Road Jack

Slip out the Back Jack

The House that Jack Built

Black Jack

REBEKKA FRANCK SERIES

One, Two…He is Coming for You

Three, Four…Better Lock
Your Door

Five, Six…Grab your Crucifix

Seven, Eight…Gonna Stay up Late

Nine, Ten…Never Sleep Again

Eleven, Twelve…Dig and Delve

Thirteen, Fourteen…Little
Boy Unseen

Edwina

BLACK JACK

JACK RYDER #4

WILLOW
ROSE

WILLOW ROSE

PROLOGUE

BLACK JACK: A card game in which the player attempts to approach twenty-one, but not exceed it.

WILLOW ROSE

[AUGUST 2010]

Having a baby was by far the greatest thing to have happened to Susan Murray. She knew it would be, since they all said so, literally *everyone* who touched her stomach told her that it was the biggest thing she was ever going to experience in life.

And she believed them.

But they hadn't told her the entire truth, had they? They hadn't exactly told her how hard it was going to be, nor had they mentioned the many endless sleepless nights. Well, that's not exactly true, her friend Marley had said she would lose sleep, but she had added that it *would be totally worth it.*

She hadn't mentioned the fact that Susan was going to constantly feel like she'd been run over by a dump truck. Nor had she mentioned that she and her husband, Bob, were going to be yelling at each other in the middle of the night because she simply couldn't take being woken up, yet again, because the baby had to eat.

And so far it had been only twenty-one days.

Susan sighed and looked at her husband sitting across the table from her, while shoveling in granola and yogurt. In front of her lingered a bowl of cereal that she was way too exhausted to eat. She had Chandelle in her arms, as she was still breastfeeding and had been all morning.

Doesn't this baby ever take a break?

Susan knew she was supposed to sleep whenever the baby did, but so far she had hardly slept at all. Not more than an hour here and there.

"Try and eat something," Bob said flatly, leftover milk in his beard. "You need the strength."

Susan grabbed the spoon in her one free hand and leaned over to eat. But as she did, the baby started to fuss.

"She's doing it again," Susan said with a deep sigh and dropped the spoon back in the bowl. She gazed, frustrated, at her husband, even though she knew he couldn't do anything about it. "It's like she can't suck properly."

Bob sighed and looked at his watch. "Listen, babe, I have to get to work."

Of course he did. For the first time in their

marriage, Susan was actually jealous of him. She used to be a teacher, but when she married Bob and became pregnant, he told her it was time to quit, that now she was becoming a mother and had to take care of their child.

Susan had loved the idea. She wasn't very fond of teaching. It hadn't quite lived up to her expectations. Kids could be monsters from time to time.

But right now she would take a day with her second-graders anytime over this. The thought of spending yet another day alone with this small baby, doing nothing but breastfeeding and changing diapers all day, was devastating. She missed leaving the house; she missed talking to her colleagues at the school.

She even missed the kids.

Bob got up from his chair, grabbed his car keys, and kissed Susan on the forehead. That was the most intimate they had been for weeks.

"It'll get better," he whispered. "I know it's hard right now, but that's to be expected, right? Everyone goes through this, but they all say it'll get better."

Susan nodded and closed her eyes while thinking *easy for you to say, you don't have to stay inside all day while someone is literally sucking the life right out of you.*

"I'm really proud of you," he said before he closed the door behind him and left her alone once again.

Chandelle fussed in her arms, struggling to get enough out of her breast. Susan hushed her and stroked her head gently.

"There now. Just take it easy. It'll get better."

And just as she said the words, Chandelle reached out and grabbed Susan's finger in her hand and held on to it. The emotion rolling through Susan's body was overwhelming, overpowering, and soon she found herself crying, sobbing in happiness, completely forgetting the sleepless hours and the loneliness. At least for a few seconds.

Yes, having a baby surely was the greatest thing that had ever happened to Susan. And even though it was tough right now, she was going to long desperately to have this time back for many years to come.

[AUGUST 2010]

"I think something is wrong."

Susan held the phone close to her ear, her heart pounding in her chest, Chandelle in her arms, fussing and crying. Susan tried to swing her from side to side to calm her down, but it didn't work.

"You always say that," Bob said from the other end.

"No, this is different. Something is off with her. She's burning up," Susan said, flustered.

"So, she has a fever? Well, that's normal in babies. They have to get used to the environment outside the mother's womb. Babies get sick and they can endure a much higher fever than adults."

Susan nodded quietly while her husband spoke. He was, after all, a doctor. He had his own practice close to where they lived in Savannah. He saw many worried mothers come in with their babies.

"It's probably just a virus," he said. "There's a lot of that going around these days. We'll monitor it. She'll probably snap out of it in no time."

"Okay," Susan said.

She hung up and took Chandelle to the living room, where she sat down and tried to breastfeed. But Chandelle suddenly wouldn't eat.

"That's not normal," Susan mumbled to the baby, who was now crying louder than before. "You usually always eat, almost all day long. What's wrong with you, baby girl, huh?"

Susan tickled Chandelle on her stomach. When that only made her cry louder, she checked her diaper, but it wasn't even wet.

That's odd. She hasn't peed since last night.

"It's probably just a virus," Susan repeated her husband's words, while trying to calm the baby down.

But nothing worked. Soon, Susan felt the frustration rise in her body and she started to walk around the house, swinging the baby in her arms, hushing her, but still nothing worked. She tried putting her down for a nap, thinking the virus and fever were probably making her exhausted and she probably needed a nap, but putting her down made Chandelle scream even louder.

Susan let her stay in the bed for a few minutes, sneaking out of the room, thinking it would be easier for Chandelle to fall asleep if her mother wasn't in the room, but after ten minutes of standing outside the door to the nursery listening to the baby scream her lungs out, Susan couldn't take it anymore.

She stormed inside and grabbed Chandelle in her arms and held her close. The baby suddenly stopped crying.

Susan took in a deep breath.

Finally. Finally.

But the joy only lasted a few seconds before Susan realized there was a reason the baby had stopped crying.

She had become unresponsive.

The baby wasn't looking at her at all. She wasn't crying, she wasn't babbling, she was hardly breathing. But she was burning hot. Susan let out a small shriek.

"Chandelle?"

Oh, my God, oh, my God!

[AUGUST 2010]

Bob was held up at his practice and arrived at the hospital an hour after Susan and Chandelle did. He rushed into the room where Susan was sitting, holding her baby's small lifeless hand. As her eyes met his, Susan stood up.

"What did they say?" he asked.

"She has an infection. Apparently, she swallowed fluid during delivery and that caused it," Susan said. "She had a one-hundred-and-four-degree temperature when we got here. They hooked her up to antibiotics."

Bob breathed a sigh of relief. "Good gracious."

"We barely made it," she said between sobs. She had been holding her tears in for so long now, there was no holding them back anymore.

Bob grabbed her in his arms and hugged her. "Hey. Take it easy. She's going to be all right. The antibiotics will help, and before you know it she'll be back home with us again."

"I just can't…I was so scared, Robert. I was terrified."

Susan only called her husband by his birth name when she was troubled or if he had done something she didn't approve of or hurt her somehow. Otherwise, it was always Bob, or Bobby, or Babe. She did it because she wanted him to know she blamed him a little for this happening. Because he didn't react when she asked him to in the first place. Because it could have gone really wrong if she hadn't walked back into the room and picked Chandelle up when she did. What if she had waited a few more minutes outside the door? What if Chandelle had gone quiet like she did and Susan had believed she had simply fallen asleep? Then what? Just because he kept telling her it was a virus, a simple virus that she *would beat in no time.*

"I know, I know," he said. "But it's all over now. She's in the best hands here. I know the pediatrician, and he is excellent. She's getting the treatment she needs and she'll be better in no time."

Susan couldn't help feeling angry with him. How could he be so casual about all this? Didn't he realize their baby almost died?

"Look at me," he said and grabbed her by the shoulders.

Reluctantly, she obeyed.

"Chandelle will be just fine. I made a mistake. I'm sorry; it won't happen again. From now on, I will take you seriously every time you fuss, all right? Could we focus on our baby now and the fact that she's still here?"

Susan's sobs subsided. She looked into the eyes of her beloved husband, who had known her since they were both in high school. "You're right," she said with a deep exhale.

"Now, why don't you and I go downstairs and get something to eat?" Bob said with a gentle smile.

"I can't," she said.

"You have to eat, Susan. You need your strength."

She sighed and looked at her baby. "But can we just leave her?"

Bob chuckled. "Well, of course we can. All the nurses are here and the doctors too. She's sleeping right now. She needs all the rest she can get. Plus, all these machines right here will go off if anything is out of the ordinary. She is in the safest place in the world."

Susan looked at her girl, who seemed so peaceful. Her small chest was heaving up and down as she breathed.

"I still don't feel like…"

"How about you and me go down there and buy a couple of sandwiches, then come back and eat them here, huh? Would that do?"

Susan nodded. "All right. I am kind of hungry."

[AUGUST 2010]

She slept in the baby's room. Bob went home to get enough sleep to be able to go to work the next day, since they knew Chandelle was going to be fine. It was hard to sleep in a chair, but, if she had learned anything these past twenty-two days, it was to get by without much sleep. She kept waking up with a start, looking at the baby, then realizing that Chandelle was still fine before she fell back asleep again.

Every hour a nurse would come in and check on Chandelle. They tried to do so without waking up Susan, but not with much success.

It wasn't until they were changing shifts around two a.m. that Susan gave in to the pressing feeling of having to go to the bathroom. She only stayed in the bathroom for a few minutes. Once she was done, she opened the door to the room and looked at the crib with Chandelle in it, then at the instruments monitoring her progress. She looked at them for a few seconds before it sunk in.

They are all turned off!

Susan ran to the crib and looked inside. It was empty.

Where's my baby?

Frantically, Susan looked around the room, as if expecting to find Chandelle on the floor or somewhere else, before she stormed out into the hallway. Hyperventilating desperately, she approached the nurses' room. The door was locked, as usual, during changing shifts.

Susan knocked. The panic made her hands shake.

"Hello?"

The door was opened and a nurse looked at her. She was about to get angry, but seeing the desperation on Susan's face made her change her mind.

"Did anyone take Chandelle?" Susan asked.

"Excuse me?"

"My baby," she continued, finding it hard to say the words. "Chandelle Murray. She's…she's not in her crib. I thought maybe something happened, maybe you took her for some examination or something."

The nurse's eyes stared at Susan, scrutinizing her. "I…I just got here. Let me just check with the others."

The door was closed in Susan's face. The wait was unbearable. A million thoughts ran through her mind until it was opened again. The nurse shook her head. "No one in here knows anything about it. Are you sure she's not in her crib?"

Susan stared at the small woman. Was she kidding her?

"You think I would make something like this up?" she asked.

The nurse shook her head. "Of course not. But maybe you dreamt something. Let me come with you and check."

"I'm telling you she's not there!" Susan cried after her, as the nurse took off towards Chandelle's room.

Oh, my God. They have no idea where my baby is!

The nurse opened the door and trotted inside, Susan on her tail. "That's odd," she said, as she saw the empty crib and all the shut off instruments.

"I was just in the bathroom. When I walked in there, she was still in the crib, sleeping. When I came out, she was gone!"

"She was given antibiotics, right?" the nurse asked.

"Yes," Susan said, her hands sweating in anxiety.

"Well, those are gone too," the nurse said. "One of the other nurses must know something. A baby doesn't just disappear from a hospital. Wait here a minute."

PART ONE:

HIT: To ask for another card.

1

[MAY 2016]

Oddly enough, no one noticed her. Not one single head on the streets of Savannah turned to look at the little girl as she strolled across the historic part of town. Tourists were everywhere, staring at the beautiful old houses, talking about the Spanish moss falling from every tree, telling each other the old scary stories about how the moss was filled with small critters, *the chiggers*, that would make you itch, or even crawl under your skin and spread all over your body. Or about frogs and snakes and spiders that liked to hide in it.

"Spanish moss was given its name by French explorers," a tour guide told a flock of tourists, as the girl walked unnoticed past them. "Native Americans told them the plant was called *Itla-okla* which meant "tree hair." The French were reminded of the Spanish conquistadors' long beards, so they called it *Barbe Espagnol*, or "Spanish Beard." As time went by, Spanish Beard changed to Spanish moss."

The girl heard the words as they fell, but she didn't register any of them. She walked past the flock and continued down a broad boulevard with large trees and old houses on each side. People she passed in the street didn't know where she was going or even care, but she knew. She knew where she wanted to go.

What she didn't know was exactly where to find what she was looking for.

As she passed them, she felt like the big houses were staring back at her from the empty dark windows, and she hurried through the streets. With a chill, she imagined the Spanish moss was long arms and claws reaching out for her, trying to drag her back…back… back inside.

The sunlight was very bright and hurt the little girl's eyes, but not enough to make her stop. Her skin was pale and her arms and legs burning in the small dress she was wearing. The girl started to run, but her delicate bare feet hurt from hitting the hard surface of the pavement, and it made her stop. She tried to read the street signs, but she soon realized she couldn't. A man with a suitcase passing her finally looked at her, and she hid her face so he wouldn't see her properly, and maybe recognize her, because what if he was friends with *the Doctor*; he could be, after all, couldn't he? If he was, he could tell that the girl had been seen, where she was, but the man walked on, not even slowing down to get a proper look at her.

The girl took in a deep breath and realized she couldn't be far away from her destination. She could smell it in the air.

The girl walked on, passing a couple of old squares and a park, then a series of old shops, where she stopped and glanced through the windows, eyes wide open and in awe. Never had she seen anything so stunning. All those things in the windows and especially all those books.

The girl laughed and looked at the blue sky above. It was so spectacular it was almost overwhelming. How can the roof be this high? So many years she had wondered what it would be like to look at it, being outside, looking up and not staring at it through the window glass until the Doctor yelled at her to *get away from the window*.

The girl made a grimace, then shivered at the thought of the Doctor pulling her arm harshly while scolding her for *risking being seen*.

While remembering the Doctor's words, the girl sped up. She knew the Doctor would be looking for her soon, wanting to drag her back…inside.

As she turned one more corner, she heaved a sigh of relief. There it was. Right in front of her. As blue as the sky above.

2

[MAY 2016]

"I was thinking this would be a good place."

Pastor Daniel looked at us with his arms stretched out. He had taken us to one of the small parks in the middle of town, or squares as they were called. Savannah was filled with them. Twenty-four in total, I had been told. The town was sort of built around them. They were all beautiful, but this one in particular.

"I was thinking we could do the ceremony right here," he said, and walked to a small pavilion in the middle of the square. "You—Jack—would stand here, with your ring-bearer, Austin, at your side and wait for the bride. Then you—Shannon—you come walking from down there, from behind the tree, so no one sees you prematurely; while the music plays, you walk up here with Angela and Abigail as your flower girls, spreading roses out on the grass for you to walk on. How does that sound?"

Tyler burst into a loud scream as soon as Pastor Daniel looked at me with that big smile of his. I looked down at the baby and tried to bounce up and down a little to calm him down. Shannon reacted to his cry immediately, giving me a tired look. She had strapped him around my stomach in the sling to give her a break for once. Tyler was now almost three months old and, so far, he hadn't slept one full night.

"So, what do you think?"

"I love it, Pastor Daniel," Abigail exclaimed. "I think it is perfect."

"And the bride and groom to be?" he said, looking at Shannon and me.

Shannon smiled, exhausted. "It looks great, Pastor."

It was her idea that we have the wedding in Savannah. It was her favorite city and she simply loved the old houses and the atmosphere here, she had said, when I tried to argue for an ocean wedding on surfboards. "It's the most romantic city in the entire country," she said, and how could I argue against that? The ocean was my choice, but I had to give her that it wouldn't be as beautiful and the water would destroy her dress and hair. Austin had been on my side and I have a feeling so was Tyler, but the girls had finally won. They wanted the romantic stuff and so they'd get it.

Savannah had another advantage. No one knew

or suspected that Shannon King, the famous country superstar would get married in some small park in the middle of town, so with a little luck we could avoid the paparazzi and other unwelcome guests. It was only going to be us, our kids, my parents, and Shannon's mother and sister, Kristi, with her husband. Shannon hadn't invited her second sister who lived in New York. I didn't know why and Shannon made it clear I shouldn't ask.

It was supposed to be a small, private wedding. We hadn't told anyone, not even my best friends or colleagues at the Sherriff's office. Not even Sherriff Ron or even my partner Beth. They were going to get the surprise once we got back. All I said was we were going on a vacation for a week to the Bahamas. Just in case any snoopy reporters called and asked for me, suspecting something. Sending them off to the Bahamas would make sure they wouldn't make it here once they found out.

"Don't you think, Jack?" Shannon smiled at Tyler, even though she was addressing me. It had been like that a lot lately. I didn't get much eye contact from anyone. I simply wasn't as cute as Tyler, I had to realize.

"Yes. I think this place would make a great wedding."

"Great. It's settled then," Pastor Daniel said. "I will make all the arrangements and then we'll have the ceremony this coming Saturday at five o'clock."

We had exactly a week to get ready. Not that we had much we needed to do. Shannon had a dress made for her and the same tailor made my suit and clothes for the kids. It was already taken care of. We had found a small restaurant to have the dinner afterwards. Our guests would arrive just before the weekend, so that meant we had an entire week to explore Savannah and enjoy each other's company.

Tyler burst into yet another loud scream and Shannon grabbed him. "Here, let me take him. I think he's hungry."

"Didn't he just eat?" Austin asked.

While Shannon unwrapped the baby from me, I looked at my big son. I couldn't believe he used to be this small and demanding. I couldn't believe I'd had baby twins and that I actually survived it.

3

[APRIL 1990]

"Hello? I'm looking for a Kimberly Milligan?"

"This is she," Kimberly said. "Who's this?"

"I'm sorry. This is Jonas Anderson, attorney-at-law in Savannah."

Kimberly lifted an eyebrow while her husband Joseph looked at her from across the living room, where he was doing homework with their daughter, Rosa.

"Savannah?" she asked, puzzled.

"Yes, ma'am. Savannah, Georgia."

Joseph shaped *a who is it?* with his lips and Kimberly shrugged visibly. She honestly didn't know. She had never been to Savannah. She had never even been out of Wyoming.

"How may I help you?" she asked, thinking this was probably just someone trying to sell her something. Kimberly prepared herself to hang up.

"I think I might be the one who can help you," he said with that heavy southern accent.

Here it comes. What is it this time? Insurance probably.

Kimberly rolled her eyes, waiting for it to come, but it never did. No sales pitch, no *This is exactly what you need*…instead, the man on the other end said something that would change Kimberly's life.

"I am sorry to inform you that your Aunt Agnes Vann, a long term client of ours, has passed away."

Aunt Agnes? Who the heck is she?

"And you are mentioned in her will."

"I'm what?" Kimberly exclaimed. "But I never even met the woman."

"Nevertheless, she has left you her home here in Savannah."

Kimberly grabbed a chair leaned against the wall of their small rental apartment and sat down. "And you're sure about this?"

"Positive," the man said.

"But, why? Why would she leave me anything?"

"I have no way of knowing my client's intentions, but this is what she wanted. She wanted you to have the house."

"I…" Kimberly clasped her mouth as the realization slowly sank in. She still couldn't believe it. A house?

Her aunt had left her a house?

"I'm asking for you to come to my office and we'll have all the paperwork done so that you can take over the house," he continued.

"I…we will be there."

Kimberly hung up. She stared at the phone a long time before she finally lifted her eyes and looked at Joseph and Rosa. Her eyes filled with tears. For so many years, they had struggled to make ends meet; for so many years they had wanted to get a house, a home they could call their own, but the banks always turned them down.

"Who was that, Mommy?" asked Rosa.

Kimberly looked into her beautiful blue eyes. Her baby doll, as she liked to call her because she looked so much like a live doll with her blond curly hair. Only nine years old and already a heartbreaker.

"It…it was a man," she said, as she grabbed Rosa and pulled her into her lap. She removed a lock of hair from the girl's face and pushed it behind her ear. "This was a very nice man who told us that we now own a house. A real house."

Rosa let out a loud shriek. Kimberly looked up at her husband, who was smiling widely.

"A house? But how?"

"Some aunt I never knew died and left it to me," Kimberly said. "But there is one catch."

"There always is, isn't there? What is it?" he asked.

"It's in Savannah, Georgia."

Joseph threw out his hands. "That's not a catch. I always wanted to go to Savannah. Now we own a house there? I can't wait to go."

"So, you want to move there?" Kimberly asked.

"Yes! I can easily get work down there and so can you! Let's do it. It would be a new start for us as a family. We would have a house. A real house!"

Joseph grabbed Kimberly and Rosa in his strong arms and lifted both of them in the air with a loud laugh. The girls whined.

"We're going to Savannah. We're going to Savannah!"

4

[MAY 2016]

Shannon looked at herself in the mirror.

"How does it feel up here over the chest?" the woman next to her asked, pulling the dress in on the sides. She was a very skilled tailor, hired by Sarah, standing right behind her, watching her every move.

Sarah was Shannon's new personal assistant. It was Jack's idea to get a PA once the baby arrived, so Shannon wouldn't have to take care of anything besides the baby. Sarah could handle everything else, along with Shannon's manager. Sarah had only been in her life for four months, but Shannon already loved her dearly. Not only did she take care of every detail, she also knew how to make Shannon look spectacular, no matter what the occasion was. She couldn't think of anyone better to take care of the details of the wedding.

"It's a little tight," Shannon said with a sigh. Losing the weight after giving birth the second time sure hadn't been as easy as when she had Angela. Of course, she was a lot younger then.

"Could you loosen it a little up there, then?" Sarah asked the tailor.

Sarah looked at Shannon's reflection over her shoulder. "Don't worry about it. It's only natural that they're a little big when you breastfeed. As soon as you stop, they'll get smaller, and before you know it you'll wish you had them back." Sarah laughed.

Sarah was older than Shannon and her children had both gone off to college when she applied for the job. Sarah was a big girl. She had a lot of authority and clout when she spoke, and Shannon had noticed that people really listened when she opened her mouth. And she always got the job done, no matter what it was. Shannon liked that she was older and that she didn't have a family waiting for her. Her husband had left her when the twins were just babies. She didn't miss him one bit, though. He was more in the way than of help, she said, laughing during her interview.

"I don't mind the breasts," Shannon said. "Jack loves them. No, it's more the stomach and the wider hips. I guess I just need to be more patient."

Sarah shrugged. "Yeah, and then maybe accept that your body has changed since you carried your second child. You've always been gorgeous. You still are. Look at yourself in that dress. Jack is going to pass out," Sarah said, and forced Shannon to look at herself. Shannon still thought she looked terrible, like a big pile of whipped cream. She missed her old body terribly.

"I need you to take it off so the tailor can correct it," Sarah said, and helped Shannon pull the dress off.

Shannon walked to the window and looked out into the yard of the house they had rented in Savannah for the week. It had been many years since Shannon had last been in this town. None of them had any ties to it and that made it easier, Shannon believed. She had an aunt who once lived here, but that was all. Jack had no family here either. It was perfect.

The kids were playing hide and go seek in the funny yard that almost looked like a maze from where she was standing on the first floor. She spotted Angela hiding behind a statue and felt a pinch in her heart. How she hoped Angela was going to be happy with this new family. Everything was changing very fast right now, and she wondered if it was rough on her firstborn.

Austin was done counting and Shannon watched as he started his search for the girls. Jack's son was Shannon's favorite of the twins. Abigail was sweet too, but she had an attitude and a way that she would never have let her have had it been her own daughter. Of course, she was Jack's daughter, and every time Shannon said something or even hinted something, Jack would get mad at her, so she tried to stay out of it.

Emily was another matter. Shannon spotted her

sitting on a swing in the yard, looking down at her feet. She wasn't well. It had been a year now since she started losing weight. She was still very skinny and not eating much. Shannon had walked in on her one day when she was exercising in her room and caught a glimpse of her in a tank top where the bones in her back poked out. Usually, she wore big shirts and pants, so no one could see how skinny she really was, and it worried Shannon. She saw how she tried to pretend like she was eating when they had dinner together, but all she did was push her food around, or sometimes she would even hide some of it in her napkin. Jack didn't see it, but Shannon did. Shannon had carefully asked Jack one day if he thought maybe Emily needed some professional help, but he had told her that wasn't necessary. Emily was fine.

"I'll talk to her," he said.

But once he did, all the girl told him was that she was fine and happy and looking forward to the wedding. But Shannon knew she wasn't fine.

Shannon sighed and spotted Angela, who had now been found by Austin and was giggling with joy. Shannon chuckled. It was so obvious how much she liked Austin; she only hoped it wouldn't cause any problems for their little family.

Sarah approached her and stood next to her while both of them looked out the window, just as Jack came out in the yard with a cup between his hands, while looking at the kids. That meant Tyler had finally fallen asleep, Shannon thought with relief. Having a baby was a lot harder than she remembered. Or maybe it was just Tyler who was different than Angela. Shannon remembered Angela as the easiest child in the world. She hadn't been quite prepared for this.

"Look at them. What a beautiful family. You're a very lucky woman," Sarah said. "Don't you ever forget that."

5

[MAY 2016]

Everyone was crying at the house. It was nothing but misery. The Doctor looked at the girls sitting around the dining table in the living room. They were all crying heavily, sobbing with tears while they were being served their soup. Especially Millie was inconsolable. She was, after all, Betsy Sue's best friend. The Doctor didn't know how she was going to do without her at the house.

"There, there my little ones," the Doctor said and walked up behind Millie. She knelt next to the little girl. "I know you're sad that Betsy Sue is gone, but do try and eat, will you?"

Still, no one touched the soup. It annoyed the Doctor, even though it was understandable. The Doctor felt sick as well, sick with longing and deprivation. At first, she had believed the girl was just hiding, but after searching the entire house, the Doctor finally realized with terror that Betsy Sue had done the unthinkable.

She had gone outside.

"I want her back too," the Doctor cried, when Millie burst into another loud bone-piercing sob.

The Doctor walked to the window, carefully pulled back the curtain, and looked outside. It was getting dark out there now in the street. Ravens were picking at the windows of the house and startled the Doctor. With a gasp, she let go of the curtain and pulled back.

"Don't let them see you. Don't let them see you," the Doctor whispered, arms hugging her chest, hands shaking.

The weeping from the girls grew stronger. It was alarmingly loud now, and the Doctor felt like her head was about to explode. The Doctor lifted both hands and held them to her ears to try and block out the loud sounds.

"STOP IT! STOP IT!"

But the girls wouldn't stop. Worst of all was Millie. The Doctor couldn't stand it anymore and grabbed the girl by the arm and pulled on it hard.

"Go to your room!"

There was a loud sound, like a crack, from her arm, and the little girl screamed even louder, but now the screams were different, now they weren't of sadness but screams of pain.

"You're hurting her!" Daisy yelled, and the Doctor let go of her arm, which was twisted at the shoulder, completely dislocated. The Doctor gasped.

"Oh, no! I am so sorry, Millie. I am so terribly sorry."

The girls all surrounded Millie and helped her get up. The Doctor felt terrible. "I am so sorry." The looks from the girls were of contempt and anger as they dragged their friend to her room. Only Miss Muffit was still sitting at the table when they had all left. Meanwhile, a bus stopped outside the door on the street and the Doctor could hear the tour guide's loud yelling in the microphone.

The Doctor watched the tourists from behind the curtain as the guide explained about the house, how it was rumored to be haunted. The Doctor sighed and looked back at Miss Muffit. Tears were streaming from her eyes.

This had gone too far.

"I'll get her back. I promise you, all of you, I'll get Betsy Sue back. Don't you worry."

6

[MAY 2016]

"The Hampton Lillybridge House was built in 1797," our tour guide Jessica said and pointed. I looked at the three-story house; it did look very creepy in the darkness. It was evening, and Shannon and I had decided to take a haunted house bus tour around Savannah, while Sarah took care of the kids and especially Tyler. It was the first time Shannon had been away from our son, and I could tell she was troubled. Mostly by the way she kept checking her phone over and over.

"It's beautiful, don't you think?" I whispered to her.

She nodded distantly.

Our tour guide had started the trip by telling us that around seventy percent of all houses in Savannah were considered to be haunted. I didn't believe in this type of stuff, so I found the stories she told us quite amusing, but Shannon didn't seem to take them as lightly as me. Maybe she was just worried about Tyler. I couldn't figure out what it was, but she didn't seem to be enjoying this ride as much as I was. I was just thrilled to be alone with my bride-to-be for the first time in three months.

"This house was cursed from the start, when a worker was killed during preparations to move the structure," Jessica continued. She was dressed in an old-fashioned dress herself, probably to create the right atmosphere for us. I thought it was quite funny how all the houses simply had to have a haunted story to them; I had even read it made their value go up if they had such a story.

"A year after that, when construction resumed, workers found a crypt on the property where the house was to be moved. Not wanting to delay any longer, the construction foreman went ahead with it anyway; the house got moved, and to this day it still sits on an old unopened crypt."

"Uh," Shannon said, shivering.

I saw it as an opportunity to put my arm around her and pull her closer. It was kind of chilly tonight, at least compared to what we were used to in Florida at this time of year. But it was still beautiful.

"It is said that weird things happen on a regular basis in this house; furniture gets moved around, items disappear and reappear, doors get mysteriously locked and lights go on and off at random. Some tenants have said this is the work of a small boy who sometimes appears in a green suit, and that you can hear him giggling after one of his practical jokes."

I chuckled at the last part, thinking even ghosts have bad humor apparently. Shannon moved closer to me in the seat, then checked her phone again.

"He's fine," I whispered. "It's only a few hours. He's probably sleeping so he'll be awake all night after we come home."

"Don't say that!" she said.

I laughed again and kissed her cheek. She smelled divine as always. She was wearing a big hat and a pair of fake glasses so no one would recognize her. I was getting used to that being the deal whenever we went out. She even sometimes wore a wig. I didn't mind. As long as it gave us the privacy we wanted.

"Savannah's history is rife with horror stories, including several major fires and a yellow fever plague that killed ten percent of the population at the time," Jessica continued talking about this tragedy like it was the most exciting thing in the world. "It was a fire that claimed the lives of the girls at our next stop: The Old Orphanage located at 117 Houston St."

I turned my head and looked at the old house. A three-story brick house with the traditional Savannah porches wrapped around it. It seemed peaceful enough, but then again, they all did.

"The building served as the female orphanage with seventeen girls living there. In 1827, tragedy struck. A fire broke out in the orphanage. Rescuers thought they had gotten all the girls out until they did a headcount and found out that some of the girls were missing. One spectator spotted two girls frantically trying to escape through an attic window while the place burned to the ground. Eleven girls died during the fire when the building's roof collapsed. To this day, the people who live around here claim they can hear the sound of girls singing and playing. People living in the rebuilt house have told stories of waking up in the middle of the night with two girls standing at the foot of their bed."

"Ugh," Shannon said and shuddered again.

I had to admit this story gave me the chills as well. The thought of these young girls trapped inside a burning building gave me goosebumps.

Because it was real.

7

It took them a few weeks to get all their stuff packed and arrange everything for the move. Kimberly and Joseph Milligan were as excited about this big move as they had been when they found out they were expecting Rosa.

This was a new beginning for them and just what they needed. As they drove up the small street in the historic downtown of Savannah, Kimberly's breath was taken away by the beauty of the town.

"I didn't know anything like this existed," she said. "I mean, I've seen it on TV and all, but that doesn't compare to real life at all. These houses are stunning, and the trees, wow, I can't stop staring at them; what's all that grey stuff hanging from them?"

"They call it Spanish moss," Joseph said, and took a turn right into another little square surrounded by the most exquisite houses. Two, three some of them even four stories, all with porches and balconies, and entrances elevated from the street, from back when there were no cars and the streets were filled with horse excrement. At least that's what Joseph had explained to Kimberly.

"Ah, so that's Spanish moss. Wow. It makes the street look really creepy."

"We're here!" Joseph said and stopped the car.

Kimberly looked out her window. The house was located on one of Savannah's famed squares, this one a small park shaded by live oaks with crossing paths leading to the surrounding streets, and benches on all sides of a flowerbed. It was so pretty.

"Is this it? No. It can't be!"

Joseph whistled and nodded. "It's the address all right."

Their house was a red-brick mansion, with balconies surrounding it everywhere. It had green shutters framing all the tall windows. It had a pair of curved staircases with wrought-iron rails leading to each side of the front porch. High columns supported the balcony on top.

"But it's the most gorgeous one of them all!" Kimberly almost yelled.

"It sure is."

"Is this our house, Mommy?" Rosa said from the

back seat.

"I guess so," Kimberly said. She spotted a man waiting at the end of the stairs leading to the front door. And what a front door that was!

"That must be that lawyer-guy that called me. I asked him to meet us here so we can sign the papers and take over the house right away," she said and jumped out of the car. Joseph and Rosa followed her closely.

"Whoa. This house has four stores, Mommy."

Kimberly chortled and decided to not correct her. Instead, she walked up the stairs where a smiling man with a brown briefcase waited. He presented himself once again as Jonas Anderson, attorney-at-law in Savannah, and Kimberly shook his hand.

"Is this really it?" she asked, smiling from ear to ear. "Are you sure?"

The attorney chuckled lightly. "Yes, ma'am. This most certainly is it."

"Wow," she said and looked up at the many balconies above. Kimberly had grown up living in a small apartment and had been living in one with her husband as well up until now.

"I can't believe it," she said.

Jonas Anderson lifted the key and dangled it in front of her. "Here are the keys to your new home."

Kimberly grabbed them and looked at her husband. "This is finally it, babe. We finally have a house we can call our own."

"There is, of course, the paperwork that..." the attorney said, but Kimberly wasn't listening anymore. She took the key and put it in the lock, turned it, and opened the double doors fully and dramatically.

"Wuaaav," her daughter exclaimed, as they stepped inside into the giant hall that seemed big enough to fit their entire apartment complex where they lived before.

Kimberly walked across the marble floors till she reached the stairwell. With a cautious finger, she touched the railing that twisted its way up to the next floors. Then she turned and looked at her family, tears springing to her eyes while she—with arms wide open—exclaimed:

"Welcome home."

8

[MAY 2016]

We ended the night with a late dinner at one of the restaurants at the harbor. The food was very good and we enjoyed having a little time together for once. Shannon eased up a little after calling Sarah, who told us that Tyler was sleeping heavily and all the other kids, except Emily, had gone to bed too, exhausted from playing outside all afternoon.

I reminded myself to buy something nice for Sarah as a thanks for all her help. I knew Shannon paid her well, but still. It was very nice of her to help us out like this and give us this night out.

We took a stroll on the boardwalk by the water and went into a few of the souvenir shops till we found some strange small statue to give her. I thought it was very ugly, but Shannon called it art, and I decided she knew best.

As we walked outside again, ugly statue hidden in the bag, we decided to go down to the water and keep walking. I wasn't quite ready to go back home yet. I wanted to make the most of the night, even though I was exhausted. I hadn't been up this late in three months.

"What a lovely night, don't you think?" Shannon said with a sigh, as we watched the moon rise above the water, causing it to glitter. Big ships were docked and the sound of the water hitting against them was calming to me.

I put my arm around her and kissed her. I felt emotional and very happy at this moment.

"Yes," I said.

"Right now, everything is perfect, isn't it?" Shannon asked.

"It sure is."

We had stared at the gorgeous moon and water in front of us for a few minutes, when a sound made me turn my head to our right.

"What is it?" Shannon asked.

"There's someone there," I said and let go of her. I took a couple of steps towards the figure. Someone was sitting on the dock, legs dangling over the edge.

"It's a little girl," I said to Shannon. "What's a little girl doing out here this late?"

"Maybe her parents went into one of the shops and will be right out," Shannon said, and turned to look at the souvenir shops behind us.

I approached the girl. She had her back turned to me and was staring out over the water.

"Jack, we should be getting back," Shannon said. "It's getting late."

"I'll be right there. I just need to make sure she's all right. I don't like that she is sitting this close to the water. If she falls in, she won't be able to get back out."

I walked up to her and knelt down next to her when I heard that she was singing. I recognized the song immediately as Willie Nelson's *Blackjack County Chain*, and I chimed in. I never would have done that before I met Shannon, but she had gotten me confident about singing, and even told me I wasn't completely tone deaf, as I had always believed I was. I enjoyed music and singing and it was a side of me Shannon had cultivated.

The girl stopped and looked up at me. In the weak light from the moon, I could tell she was young. Not as young as the twins and Angela, but only a few years older.

"That's quite a song for such a small girl to sing," I said.

The girl stared at me for a long time, then her eyes left me and returned to the water.

"The Doctor used to sing it," she answered.

"The Doctor? Who's that?"

The girl didn't answer.

"What's your name?"

"I'm not allowed to talk to strangers."

"Of course not. Good answer. Where are your parents?"

"I don't have any."

My heart sank. "Really? Then are you just here all by yourself, then?"

She looked at me. "No. Of course not."

"So, who's here with you? The Doctor?"

"Yeah, sure," she said.

"Where is he?"

The girl looked at me again. She was biting her lip. "He…he just went for a walk. Will be right back, he said."

"Jack?" Shannon called from behind. "Can we go now? I want to get back to Tyler and I'm getting cold."

"One second," I yelled back. I didn't like to leave this little girl out here all alone. I didn't buy the story of the doctor and his walk one bit. Something was off here. "Do you know I'm a police officer?" I said. "My name is Jack."

The girl turned her head towards me again. I reached out my hand so we could shake, but she left it hanging.

"I'm Betsy Sue," she said.

9

[MAY 2016]

"So, tell me, Betsy Sue. I notice you're not wearing any shoes. Where do you live?"

"Around."

"I bet," I said. "Do you know your address?"

She shook her head without looking at me. I could hear Shannon sigh behind me. I felt torn. I could just get up and leave her, that seemed like what she wanted, but something told me not to; my gut told me it was a bad idea.

"A phone number?"

Head shaking again.

"Jaaack, come on!"

"I'll be right there."

"You should go, you know," Betsy Sue said. "Don't want to keep a lady waiting."

"You're right," I said with a light chuckle. And then it struck me. This girl knew country music. "Say, do you know Shannon King?"

The girl turned her head and looked straight at me. "Yes. She's my favorite singer!"

Bingo!

"Well, that's her. But don't tell anyone," I said, putting my pointer finger over my lips.

"That is Shannon King?" The girl turned her head and looked back at Shannon standing underneath a streetlamp wearing her big hat.

"Yes. And she's my girlfriend. We're going to get married here in Savannah next Saturday."

"Lucky you."

I snickered. "Thanks. Say, would you like to meet her?"

Even though it was dark and the only light came from the moon, I could still see the girl's eyes become big and wide.

"I'm guessing that's a yes," I said.

I got up to my feet and reached out my hand. She grabbed it in hers and let me pull her up. We walked towards Shannon, who looked at me, confused, then smiled when she saw the girl.

"Shannon, meet Betsy Sue; she's your biggest fan."

"Well, hello there, Betsy Sue," Shannon said and reached out her hand. Betsy Sue looked at it and embraced Shannon in a big hug instead. Shannon laughed, startled.

"Say, are you hungry?" I asked.

Shannon gave me a look. I knew we had to get back, but I had to find out where this girl lived so I could get her home. The harbor was almost empty except for one bum sleeping it off on a bench. This was no place for a little girl. I was guessing she had run off from home and it was vital for me to get her back. These streets were hardly safe for such a small girl at night.

"We can't leave her here," I said.

"Of course not," Shannon said.

"Let's grab a burger somewhere," I said. "I'm sure we can find somewhere that's open. Do you like burgers?"

The girl looked puzzled. "I don't know," she said.

"You don't know?" I said, laughing, and looked at Shannon. "All little girls like burgers!"

"Okay."

I pondered over her answer, then Shannon grabbed her hand in hers and we walked till we found a diner that was open. I ordered a burger and fries for the girl, the burger plain, with only cheese, like my kids always wanted.

"And loads of ketchup," I said to the waitress. "And coffee for us."

"Not me," Shannon said. "I can't sleep if I drink coffee this close to bedtime."

"Then just for me," I said. "And a soda for the girl.

What do you like?"

Betsy Sue stared at me, then shrugged.

"We have Coke, Sprite, Fanta, Lemonade, and iced tea," the waitress said.

"Do you have water?"

"Sure thing, sweetie pie," she said and winked at Betsy Sue.

"So, Betsy Sue. We need to find out where you live," I said, as soon as the food had arrived.

Betsy Sue just stared at it like she wondered how to attack it. It was nothing like the reaction I had expected. My kids were always throwing themselves at their food when it was served.

"Aren't you hungry?" Shannon asked and hugged her hand in hers.

"Yes. But…"

"But what?" Shannon asked gently.

The girl's eyes hit the edge of the table. "Usually we have to wait."

"Wait for what?" I asked, thinking this was the strangest child I had ever met. In the light from the diner, she looked so pale I couldn't believe it. Her skin was almost see-through, like paper, and I could see all the veins underneath it. She looked suddenly a lot younger than I had initially thought she was. It was just that the way she spoke and acted made her seem older.

"Maybe you're used to saying a prayer before you eat?" Shannon asked. "We always did that at my house."

"Nope. Never at my house," I said. "But we can say one if you like. Would you like that?"

The girl nodded. We closed our eyes and held hands while Shannon led us all in the prayer she grew up with.

"Amen," she ended.

When I opened my eyes, I realized Betsy Sue hadn't closed hers at all. She was staring at us.

"No prayer?" I asked. "Then what do you usually wait for before you can eat at your house?"

Betsy Sue's eyes met mine as I sipped my coffee. There was something in them, something in that look that caused a chill to run down my back. I couldn't put my finger on it, but something was really wrong with this little girl.

"The ghosts."

I almost choked on my coffee and some of it spurted out. I wiped it off from the table with my napkin. "I'm sorry."

"Did you say ghosts?" Shannon asked.

The girl nodded.

"You have to wait for the ghosts to do what?"

"To sit with us," she answered. "Once they're there, we can all eat."

I took another sip of my coffee, then said, "Well let's just say the ghosts are here right now, sitting at the end of the table so you can eat, alright?"

The girl shrugged. "Okay." Then she finally picked up her burger and took a bite. She never put it down again. Soon she was eating so fast I was beginning to worry she might choke.

"You sure were hungry," I said, as the burger disappeared, and soon after the fries went the same way. "So, tell me. What were you doing at the harbor?"

The girl swallowed a bite. "Looking at the water."

"Yes, I know you were looking out over the water, but were you waiting for someone? Why were you there?"

"I wanted to see the ocean."

"Yeah, all right, but I mean…you have seen the ocean before, right?"

The girl shook her head with food in her mouth. I had never seen a little girl devour a burger and fries that fast. Not even my own twins. They usually made it a little more than half way, and then gave up. I was beginning to wonder when this little girl had eaten last.

"How can you never have seen the ocean when you live in Savannah?" I asked.

The girl shrugged. "I don't know."

"Maybe she's not from here after all; maybe she's just visiting," Shannon said, then addressed Betsy Sue again. "Did you come here by car or airplane?"

The girl stared at Shannon like she had no clue what she was talking about.

"I don't know."

Could she be mentally challenged? I started to wonder. Maybe she had run off from some institution somewhere. There was something in the way she spoke, like she had a speech impairment as well.

"What do you want to do?" Shannon asked, as we paid for the food and my coffee.

"It's late," I said, while putting down a tip. "Let's take her back to our place, then I'll make some calls to my colleagues around here and ask if anyone is missing a little girl. We've got to find out where she came from."

10

[SEPTEMBER 1990]

It took Joseph only two interviews before he landed a job as a music teacher at a local school in Savannah, a dream position for him, as it gave him the time to pursue his own music and teach young kids about his big passion at the same time.

For so many years he had struggled as a musician, doing gigs here and there in bars and restaurants or at festivals, but never really making ends meet. With this job, he was finally able to provide stability for his family, and Kimberly could stay home and not work anymore.

It was perfect.

Meanwhile, Kimberly had a lot to do, taking care of this new big house. She decided to homeschool Rosa, as she herself had always been homeschooled. Rosa loved being at home all day and having extra time with her mother. As soon as she was done with her assignments and classes for the day, she would go into the back yard and play or on rainy days like today, she would go to the attic and play.

"Don't get your dress dirty," Kimberly yelled after her, but the girl was already long gone. Why she loved that attic so much, Kimberly never understood, but she could spend hours on end up there.

Meanwhile, Kimberly did the laundry. She walked to the basement with the big full basket under her arm. She divided the clothes into colors and whites, then put the first load in and started it. The old machine made a loud noise and drowned out everything.

Kimberly whistled as she walked up the stairs to check on her bread baking in the oven. The kitchen smelled divine and she took it out, burning her finger as it slipped when she put it down.

"Ouch."

Kimberly blew on her finger, and then went to the sink to run water on it. She was holding it under the faucet when she heard a sound and turned to realize a raven had found its way inside the kitchen. There were so many of them all over the property, and they had even made a nest in the attic, which she had asked Joseph to remove a thousand times.

"Shoo!" she yelled, still holding her finger under the cold water. The bird didn't react. It flew up on the kitchen counter and sat there, then made a gurgling croak while staring at her bread. The sound was rising in pitch and soon it became very loud.

"Shoo!" Kimberly yelled again, but the bird didn't react. It started to pick at her bread.

"STOP!"

The bird picked and destroyed the newly baked loaf of bread in a matter of seconds, crumbs flying everywhere. Kimberly picked up a wooden spoon and threw it at the bird. Finally it moved, but it didn't fly away. Instead, it flew towards her very fast and grabbed her hair between its claws, then pulled it violently.

"Ouch! You bastard!"

Kimberly pulled her finger out of the water and grabbed a kitchen knife.

"CR-R-R-UCK, CR-R-R-UCK, CR-R-R-RUCK," the bird screamed and flew up under the ceiling, while the knife missed it, but cut off a huge lump of Kimberly's hair, which fell to the ground.

Kimberly gasped and picked up her long hair between her hands, then looked at herself in the mirror.

"My beautiful hair," she sobbed, when she realized she had lost all the hair on the right side of her head. Now she'd have to cut off the other side as well to make it even.

Meanwhile, the bird sat under the ceiling, croaking. Kimberly groaned in anger, yelled at it, then picked up a broom and tried to reach it. The bird took off, flying under the high ceiling towards the front door, croaking loudly, sounding exactly like it was laughing at her.

Like it was mocking her.

11

[MAY 2016]

"We can't just keep her here!"

Shannon was angry. She looked at Jack, who had been on the phone for at least an hour, talking to his colleagues at the nearest police station, but no girl had been reported missing, they told him.

"I'm sorry," he said. "They don't have anywhere better for her to spend the night. Besides, she's already sleeping. We'll take her down to the station tomorrow and they'll call DCF. For now, she's fine."

Shannon bit her nails. She didn't like it. Ever since Jack went over to that little girl at the docks, she'd had this sensation, this feeling of dread inside her stomach that she couldn't escape.

Jack got up from his chair and walked to her. He grabbed her face between his hands and kissed her.

"It'll be fine," he whispered. "We're doing something good here. She would still be out there if we hadn't taken care of her. God only knows who she would run into down there or on the streets. We helped her. We're the good guys, remember?"

Shannon eased up. She needed to trust Jack more, she knew that. It was an issue she was working on. Trust. It sounded so easy. Just a five-letter word. Still, it was the hardest thing for her to do. To trust another human being, especially a man. She hadn't exactly had much luck doing so earlier in life.

"I know."

"Now, Sarah has gone to her room, all the kids are asleep, and I mean all of them, even Tyler; do you know what that means?"

"We're alone," Shannon said.

"Exactly."

Jack leaned over and kissed her neck. He continued down to her shoulder, where he pulled off her shirt, talking in-between kisses. "So…Shannon King…soon to be *Mrs. Ryder*…what…do…you…say to…the two of us…making all…the love…tonight?"

Shannon giggled and closed her eyes. It felt good to feel his lips on her body again. It had been so long. She leaned her head back. Jack stopped. "Wait, you're not too tired are you? I don't want to pressure…"

He didn't get to finish. She grabbed him by the neck

and pulled him towards her, and soon after they both tumbled towards the couch where they made love. *All the love*, like they always called it. It was taken from some movie, neither of them could remember which one. It might also have been a cartoon. Shannon never knew these crazy days anymore. But she did know that she loved Jack. She loved him and the family they were building together. She loved her life more than ever before.

"So, what do you think is with this girl?" Jack asked when they were done and were lying on the couch of the rental house.

"What do you mean?"

"She's strange, don't you think?"

Shannon nodded. "Sure do."

"I mean, show me one kid in this country that doesn't know if they like a burger or not, or even what flavor soda they like."

Shannon laughed lightly. "That is really odd, yes."

"And that story of the ghost?" Jack asked, while putting his pants back on. He left his shirt off, since they were going upstairs to bed in a few minutes anyway. "And she kept talking about the Doctor, like this doctor was her parent or something. I think she ran away from an institution around here. I mean, that is the only explanation, right?"

Shannon yawned. She was seeing dots in front of her eyes now. It was past midnight. She hadn't been up this late since she became pregnant. Tyler had been sleeping all evening, Sarah said, so there was a really good probability that he was going to wake up very soon and ask to be fed.

"Sure."

And there it was. The sound of Tyler crying on the monitor. On the screen, she could see that he was wide awake. Shannon's eyes met Jack's.

"Oh, no, "she said.

Jack shrugged. "Better now than after you've fallen sleep, right? Maybe if you feed him now, you'll get to sleep afterwards."

Easy for you to say when it's not you who has to get up at night.

Shannon got up with a growl and went up the stairs. While she was walking up, she realized that Tyler had suddenly stopped crying. Puzzled, Shannon opened the door to his room anyway. Inside, she spotted Betsy Sue. She was standing by the crib, leaning over it. Shannon gasped and the girl turned her head, then smiled. That was when Shannon realized the girl had put her finger into the baby's mouth and Tyler was eagerly sucking on it.

"I used to do this to Miss Muffit all the time," she said, her light blue eyes staring at Shannon from her ghostly pale face. "It always calmed her down."

12

[MAY 2016]

Two officers came to the house the next morning. I had spent hours the night before trying to calm Shannon down after she walked in on Betsy Sue. Shannon insisted that one of us stay in the nursery to make sure the girl didn't go in there again. I thought she was freaking out for no reason, but that wasn't what she needed to hear.

"This girl is creepy," she kept telling me. "I don't trust her. I tried to be nice; I tried to embrace her, but this… this is awful what she did, Jack."

"She probably didn't know any better," I tried to defend her. "Apparently, she was used to doing it to her sister, and that used to make her stop crying, so she believed that it was okay. Cut her some slack."

But it didn't help. Shannon had decided the girl was sick or a weirdo and that she was not to be trusted. So I ended up sleeping in a chair in the nursery.

When the officers arrived, I hadn't even showered, and I felt like someone had run a truck over me.

The two officers, a man and a woman, showed me their badges. "Are you Detective Ryder?"

I nodded and let them inside. I straightened my hair with my hand and tucked my shirt in my trousers. Tyler was crying upstairs. Shannon was with him.

"Just give me a second, will you?" I asked them and walked into the kitchen where all the kids were eating cereal with Sarah. Betsy Sue was sitting with them at the breakfast counter, staring at her cereal bowl like was it the Holy Grail. Abigail and Austin were fighting over a spoon, and Angela was chatting about her being a flower girl at the wedding to Sarah, and explaining how she was going to throw the rose petals.

Betsy Sue seemed awkward as she sat there all quiet and pale. If I didn't know better, I would have thought she had never seen other children before, but of course she had. As far as I knew, she at least had a sister, but maybe the children she had known hadn't been as vocal and rowdy as our kids. She didn't seem uncomfortable with it, though. It seemed to amuse her.

"Could you take them to the park afterwards?" I asked Sarah pleadingly. "We need to figure out what is going to happen to Betsy Sue."

Sarah nodded. Abigail and Austin yelled in happiness.

"Yay, the park!"

Abigail looked at Betsy Sue. "I'm sorry you can't come with us," she said. "Maybe next time?"

I didn't see Emily anywhere and assumed she was still sleeping, teenager as she was.

I turned and looked at Betsy Sue, then smiled. "There are some people here to see you."

Betsy Sue followed me to the living room where the two officers were waiting patiently. I asked them if they wanted coffee, but they refused. They presented themselves as Detective Bellini and Detective Nelson from the Special Victims Unit. I explained to them really quickly how I had found Betsy Sue by the water, sitting on the seawall at the harbor, her feet dangling dangerously from the edge and told them that I was worried about leaving her so late on the streets. They both nodded while listening. The female detective, Bellini wrote down what I told them.

"So far, all I've gotten out of her is that she is from Savannah and that she has a sister called Miss Muffit, I don't know what kind of name that is, but I'm thinking it must be some kind of nickname or something. But, then again, I don't know if it's her sister or not, I just know that she knew her as a baby. She might have run away from some institution or something. She told me she has no parents and apparently she has lived with a doctor."

Detective Bellini nodded again and wrote it down, then looked up at me. I sniffled, my eyes darting between the officers.

"We haven't had anyone report this girl missing, and we've reached out to all institutions and foster homes in the nearby area this morning, but no one seems to be missing a girl," Bellini said. She lifted her hand and touched her hair, showing off a very big ring on her finger with a heavy green stone.

"That's strange," I said.

"If you don't mind, we'd like to talk to her ourselves a little bit," Detective Bellini said.

"Of course not," I said and got up. "I'll go check on the baby and his mother while you do."

13

[MAY 2016]

"She won't talk to us."

Detective Bellini had come upstairs where Shannon and I were sitting while she was breastfeeding. She knocked on the door and peeked inside.

"Excuse me?" I said and got up.

The detective shook her head. "She refuses to say anything. You say that she spoke to you two last night?"

"Yes," Shannon said. "She spoke to us a lot, even."

I looked at Shannon. "She spoke to you mostly. She likes you."

"We can't seem to get through to her. We called DCF and they will send someone over. It might take a little while, though, since it's Sunday and all. And I don't want to take her to the station. It might be too much for her right now. She seems quite shocked. And you don't know what happened to her before she came here?"

"No clue."

"I've called the station and they they're going to be knocking on doors. Maybe her parents simply slept in and haven't discovered that she's gone yet. But is it okay if she stays here at your house till someone from DCF arrives? It shouldn't be more than an hour or so."

I looked at Shannon and could tell she wanted to get the girl out as soon as possible. I decided her needs were more important now. "Maybe we should…"

"Of course she can stay," Shannon interrupted me.

I smiled, relieved.

"What?" Shannon asked me when Detective Bellini had left us. "I'm not a monster. Besides, it's just a for a few hours, right?"

I chortled. "I didn't think you were." I leaned over her and kissed her gently, then leaned down and kissed Tyler.

"Careful not to wake him up," she whispered. "He finally fell asleep."

"He looks so peaceful when he's asleep," I said.

"I know. Let's keep it that way, shall we?"

I laughed lightly, then sneaked out and went down the stairs where a woman from DCF had already arrived. She had pulled up a chair next to Betsy Sue.

The girl wasn't looking at her, but simply staring at her feet.

"That was fast," I said.

"She lives in the neighborhood," Detective Nelson said.

"So these nice people tell me your name is Betsy Sue," the lady said. "Is that true?"

Betsy Sue didn't react. She kept staring at her feet and her long, dirty striped socks.

"Is that your real name or a make-believe name?" the lady asked.

Still no answer.

"You know most people have a last name too. Do you have that?" the lady tried. She seemed a little harsh in the way she spoke to the girl. I wasn't sure Betsy Sue was going to react well to her approach.

I was right.

"Listen, if you don't tell me who you are, then I can't find where you live. These nice people tell me you said you don't have any parents. Is that true? Or were you just wishing you didn't have them?"

Still no answer.

The lady got up and walked away. She approached the officers. "I'm not getting anywhere with her. My guess is she is a runaway, and that she will do whatever it takes to make sure she doesn't get sent back there. We see that often. Unfortunately, she will have to go back, but we will have to look into her family once we find them. For now, I need to have her checked by a doctor to make sure she hasn't suffered abuse, then I'll have to find a temporary place for her to stay until the parents show themselves."

As the lady spoke, my eyes met those of Betsy Sue. There was something in them, a begging, a pleading for my help that I couldn't escape.

You can't send her off with that awful woman. You can't send her off to some home somewhere.

Exactly what it was that made me open my mouth and speak, I don't know. It could have been her begging eyes; it could have been my pounding heart that simply couldn't stand this. I did it, even though I knew that Shannon was going to kill me. When it came to children, I had a soft heart. I had to help. I simply couldn't do nothing. I would hate myself afterwards.

"She can stay here with us as long as needed," I said.

14

[OCTOBER 1990]

It started as just an itch. Then there was another one. All on Rosa's legs. Soon they turned into big blistering bumps that she wouldn't stop scratching, especially at night. Kimberly could hear her in the room next to her, scratching all night long, and in the morning she would wake up with even more bloody bumps on her legs.

"What is this?" she asked Joseph and showed him Rosa's legs.

Kimberly cleaned the blisters thoroughly every day to make sure they didn't get infected, but they stayed swollen and Rosa kept crying.

"I…I have never seen anything like this before," Joseph answered. He knelt next to his daughter while inspecting her legs.

"I have them on my back too now," Rosa cried and lifted up her shirt.

Kimberly gasped. Rosa's back was covered in red blisters.

"Could it be mosquitoes?" Joseph asked.

"Should we take her to the doctor?" Kimberly asked anxiously. They didn't have insurance and could hardly afford a doctor's visit right now.

Joseph bit his lip, then shook his head. "Let's give it a couple of days and see. Maybe she's just allergic to mosquito bites. I'll drop by the pharmacy on the way home and get her something for it. Don't worry." He leaned over and looked into Kimberly's eyes, then kissed her gently.

Kimberly eased up. Joseph was right. It looked like an allergic reaction. A little medicine and that should take care of it.

Luckily, he was right. When he came back later that same day he brought her Benadryl, and an hour later, the swelling had gone down visibly. Kimberly sighed, relieved, as she saw the improvement, and all night she tried to listen for her the sound of her daughter scratching behind the wall, but she was completely quiet.

For a few days, it seemed like everything had gone back to normal, until one afternoon when Kimberly was in the kitchen, peeling potatoes for their dinner, when her daughter suddenly screamed from the living room. Not a whine of joy because she was playing or even a scream because she had fallen and hurt herself.

No this was worse; this was deeper and contained an anxiety so deep, it immediately made Kimberly throw everything she had in her hands down and rush in.

In there. In the middle of the living room, stood her daughter, staring at her with utter terror in her eyes. As Kimberly looked down at her legs, she saw why. They were completely covered in small black insects.

"Help me, Moom, help me!"

Kimberly stood, frozen. Never had she seen this many bugs in one place. And they were all crawling on her baby! Kimberly ran back to the kitchen, grabbed her broom, and ran back. She tried to wipe the insects off her daughter's legs, but more appeared as she did. Kimberly screamed as loud as she could while wiping them away, trying to kill them. But it didn't help. The bugs were biting Rosa and she was screaming in pain. Soon they were on Kimberly as well, and that was when she realized they were coming up from the wooden floors. Thousands of them crawling up.

Out. We've got to get out of here!

Kimberly grabbed her screaming daughter, lifted her up with bugs falling off her body, and stormed out into the yard. She threw Rosa in the grass and dusted off all the bugs from her own legs before she could get the rest off of Rosa's legs as well. They rolled in the grass, whining and wiping their legs till all the bugs were off. Then Kimberly grabbed her daughter by her hand, and together they ran onto the street where they found a payphone and called for help.

15

[MAY 2016]

We took Betsy Sue to the ER. I rode with her in the police car, since she refused to leave the house without me. When they told her she had to go, she grabbed my hand in hers and didn't let go again. So what else could I do?

She still hadn't spoken a word to anyone since last night and I was beginning to think she wasn't going to. I wondered if she would even speak to me again. I looked at her pale face and saw how she covered her eyes from the light as we pulled onto the street.

Right after I made the promise to the lady from DCF, I told Shannon that Betsy Sue was going to stay with us…maybe even for a few days. She had finally managed to get Tyler down for his nap when I spoke to her in the hallway.

"She's staying? But? Why?"

"We have to help her. We simply do. Just trust me on this," I said. "They have nowhere to place her while they look for her parents."

"But, why us? Why can't someone else take her? How about that woman detective?" Shannon asked, but knew very well the answer.

"I have to know she's all right," I said. "She trusts me. She trusts us. We're the only ones she has spoken to, remember? I've got to help this girl. I sense she is in trouble. Just let me do this."

Shannon exhaled deeply. "All right. Guess I put this on myself by marrying a man who actually cares, huh?" she said and kissed me. "But she can't put her finger in Tyler's mouth again. That was so disgusting."

I kissed her and promised her it wouldn't happen again.

We arrived at the ER around ten in the morning. Detective Bellini had called in first and the doctor was waiting for us when we arrived. Betsy Sue and I were taken to a private room. The doctor came in. I felt her hand hold on to mine tighter. The little girl was a lot stronger than she seemed.

"Are you her parent?" the doctor asked.

"No, I'm a detective," I said.

"Only parents or legal guardians present, please," he continued.

I tried to let go of Betsy Sue, but she tightened her grip with a loud roar. I looked into her very light deeply set blue eyes.

"I'm sorry, Betsy. You've got to let go of my hand now. The doctor needs to examine you," I said.

Her eyes stared into mine. I saw fear bordering on utter terror. She shook her head and snarled. I glanced down and noticed her hands were shaking while holding onto mine. I realized the presence of the doctor made her scared.

Of course. There was a doctor she kept talking about last night. Was she afraid of him?

"It's okay, Betsy Sue. This is a nice doctor. He's not going to hurt you."

The girl didn't believe me. She kept her eyes locked on me and both her hands holding onto mine in a very tight grip, her knuckles turning white with restraint.

"I'm sorry," I said, looking at the doctor. "She doesn't seem to want to let go of me. I have a feeling she might be afraid of doctors."

He nodded. Luckily, he was a nice guy. "Very well, then. I guess I can let you stay. Don't want to scare the poor thing, right?"

I smiled and nodded, wondering what I had gotten myself into.

16

[MAY 2016]

The detectives and the lady from DCF finally left late in the afternoon, after hours of unsuccessfully trying to get Betsy Sue to talk to them.

"We'll be back tomorrow morning; we have a child psychologist affiliated with our department," the DCF lady said.

All day, ever since she'd gotten ahold of my hand, Betsy Sue hadn't let go of me. Not until the second after they were all gone, then she finally loosened her grip and I pulled my hand away.

Betsy Sue got up from her chair that she had been sitting in all afternoon while the detectives and DCF questioned her. I had watched her grow smaller and smaller in the chair, refusing to even look up at them.

Now everything changed. The girl stood up and smiled.

"Can I go play in the yard?" she asked.

I stared at her, completely stunned over this sudden change in her mood. "Now you're talking?"

She nodded like it was the most natural thing in the world.

"Why wouldn't you talk to the detectives or the lady who was here from the DCF? Or even the doctor? They're all trying to help you."

Betsy Sue answered with a shrug.

"But you don't mind talking to me?" I asked.

She nodded with a smile.

"Why me?"

"I like you."

"Why do you like me? We hardly know each other?" I asked, puzzled.

"Because the ghost likes you."

"Excuse me?"

"The ghost. He likes you."

"What ghost? What are you talking about?"

Betsy Sue laughed. It was the strangest sound I had ever heard. It sounded more like a bird's croak. It creeped me out a little. "The ghost in this house, of course. The little boy."

I stared at her. I had no clue what to say.

"See, he's right there behind you. He's been following you around all day, standing right next to you when you were sitting in that chair. He likes you. I can tell. He doesn't want to leave your side. Just like me. Ghosts can sense these things, who's a good person and who isn't."

Betsy Sue stood in front of me while I figured out how to deal with what she had just said. I opened my mouth a few times to say something, but then stopped myself. It was all so strange.

"Can I go play?"

"Sure," I said. I could hear the other kids in the yard, probably playing hide and go seek again. I could do with a little break from all the weirdness.

Betsy Sue took off and I walked into the kitchen, where I found Shannon with Tyler in her arms. She was eating some toast. "I got hungry," she said.

I chuckled and grabbed myself some coffee while the kids shrieked in the yard. I realized I hadn't seen Emily all day.

"Is Emily still in her room?" I asked.

"She went for a run," Shannon answered, mouth full of toast and butter. "I didn't even think about what to eat for dinner. I am sorry. I am such a bad housewife."

"Let's order in," I said.

"You don't want to go out instead?"

I sipped my coffee and looked at the kids in the yard. Betsy Sue was screaming loudly and dancing. Clouds had gathered in the sky now and it was getting darker.

"Not with her," I said. "I think it's best we stay home."

"You're the one who wanted to save her," Shannon

said. "Just sayin'."

"I know," I said. "I know. It's just…the more time I spend with her, the weirder she gets."

"So what did the doctor say?"

Tyler fussed and Shannon hushed him. I put him in his playpen.

"It's the oddest thing," I said. "He said she seemed to be fine. No abuse, nothing seems to be wrong with her, except that her eyes are unusually sensitive to light, and—get this—it's almost as…as if her skin has never been exposed to sunlight before. She has a severe lack of vitamin D. It reminded me of the case of the Fritzl kids in Austria."

"The kids that were kept in a basement all their lives?" Shannon asked.

"Exactly. They too had that pale skin and eyes sensitive to light. I remember reading about it and how health experts said a chronic lack of sunlight and exercise could leave the children's bones pliable, their muscles weak, and their eyes overly sensitive to strong light. I asked the doctor if it could be because she had never been exposed to sunlight and he said that those were the symptoms, but that he believed it was impossible. That would mean she had never even walked outside or been out in a yard to play."

"Remember what she said about the ocean?" Shannon asked, while putting more bread in the toaster.

"Yeah, it got me thinking. She had never seen the ocean before; she had never eaten a burger before or even had a soda."

"You think she was locked up?" Shannon asked.

"It would explain a lot of things. Like the ghosts or imaginary friends that she's talking about, and the lack of knowledge about anything."

"But there was a baby she talked about," Shannon said, as the bread popped out of the toaster.

"Miss Muffit, was that her name? Who calls a child that?" I asked.

"A person who locks up their children and lets them wait for ghosts to arrive before they can eat."

I grabbed a barstool and sat by the counter. I looked at Shannon, who had buttered yet another piece of toast. I liked her weight gain after giving birth, but I knew she wasn't feeling good about it. She had this idea that just because she was a superstar, she couldn't allow herself to even add a few pounds without the magazines being all over it. I told her it was ridiculous. Everyone knew she had just had a baby. No one could expect her to look like her old self. The breastfeeding made her eat more, and I knew she was going to be mad at herself afterwards, but I enjoyed watching her sink her teeth into the buttered toast with a low groan.

"It would explain why we can't find her," I said. "The mother, I mean."

I leaned over to get a bite of her toast and she let me taste it, slightly reluctantly. I laughed and chewed.

"You mean she's mentally ill?" Shannon said.

I nodded. "Yeah."

"Who says it's a woman? What if it's a man?" Shannon asked.

I looked at her, stared into her beautiful eyes. I couldn't wait to make her my wife.

"Of course," I said. "*The doctor.*"

I could hear the kids yelling my name. "I'd better check and see what's going on," I said and got up.

I walked outside, where I found Abigail and Austin storming towards me, faces filled with excitement.

"What's going on, guys?" I asked.

"You gotta see this, Dad," Abigail exclaimed. "Come."

Abigail and Austin each grabbed a hand and pulled me further into the yard. They dragged me into the maze behind the high bushes, where I spotted Betsy Sue sitting in the grass. She was surrounded by birds, all black ravens. One even sat in her hand and she was talking to it, looking straight into its eyes and petting it on the back. Hundreds of other ravens were swarming her.

"What is she doing?" I asked.

"They bring her stuff," Abigail said. "Look. They already brought her this."

She pulled me towards a small pile in the grass and picked some things up. One blue earring, a tiny light bulb, a paperclip, and a rusty screw.

"They're treasures, Dad. They bring her treasures. She's just like Cinderella."

8 8

17

[MAY 2016]

"We need to find out where she came from, and fast," Jack said, as he returned from the yard.

Shannon was standing in the doorway leading to the yard, watching all the birds gathering behind the bushes, making an awful noise. Shannon had been terrified of birds since she was a child and one got stuck in her hair on her way to school. It pulled out big lumps of her hair and scratched her scalp to blood before it finally got out. Ever since, she had stayed far away from all flying creatures.

"What's going on with all the birds in the yard?" Shannon asked.

Jack sighed and ran a hand through his curly hair. It was getting long. Shannon liked it long; she liked Jack when he looked rough and unshaven and had asked for him to look like that for the wedding. He was a surfer and she wanted him to look like one.

"It's the girl. Apparently, she's a bird friend," Jack said. "I don't know. There's just something about her… it freaked me out a little. I'm just being silly, right? Tell me I'm acting stupid."

"I can't. I hate birds and think it's totally creepy."

"Same here."

"They're not coming in the house," Shannon said, feeling a shiver just at the thought. "Or even near it."

"No, of course not," Jack said. His phone was suddenly vibrating in his pocket and he picked it up. It wasn't a number he had stored in his phone.

"Ryder," he said and walked into the kitchen to get away from the bird noise. He talked for a few seconds, then hung up and looked at Shannon. Her heart was pounding in her chest. The look on his face was one of mystery.

"They know who she is," he said.

"What?"

"They found out who she is. They took a DNA sample this morning at the hospital and they have a match."

Shannon stared at him, puzzled. "This morning? How is it even possible to do it so fast? I thought it took days at least."

"Yeah, well, they used the newest technique, an

entirely new method. I've heard about it, but it hasn't quite reached Cocoa Beach yet. It's called Rapid Forensics DNA Analysis. It's a newly developed test that makes checking DNA from people arrested for crimes with DNA samples from crime scenes stored in forensic databases almost as easy as matching fingerprints. To increase the speed of forensic DNA testing, the scientists built a chip that can copy and analyze DNA samples taken from a cotton swab. Forensic technicians can collect DNA from suspects by swabbing their mouth, mixing the sample with a few chemicals, and warming it up. The DNA-testing-lab-on-a-chip does the rest. The entire process takes only four hours. But the bottom line is they had a match with a sample of DNA in their system."

Shannon's eyes became wide. This was good news. This was really good news. "So, who is she then?"

Jack rubbed his chin like he often did when thinking. "Apparently, she's some girl who disappeared five years ago."

"Five years ago?" Shannon looked at her husband to be.

"What's wrong? You look like you don't believe me," he said.

"No. No. Not at all. It's just that, well I don't know, but Betsy Sue is around ten, isn't she?" Shannon asked.

"Yes. So?"

"You said the doctor said she had never been exposed to sunlight. If she lived with her parents for the first five years of her life, how could that be? And that she had never seen the ocean or eaten a burger?"

Jack shrugged and put the phone back in his pocket. "I don't know. Does it matter? Maybe she doesn't remember anything because she was too young. Maybe five years of lack of sunlight is enough. I don't know. It's out of our hands. They're coming to get her soon, and now we can get on with our lives and, most importantly, our wedding."

Jack walked closer and grabbed Shannon around the waist. She laughed and let him kiss her.

Jack is right. It's going to be a great relief to get the girl out of our lives. Finally, we can both focus on the wedding again.

18
[MAY 2016]

The Doctor had left the house. An urgent matter had come up. Betsy Sue hadn't come back and the girls were beyond consolation at having lost their dear sister.

The Doctor wasn't happy either. The Doctor had other plans for her, and Betsy Sue knew it. It was time to get her back.

Now, the Doctor wasn't stupid. And neither was Betsy Sue. It was hardly a surprise that the girl would try and escape after what happened to Daisy, so the Doctor had placed a GPS tracking device disguised as a Hello Kitty watch on the girl, very similar to those they used at the retirement homes to track the elderly Alzheimer's patients. Now all the Doctor needed to do to find her was to follow the directions on her phone.

It took her to an old house in the historic downtown, a two-story house with a beautiful porch outside facing the square. A woman walked her dog past the house and the Doctor greeted her in a neighborly way.

The Doctor walked up to the house and looked inside a window, then heard voices coming from the back and walked around the house. It was almost dark now, but the kids were still playing in the back.

The birds guided the Doctor. The same birds Betsy Sue always played with in the attic. The Doctor knew they would lead to her. The Doctor smiled at the thought of getting the girl back. There was no escaping the inevitable. It had to be done.

The Doctor carefully opened the gate in the fence, then sneaked inside the yard and past a few windows. The kids were yelling loudly in joy. There was no one who would be able hear the Doctor over all that noise. It was perfect. The Doctor walked closer, reached a window, and peeked in. Inside stood a man with a woman in his arms. They were kissing and chatting lovingly.

They won't see anything. Perfect.

The Doctor watched for a few minutes while the man and the woman continued their embrace. It wasn't until they let go of each other that the doctor realized who the woman was.

Shannon King. Here in Savannah?

The Doctor was about to make a move, when

something else grabbed the doctor's attention. Something right behind the couple, lying in a playpen.

A baby.

The Doctor couldn't take her eyes off of the small baby. Such a beautiful creature, such a perfect specimen. It had to be a boy, since it was wearing a blue outfit. It was the most beautiful little thing.

The Doctor was filled with an urgent feeling. The Doctor knew what had to be done. But the Doctor never had a boy before. Always girls. Girls were easy. They liked to please. They took care of each other. But this…a boy?

No, there's no way around it. You know what must be done.

Before the Doctor could react, a car pulled up and someone got out. The Doctor climbed close to the wall and hid behind it while four people walked up to the front door. The doctor peeked out just as they reached the porch, then gasped when realizing who it was.

19

[OCTOBER 1990]

"I'm telling you. It's like the house doesn't want us here."

Kimberly stared at her husband across the kitchen. She handed him his coffee and he sat down to eat.

"You're being ridiculous," he said.

"Am I now? Am I really?"

"I think you are." Joseph picked up the paper, probably turning to the sports section as he always did.

Is he wearing a suit?

"I'm telling you, Joseph. There's something wrong with this house. There's this strange smell whenever I use the dishwasher and garbage disposal, and flies are constantly circling it. There are ravens all over the place. Look at them in the yard right now; they're constantly poking at the windows, scaring me, not to mention the flock in the attic that I can't get rid of. And then there were the bugs?"

Joseph scoffed. He didn't even put down the paper to talk to her. She spotted the sports section on the table.

He never used to be this interested in the real news.

"I told you. The exterminator said it was just fleas. They were living in the cracks in the floor. He got rid of them. The birds are everywhere in Savannah, and I'll have a plumber take a look at the garbage disposal."

"We don't have any pets! How can it be fleas if we don't have pets? How would they survive?"

"Apparently this type of flea doesn't care. He said they can survive for very long without a host. They lived off Rosa for a little while, and she is apparently allergic to them. It's all just a series of unfortunate events, Kim. You've gotta let it go. It's an old house. Of course there will be stuff wrong with it."

Kimberly approached her husband and pulled down the paper to force him to look at her while she spoke.

"I'm telling you. This house is evil. I hear it at night. It's like it's laughing at me. I can't sleep because of this scratching sound. It's driving me nuts. This place is driving me nuts."

"That's because it's haunted," Rosa said, as she came into the kitchen at that very second.

Kimberly didn't like that she had overheard their

conversation. She didn't want her to be uncomfortable here. She didn't want her to be more scared after the incident with the fleas.

"Excuse me?" Kimberly said.

Rosa sat down and poured herself some cereal in a bowl with a shrug. "That's what the old lady says. The one who lives down on the corner."

"Mrs. Thomas?"

Rosa nodded. Kimberly poured the milk for her and she started to eat. "She told me everyone who has ever lived here has gone insane."

"Don't listen to nonsense like that," Joseph said. "It's just old wives' tales."

Kimberly stared at her daughter, not knowing what to say.

"It's not," Rosa argued. "The past owner killed his own three daughters. At least that's what Mrs. Thomas said. The parents went out one night, leaving their four girls at home with their nanny. When they came back, three of the girls had been killed, and so had the nanny. One girl had survived, but she was only four years old and asleep upstairs when it happened. Mrs. Thomas said two of them were still inside the house, and one was on the front porch. Mrs. Thomas says the dad killed all of them. She says she is certain he came home earlier than his wife and did it. But the murders were never solved. His wife told the police he was with her all evening. But Mrs. Thomas said he had lost it *looong* before that night. He went nuts from living in this house. You could see it in his eyes."

"Stop it," Joseph said, spitting while he talked. "Stop it with all that nonsense."

Kimberly didn't know how to react. She didn't know her aunt very well and had no way of finding out if this was a true story or not. She looked at her husband, who was now reading the business section as if it was of great interest to him. Then she wondered why she never heard him play his guitar anymore.

20

[MAY 2016]

Detective Bellini had a big smile on her face as I opened the door for them. She was with the lady from DCF and a couple I could only guess had to be Betsy Sue's parents.

Judging from their appearance, I'd say they were very wealthy people. The woman wore heavy jewelry and the man a very expensive suit. They seemed nervous as I shook their hands and they presented themselves as Mr. and Mrs. Hawthorne.

"It has been a long road for the Hawthornes," Detective Bellini told me, as we walked inside where Shannon was waiting with Betsy Sue. "Losing their daughter five years ago and never knowing what really happened to her. It gives me great pleasure to finally be able to bring their daughter back to them."

"I can imagine," I said.

We walked inside the kitchen and Betsy Sue looked up as her parents entered. It didn't look like she recognized them and soon she looked away.

Mrs. Hawthorne let out a loud shriek and clasped her mouth delicately. Mr. Hawthorne stopped and stared at the little girl like he couldn't believe that he was actually standing in front of her. He shook his head again and again. He was a tall man, trim build, once handsome, I suspect, back when he was younger. Still had a measure of vanity, since it was clear he colored his hair. His rawboned face was pleasant. His wife appeared to be one of those immaculate women who never would leave the house without makeup and hair perfectly done. She seemed to be in the beginning of her forties, while he was a lot older than her, maybe by ten years, but I could be mistaken.

Shannon grabbed Betsy Sue by the shoulders and turned her to face them. "Look who's here, Betsy Sue," she said.

The girl stared at them like they were from another planet. Mrs. Hawthorne was sobbing.

"Adelaide?" she said, and stared into the little girl's eyes, bending down to her.

The father kept shaking his head like he was in disbelief. I guessed it was hard for him to comprehend. I couldn't even imagine how it must have felt in that instant, to go through what they had. Had they given up hope? Had they come to terms with her being gone, or do you simply keep wondering, hoping you'll see her again somewhere, somehow?

It was a very emotional moment and I could tell Shannon was fighting her tears. Well, who am I kidding? So was I.

"She told me her name was Betsy Sue," I said. "I am guessing that is the name the kidnapper gave her."

The sound of the word kidnapper resonated in the kitchen long after I had said it. I guess we were all thinking the same thing:

This guy should get caught and be punished for this.

I tried to imagine what it would be like to be in the Hawthornes' shoes. To have been deprived of five years of your child's life. To stand in front of her again now and see that she doesn't recognize you, that she responds to a different name, to not know what she has been through, what kind of scars she has been left with.

It was so awful to even think about.

Mrs. Hawthorne reached out her arms towards Betsy Sue. The girl looked up at me and I nodded to show her it was okay. She still didn't move.

"It might take some time," I said.

Mrs. Hawthorne rose to stand straight up. She looked disappointed. The father still seemed baffled and was almost as pale as his daughter.

"Why?" he asked. "How? Where…where has she been?"

"Unfortunately, we don't know the answers yet," Detective Bellini said.

"And you found her?" he asked, addressed to me.

"Yes. I found her at the harbor. She told me she wanted to see the ocean," I said.

"Has she said anything else?" Mrs. Hawthorne said.

"She hasn't spoken to anyone but Mr. Ryder and Mrs. King," Detective Bellini said. "But I'm sure she'll come around. And I want to assure you that my department will do everything it takes to get this guy. You can trust in that. But we'll need your daughter's help."

"Of course," Mr. Hawthorne nodded. The realization seemed to be starting to sink in properly now. He was smiling at the girl.

"Well, Adelaide…"

"It's Betsy Sue now," his wife corrected him. "Even though that is an awful name, we should call her that if that's what she responds to."

"Sorry, *Betsy Sue,* I must say I…am extremely thrilled to see you again. More than you can ever imagine."

21

[MAY 2016]

What started out as a sweet reunion scene soon turned out to be a complete nightmare. Troubles began once the Hawthornes wanted to leave and take Betsy Sue with them. Of course, the girl refused to leave.

Her begging and pleading eyes landed on me as they pulled her arm. I tried to smile and let her know it was all right, that she was going to be fine, but the terror on her face was disturbing.

She can't stay here forever, Jack. The girl needs to be with her parents. And you have a wedding to plan, remember?

Mr. Hawthorne ended up grabbing the snarling and fighting Betsy Sue in his arms and walked out to the car with her over his shoulder. I watched with a thumping heart as they drove away with the little girl.

It felt awful.

Shannon walked up to me as I stood in the window, still looking out at the empty road in the direction where the police car had disappeared.

"You think we'll ever see her again?" I asked.

"Part of me hopes we won't," Shannon said.

"And the other part?"

"Wants to run after that car and tell them to bring her back here."

I looked at my bride to be and felt such deep love for her. She was holding Tyler in her arms.

"You feel that too, huh?"

"I couldn't stand the way they carried her away like that. And she clearly didn't know who they were. Did you see the look on her face? She was so confused. Shouldn't she be able to remember them?"

I shrugged and caressed my drooling son gently on the cheek. "I don't know. It's been five years. She was very young when she disappeared. No one knows what's going on in that little girl's mind and what she's able to remember and what she's not. I mean, being taken from her parents five years ago must have been quite the trauma for her. Maybe she blocked out all memories from before then simply to survive?"

Shannon put her head on my shoulder. Tyler was fussing and she tried to make him calm down. When she didn't succeed, I told her to hand him to me. I looked into the eyes of my beautiful baby and wondered how I would react if he was kidnapped.

I couldn't even finish the thought.

Shannon's hand landed on my shoulder. "We've done everything we can. There really isn't anything else we could have done. I mean, the girl is back with her real parents."

I nodded and kissed her. We had to let it go. Both of us.

"So, should we order in?" I asked.

"Or…" Shannon said with glistening eyes.

"Or, we could go out!" I said. "Now that Betsy Sue isn't with us, it's a lot easier."

Shannon threw herself onto one of the old couches, her iPad in her hand. "I'll find a place. Somewhere that's fun for the kids too."

"Oh, what about the Pirate House? Someone recommended that to me," I said. "It's supposed to be haunted and everything."

"What place around here isn't?" Shannon said, and I couldn't stop thinking about Betsy Sue and the boy she said was constantly by my side. I didn't believe in ghosts, yet I felt a chill run down my spine while Shannon called to make reservations for us.

22

[MAY 2016]

The Pirate's House was a restaurant that had been there since 1753. The small building adjoining the Pirate's House was said to be the oldest house in the State of Georgia. Situated a block from the Savannah River, the Pirate's House first opened as an inn for seafarers, and fast became a rendezvous for bloodthirsty pirates and sailors from the Seven Seas. Here, seamen drank their grog and discoursed, sailor-fashion, on their exotic high seas adventures from Singapore to Bombay and from London to Port Said.

At least that's what the sign at the entrance said. I was reading it while we were waiting to be seated at the very popular place. The kids were already running all over the place, yelling and acting like pirates, stomping the old wooden planks and talking to the pirate statues like they were part of the game. Well, my kids did. Angela stayed close to her mother, as always, looking dazzled and amused by Austin's goofiness.

A guy dressed up like a pirate approached them and started telling the tale of how the tunnels underneath the restaurant were used to transport shanghaied seamen to the boats. They were drugged and captured at the Pirate's House, then shuttled to waiting pirate ships via a secret tunnel where they'd wake up far out to sea.

"Stories still persist of a tunnel extending from the Old Rum Cellar beneath the Captain's Room to the river through which these men were carried, drugged, and unconscious, to ships waiting in the harbor," he told them, making his voice scary and piratish. "A Savannah policeman—so legend has it—stopped by the Pirate's House for a friendly drink and awoke on a four-master schooner sailing to China from where it took him two years to make his way back to Savannah."

"Wauv," Abigail exclaimed, while Emily scoffed from where she was standing leaned up against a wall, her bangs covering most of her face, her hoodie pulled up. She was wearing way too many clothes for such a warm evening.

"Well, it's true," I said, addressed to her. "That there are actual tunnels underneath Savannah."

I had heard about the tunnels myself, but had always been told they were used for the bodies of people who succumbed to yellow fever. Through an underground network, they were put in the tunnels and moved to prevent panic aboveground. Still another tale tells of runaway slaves hidden under the floor of the First African Baptist Church, and then ferried out of harm's way via an Underground Railroad. I didn't know what to believe. Savannah was a place of myths and legends and the Savannahians' master storytellers. With a location this steeped in history, there was no shortage of compelling plotlines and colorful characters.

This place was no different.

"Even now, many swear that the ghost of Captain Flint still haunts the Pirate's House on moonless nights," the pirate ended his tale, just as our table was ready and we were seated in a private area like I had asked for, to make sure Shannon could take off her hat and relax for a bit. And so she could breastfeed if she needed to.

I tipped the lady extra and she went away with a happy smile.

The kids got menus that they could shape into pirate hats and paper earrings and color, while Shannon and I looked at what to order. Tyler had fallen asleep on our way here and stayed in his car seat, slumped down deep in dreamland. I just hoped he would stay there until we were done eating. We could use a nice night out with the kids without his meddling for once. He was adorable, but also exhausting.

"I'm gonna get myself a steak," I said, and then added a pirated, "arrr."

Shannon laughed. The kids seemed more embarrassed, especially Emily, who was hiding behind her menu.

"I'll have some Southern Style Catfish," Shannon said. Then tried an "arrr" of her own. It received a laugh from her own daughter. Mine didn't know how to pity-laugh.

It was all the way it was supposed to be. It felt great to be back to normal again. If you could ever call this crazy family normal.

PART TWO:

PUSH: A tie; the player and dealer have hands with the same total.

23

[MAY 2016]

Shannon was happy. It had been a tough couple of days with Betsy Sue in the house, knowing her story and everything, and it hurt thinking about it. But now Shannon had finally let it go; finally, she was back with her family enjoying every one of them.

Jack's kids were being rowdy, as always, and every now and then she wanted to say something to Abigail, but she held it back. This was not the time or place. It was still Jack's battle to fight. Later, when they were more used to Shannon being around, when they moved into the new house, she might listen to Shannon.

The house. Oh, the house. They had owned the property for almost a year now. They started building the house following Jack's plans and the drawings he made with the architect, but the house wasn't done yet. It was about to drive all of them nuts. The house was there. There was a roof on and everything, but then there was the issue of the plumbing, then there was the electricity. It still didn't work properly and they hadn't been able to move in yet.

Soon, they said. Very soon.

They had said that for months now. It was getting tiresome. Shannon couldn't wait to move in and start living in the house that Jack built for her.

All good things come to those who wait.

She was hoping that they'd be able to move in before the summer, but was trying to not get her hopes up too high. Until now, they had all been living in Jack's apartment and it was getting a little cramped. Emily was spending most of her nights at the motel that Jack's parents owned next door, and that had helped a little.

Shannon ate her catfish while looking at Emily, who had ordered fish, but barely touched it. Jack didn't see it, but Shannon did. The girl cut out the fish into small pieces, and then pushed them around on her plate, making it look like she had eaten. She was getting really good at hiding it; it was almost scary.

"Can we get dessert, dad, can we pleeeeeaaaase?" asked Abigail and, as usual, she got her way. The kids were served chocolate ice cream and were soon bouncing off the walls of the small private room.

Luckily, Tyler slept through everything. At least Shannon didn't have to worry about him. Jack put his arm around her shoulder.

"Do you want a dessert too?" he asked.

"I can't," Shannon said.

"Ah, come on," he said. "You look great. No need to worry."

"I have to be able to fit into the dress," she said. "They just finished it. I can't make any more adjustments to it."

"Oh, well I could do with some chocolate ice cream myself," he said. "Arrr."

"Dad, it's not funny anymore," Abigail said. "It never was."

Jack ignored her. "How about you, Emily? You love chocolate cake. They have that with vanilla ice cream?"

Shannon could have screamed. How could he ask her that? Did he not see that she hadn't eaten? Did he not see her?

Emily shook her head and leaned back in her chair, arms crossed over her chest. Shannon felt a pinch in her heart. She could see how Emily's hands had gotten so skinny. The bones were too visible. She wondered how she looked underneath all that clothing. Shannon realized it was going to be up to her if anything was to be done about Emily's condition.

Jack ate his ice cream and they paid. Shannon put on her big hat when walking back through the crowd. All it took was one person recognizing her before hell would break loose. Shannon knew it was vital that no one saw her here. The press would hear about it and make a circus out of their wedding.

Tyler started fussing as they walked towards the entrance. The kids stopped to look at some door that another pirate told them was magical. Shannon felt the pressure of Tyler's demands and Jack saw it on her face.

"Just go out to the car with him while I gather the kids," Jack said.

Shannon carried Tyler in his car seat out through the front door of the restaurant, leaving all the chaos behind her. It had gotten chilly outside and Shannon took her jacket from around her waist. To use both her hands, she had to put Tyler down on the porch. She put her jacket on and, as she turned to grab the handle of the car seat, it wasn't there.

24

[MAY 2016]

At first when I heard Shannon scream, I thought it was part of some gimmick in the restaurant. Someone screaming…pretending to be a ghost or to have seen one. I laughed and gathered the kids. We walked towards the entrance when I heard it again. This time it was a lot more serious and I realized it wasn't part of a show put on by some people working here. This was real.

It was a nightmare come true.

My eyes met hers when she opened the door to the restaurant and stepped inside. "Did you take Tyler?" she asked, her voice trembling.

I shook my head, panic starting to emerge in the bottom of my stomach. "What are you talking about?"

"Did you take him? Did you come out and grab him?"

"No. I've been in here with the kids, trying to gather them. You took him outside, remember?"

"He's not there," she said. "He was there, and then he wasn't."

It sounded like she had lost it. Her voice was calm like someone in deep shock. I had seen it before and it scared me even more. "What do you mean he isn't there? Didn't you hold on to him?"

"I had him in the car seat, and I carried him outside to the porch. Then I felt cold and put the seat down to put on my jacket. When I reached down to grab the handle, it wasn't there. He was gone."

"Oh, my God," I said and stormed outside to the old wooden porch. I looked to both sides of me, trying to imagine being Shannon putting on my jacket.

Why on earth did she turn away from him? Why didn't she keep an eye on our baby?

"Tyler?" I asked, as if he was able to answer. I walked around the porch to the other side of the house, my heart throbbing in my chest. Cars were coming in and others leaving the big parking lot in front of the restaurant like nothing had happened. I felt like yelling at them, stopping them, and searching them for my baby.

Where are you, little man?

"Do you see him?" Shannon asked, as she came out behind me.

I shook my head and rubbed my hair frantically. "No. Where did you put him down?"

"Over there," she said and pointed at a spot next to the door. "I put him down right there, I think."

"You think? You think?" I asked, a little more aggressively than I meant to. "Please do try and remember, Shannon. Did you put him down over there or not?"

"Maybe it was over here closer to the door. I don't remember Jack, I don't remember exactly where it was!"

"Think, Shannon," I said.

I stormed into the parking lot and started searching around the cars. I spotted a lady who was unlocking her car, holding a box of food in her hand. "Hey!" I approached her. She looked afraid of me. "Have you seen a baby in a red car seat? Maybe seen someone carrying it somewhere?"

She looked at me like I was crazy. "No." She hurried up and opened the car door and got in. I sighed, trying to ease up the panic slowly spreading in my body. I stared around me. Nothing but a sea of cars lit up by streetlamps. Cars were constantly coming and going. Someone ought to have seen at least something, right? A baby doesn't just disappear, does it?

I spotted Shannon, standing still on the porch, staring at the same spot where she said she was almost certain she remembered putting the seat down. I felt anger and found it hard to control it. I ran back towards her, yelling.

"Come on! Shannon. How could you let this happen?" I yelled to her face, while raising my arm angrily.

Startled, Shannon ducked down with a shriek, protecting her head with both of her arms.

I gasped and pulled back.

Oh, my gosh. She thought I was going to hit her, didn't she?

"I'm sorry," I said. I backed up, angry at myself now for being so insensitive, given her past with a violent ex-husband. I knew better than this. I was just so scared.

Shannon whimpered, then broke into tears. "I'm so sorry, Jack. I am so sorry. I lost him. I lost our baby."

I knelt next to her and pulled her into my embrace. I was fighting my own tears, but didn't allow myself to cry.

"No. *We* lost him. And *we'll* find him. Together."

25

[MAY 2016]

"What's going on?"

It was Emily. I looked up at her.

"What happened to Shannon?" she asked. "The kids are really scared. Can they come out?"

The kids had stayed inside because I told them to when I ran out here. "Yes," I said and rose to my feet. "Maybe they can help us search for him."

Emily went inside and came out, followed by Abigail, Austin, and Angela, our three A's. They all looked terrified. Abigail was the only one with courage enough to speak.

"What happened, Dad? Did something happen

to Tyler?"

"We can't find him," I said. "Maybe if we all looked around the area? Could you guys help us with that?"

The three young ones nodded. "Maybe you could go with them, Emily?" I asked. "Just basically look everywhere."

The kids took off into the parking lot and I watched them for a little while before I helped Shannon to sit down on an old bench by the front door. A couple walked past us. The man grabbed the door handle, but his wife urged him to stop. She approached us.

"What's wrong, dear?"

She sounded like she was from up north, but I had never been very good with accents.

"I…we can't find our baby," I said. "He's in a car seat, you know the ones you can carry by the handle."

The lady nodded. "Yes."

"Well my…our baby boy, Tyler, was in one, sleeping. My wife put him down for just a second and when she reached for him, he was gone."

"Oh, my. That's terrible," the lady said. "Where did it happen?"

"Right here," Shannon said. "In front of the door."

"Say, aren't you that singer?" the lady asked, and suddenly I could see the headlines in all the newspapers tomorrow.

Shannon shook her head and looked away.

"Thank you. We'll take care of it," I said and helped

them get inside. "Don't worry."

I realized my hands were shaking as I closed the door behind the couple. Shannon had gone into complete shock and I could make no sense of what she was saying. I walked back into the restaurant and alerted the hostess, asked her to look for a baby in a small car seat. But I also told her to please be discrete about it to protect my wife.

"Let me call my manager right away," she said. "We'll have everyone looking for him."

The words kidnapped and abduction were staring to roam in my mind as I returned to Shannon, but I didn't want to succumb to them; I didn't want to say them out loud or even let them take root in my head.

Tyler has to be here somewhere, right? He simply has to be. Just stay calm now, Jack. You have to keep your cool.

"He's gone, isn't he?" Shannon suddenly said, looking up at me. Our eyes met and I felt the anxiety she was going through.

"Don't say that," I said. "I'm sure there is some explanation for all this."

Shannon was rocking back and forth, biting her nails. "Do you think that's what the Hawthornes told each other when their daughter went missing five years ago?"

"No! Don't talk like that!" I yelled. But I had no right to be angry. She was just saying what I was afraid to even think.

It did, however, make me realize we had to do something more drastic. I grabbed my phone and called Detective Bellini.

"Bellini. Ryder here. I need your help. We…" I looked at Shannon, who was shaking her head in panic, crying heavily between sobs. She got up and started searching in the bushes next to the restaurant. I fought my urge to cry. Saying the words out loud made it so much more real, so much harder to cope with. But I had to. I needed all the help I could get now.

"Tyler is missing."

"Tyler, as in your newborn?" she asked with great urgency.

"Yes." I swallowed the lump in my throat and closed my eyes. "Our three-month-old baby is gone. He disappeared outside the Pirate's House. We're in front of the house now, searching the parking lot, but there aren't many places he can have gone. I fear he might have been taken. Please, help us."

"Be right there."

"But, Bellini?"

"Yes?"

"I need you to be very discrete about this. We can't have this hit the front pages tomorrow morning."

"Of course not. I'll see what I can do."

26

[MAY 2016]

"I have a surprise for you, girls!"

The Doctor turned off the lights and all the girls in the house started to scream. Mostly in excitement. They knew something was coming. The Doctor had placed them in a circle. Meanwhile, the Doctor carried the surprise into the middle of the circle, went back to the wall, and flipped on the lights again.

"Ta-da!"

All the girls stared at the little pink lump in the car seat in front of them. The Doctor stormed back and took him out. All eyes were fixated on the baby, but no one spoke. Not until Daisy opened her mouth as the first. Typical Daisy to be the first to complain.

Always her.

"But…" she started, but got a look from the Doctor that made her stop. She opened her mouth once again, but then held it back.

"That's not…" Miss Liz said.

"That's a boy!" Millie said. "That's not Betsy Sue!"

The Doctor gave Millie a look. It made her stop whining immediately and look away. Her arm was doing better, but was still in a sling. The Doctor had put it back in place, but Millie still complained about the pain. She wasn't going to risk another incident. She wasn't that stupid.

"I know it's a boy," the Doctor said, caressing the baby's cheek. "Isn't he a beauty?"

Lacy Macey made a grimace. "Yuck, I think he's ugly."

The Doctor turned to look at the little girl with the brown curly hair. Her long eyelashes were blinking as she realized she had crossed the line for what the Doctor found acceptable. The Doctor approached her, lifted her chin up with a finger underneath it, and made her look into the Doctor's eyes. Next, the Doctor slapped her across the face, causing her head to turn forcefully to the side. It didn't return to face the Doctor before the Doctor grabbed it and turned it back.

"Now," the Doctor said with a sniffle. "What do you say to poor little…Rikki Rick?"

Lacy Macey's eyes hit the wooden floors.

"Look at him," the Doctor said. "Look at him when you say it."

The girl looked up. "I'm sorry," she said.

"I am sorry, what?"

"I'm sorry, *Rikki Rick*."

The Doctor smiled and sighed. "That's my girl."

The Doctor lifted the baby into the air like Simba was lifted up in the *Lion King* to meet his future subjects. The boy wasn't happy and started to cry. The Doctor ignored the crying.

"This is Rikki Rick, everyone. He will stay with us from now on. Be good to him and treat him like a king. Teach him everything he needs to know."

All the girls looked up, especially little Miss Muffit. But she didn't look at him with excitement or joy as the others. She didn't dance joyfully because they now had a brother among them. She didn't partake in the welcoming party for the boy. Instead, she sat in a corner, tears pouring down her cheeks.

Because she knew that since Betsy Sue didn't seem to be coming back, the countdown to her own demise had begun.

27

[NOVEMBER 1990]

Thanksgiving was Kimberly's favorite time of year. It was the one holiday where people gathered just to be together, just to be thankful for each other and what they had, and not wonder what they were going to get.

Plus, she loved turkey.

Things had been calm in the old house for several months now, and she was getting to a point where she was as close to calling herself settled in as she could get in this place.

She still woke up at night hearing strange scratching sounds and she still felt a chill run down her back when she walked into the living room. She had learned to live with the roaches in the toilet bowl from time to time and the strange smell in the kitchen from the garbage disposal. And she had accepted the ravens, as long as they stayed in the attic. She had also learned that there was a lamp in the hallway that had been here when they moved in that never turned off. Even when it didn't have a bulb in it, it was simply always lit.

She knew it and had come to terms with it. It was, as Joseph had said earlier, it was an old house and they never knew what to expect from it.

"When are we eating?" Rosa said, when she came into the kitchen that was already encased in the sweet smell of roasted turkey.

Kimberly laughed lightly at her daughter's impatience. "There are still a couple of hours left."

"Aw. What am I to do while I wait?"

"How about you go outside and play for a little bit?" Kimberly asked.

Rosa hadn't made any friends since they moved here, and that worried her. Maybe it was, after all, a bad idea to homeschool the girl, she often pondered.

"There's nothing to do out there," Rosa said.

"Don't you think you can find something to do?"

Rosa shook her head, grabbed a chair, and sat down. Kimberly found a coloring book from one of the cabinets and handed it to her, along with some crayons. Rosa started coloring.

"What is your dad up to?" Kimberly asked, wondering if he was writing another song. He and Rosa had surprised Kimberly with one last year after their dinner, singing it together.

"He's in the basement," Rosa said with a shrug.

Joseph had spent a lot of time in the basement lately. Kimberly didn't really know what he did down there for hours on end. Until now, she had let him have his own space down there, but she did worry that his instruments were all gathering dust in the music room upstairs. It had been ages since he last picked one up and played. In the ten years they had been married, she had never been able to pull him away from his instruments or make him stop singing all day long. Not a tune left his mouth these days. Not even humming or whistling did she hear from him.

Kimberly threw the potatoes in the sink. This was the worst part of the dinner, she believed. The peeling of the potatoes. Kimberly sighed when she looked at the stack. They were just going to be the three of them this year, since all their families lived upstate and couldn't afford to travel down there. Still, she thought it was a big job to peel all these potatoes. She needed to do the cranberry sauce and the gravy as well.

Kimberly looked at her daughter, who was coloring, but didn't seem to be enjoying it very much.

"Rosa?"

She looked up. "Yes?"

"Would you mind peeling the potatoes for me?"

"Sure."

Rosa stood up and approached the sink. Kimberly

helped her put on an apron and roll up her sleeves. Rosa had peeled potatoes a few times before and was actually quite fast. Best of all, she actually liked it.

"So, what do you think your dad does down in the basement?" Kimberly asked, when her daughter picked up the first potato.

In the old times, what they now considered the basement was used to quarter the help. One of the rooms had since been made into a laundry room, but there were several other rooms that had been left unused, that they had just used as storage rooms when they moved in. Joseph had once day closed the door to the biggest one in the back and she had heard him rummaging around while doing her laundry, wondering what he was up to.

"I don't know," Rosa said. "He never lets me in there."

"You think he might be building something? Maybe a new music room or a studio to record his music?" Kimberly asked.

"He doesn't play anymore, Mom," Rosa said, and put the finished potato in the pot of water Kimberly had placed next to her.

She knew the girl was right, but it still hurt to hear. Somewhere deep down inside, she had hoped that Joseph was still playing, that she just hadn't heard him.

"I know," Kimberly said.

"Doesn't Dad like music anymore?" Rosa asked.

"I don't know. Maybe he just needed a little break. He does teach it at the school, so maybe it became a little too much, you know?"

"He never used to get tired of music," Rosa said pensively, while looking out the window into the yard. It was beautiful how the sun fell on the brown leaves.

"Well, people change," Kimberly said, while secretly hoping Joseph hadn't. She missed him the way he used to be. Now he was all about reading business magazines and he wore a shirt and tie even when they were just at home on the weekends. Where he used to annoy her by strumming his guitar from morning to nighttime or playing the drums late at night, now he was so quiet, she hardly felt he was there anymore. And he was constantly talking about bourbon. Oh, the bourbon. He would buy some bottle with a name Kimberly never had heard of and talk about it for so long, how it was made, on what type of wood, and it gave it this character and that color and whatnot. She would let her thoughts drift off just to stay awake.

"I think he likes to play cards now," Rosa said.

"He does what?"

"He plays card games."

Drinking bourbon and playing card games? What was that? Joseph never used to like any of those things. Joseph was a beer-man and he hated playing any type of games, whether it was board games or card games, because he always lost.

"Who does he play with?" Kimberly asked, slightly nervously.

Their daughter shrugged. "I don't know."

Kimberly shook her head, wondering if she even knew her husband at all. This side of him, she didn't recognize at all.

"I'm done," Rosa said.

"Good job," Kimberly said. She leaned over the sink, wiped some flies away, picked up most of the peelings, and let the rest fall into the garbage disposal.

"Cover your nose," she said to Rosa.

The disposal smelled the worst when they ran it.

"Here comes the smell."

Kimberly squeezed her own nose and pushed the button. The disposal grinded and roared, then ran smoothly before it started making a very strange noise.

KRA-KUNK! KRA-KUNK! KRA-KUNK!

Kimberly sighed, annoyed. She was so sick and tired of this disposal and this kitchen in general. Now it was acting up again and the smell was worse than ever.

"Eeeewww," Rosa exclaimed.

Kimberly leaned over to stop it. Her finger hadn't reached the button before the disposal made a new loud sound—SPLUSH!—and she was covered in something wet. It went in her hair, in her face and, worst of all, in her mouth. It also covered all of Rosa's face, and when she finally stopped the disposal and looked at her, Kimberly realized they were both covered in blood.

28

[MAY 2016]

"Tell me we'll find him."

It was late at night back at the house. Shannon was sitting in the darkness, looking out at the square lit up by the streetlamps. We had looked all night in the parking lot and the restaurant. The kids and Shannon had been sent home first, before the police came, because we couldn't risk her being seen once the reporters arrived when they heard of the missing baby. Meanwhile, an Amber Alert had been sent out.

I walked into the bedroom looking for her at one a.m. I was exhausted. We still hadn't seen any trace of Tyler anywhere. Leaving the place was the hardest thing I'd had to do, but Bellini told me to go home and take care of my family, that she and her colleagues would keep looking all night.

I sat next to her on the wide windowsill. I felt awful. I rubbed my eyes. "We'll find him," I said, my voice hoarse from calling the boy's name, even though I knew he wouldn't answer.

"Why do these things keep happening to me?" Shannon asked. "First it was Angela, now Tyler?"

The burden of guilt fell heavy on my shoulders. "I'm afraid it has to do with me," I said, heavyhearted. This was exactly why so many people in my line of work got divorced. "Remember last year what happened to Austin? It's my work. I'm an easy target. I'm so sorry, Shannon. It's my fault."

Shannon finally looked at me. "You think Tyler was kidnapped?"

I shrugged. "I don't know how else to explain his sudden disappearance."

She crept closer, leaned over, and kissed me. The kiss startled me. I thought she would be upset with me. That she would be ready to leave me.

"I can't believe you never even once asked me if I had been drinking," she said. "Most men would have asked that as the first thing, given my story."

"It never occurred to me," I said.

"That's why I'm marrying you. You always think the best of people. You bring out the best in me."

I swallowed hard. Could this really be? Could she really love me despite my work? "We *will* find him," I said, this time more convincingly than the first.

Shannon nodded, tears springing to her eyes. "You think this is related to Betsy Sue, don't you?"

"It's a very strange coincidence if it isn't."

"True," Shannon said. She paused. We sat in silence for a little while before she spoke again.

"So, you think it was kind of a way of punishing us for taking Betsy Sue back to her real parents? Tit for tat or an eye for an eye?"

I sighed. "Something like that, I'm not quite sure. Is it too crazy? I'm too tired to think. You wanna lay down with me for a little while?"

Shannon nodded. We both walked to the bed and lay our heads on our pillows. I held her in my arms while she cried.

"I miss him so much," she whispered through tears.

"Me too. Try and get some sleep. Tomorrow is a new day," I said.

Shannon closed her eyes, but she didn't fall asleep. Neither did I. I stared out the window at the streetlamp outside, making my plan for how to get our boy back.

29
[MAY 2016]

They had placed two officers from the Savannah Police Department to guard the gate. The mansion behind them seemed to be twice the size of the house I was building back home in Cocoa Beach for me and my family. *Maybe even bigger than that*, I thought, as I approached it. It was located in the historic downtown and in walking distance to the place we were renting for the week.

"I'm sorry, sir. No visitors today," the officer told me, as I parked the car and walked up to the gate.

"I know them," I said. "I want to talk to them."

"I'm sorry, sir, but the family has requested peace and quiet."

"I understand that, but could you just press that

buzzer and tell them I'm here? My name is Jack Ryder," I said.

"Sorry, sir. I can't do that."

I pulled out my badge and showed it to him. He shook his head. "I'm sorry, *Detective*, but I have my orders."

I groaned. I was so tired after not sleeping all night. As I was about to turn around and leave, a car drove up to the gate. Mr. Hawthorne poked his head out. "Detective Ryder?"

I turned around.

"You can let this man in," Mr. Hawthorne said to the officers.

He pushed the buttons and opened the gate. He drove in and I followed him on foot. He approached me as I reached the front door.

"Hello again, Detective Ryder," he said and shook my hand. "I'm so sorry about the guards at the gate, but the press has been all over us since Adelaide…since *Betsy Sue* came home, and I can't be too careful. They still haven't caught the guy and you never know if he's lurking out there, trying to steal her back. Come on in. I'm sure Heather will be very excited to see you again. We feel like we owe you everything."

I was quite baffled to be greeted like this. I followed Mr. Hawthorne inside where his wife, Heather, was waiting in the living room.

"Oh, Ron. I'm glad you're home," she said.

When she saw my face, she seemed everything but as excited as her husband had said she would be.

"Hello, there…Detective," she said, cautiously approaching me.

"Ryder," I said. "You can call me Jack."

"All right…Jack." She looked nervously at her husband and rubbed her hands together. "Can I get you anything? Water? Coffee?"

"You don't have to trouble yourself on my behalf," I said. "Mr. Hawthorne was so kind to let me inside."

"Call me Ron," he said from the other end of the living room, where he was already pouring bourbon into two glasses. It was barely ten in the morning and way too early for me to be drinking that kind of strong alcohol.

"Forget the water and coffee," he said and handed me the bourbon. "The boys need something stronger, don't they?" He laughed and lifted his glass for me to salute him. I did and barely sipped my bourbon while he emptied his. Heather stood behind him, rubbing her hands together anxiously.

"So, what brings you here, Detective…Jack."

I cleared my throat. "I wanted to check in on Betsy Sue. See how she was doing. Has she been talking?"

Heather drew in a deep breath, then shook her head, her eyes hitting the floor as she spoke. "No. We can't get her to speak at all."

I nodded and looked at the glass in my hand,

wondering if it would be impolite to put it down now. I held on to it for a little longer. "I thought so," I said.

I stared at them, wondering if I should tell them about Tyler, but something told me not to. I don't exactly know why, but I decided to not do it, at least not yet. They wouldn't be able to help me anyway. I hoped their daughter could.

"Could I see her?"

Heather shook her head. "No. Today is not good."

Ron poured himself another bourbon and let his wife answer for them. "Why not?" I asked. "Is she not feeling well?"

"No. No. She's fine. It's just…well, we're trying to get her to forget everything from her past, and you play a big part of it. Seeing you might rip up some memories that…" Heather stopped talking and I sensed something behind me. As I turned, I saw Betsy Sue. She was standing right behind me, her blue eyes staring up at me from her still very pale face.

"My God, you scared me," I said and put a hand to my chest. My heart was pounding behind it.

"I've told her to not sneak up on people like that," Heather said. " She does it all the time. Scares me half to death every time."

I knelt in front of her and wiped a lock of hair away from her face. "How have you been, pretty girl?" I asked.

She didn't answer.

"It's no use," Heather said. "She refuses to talk to anyone. The police, the psychiatrist, us, anyone."

"Except she did talk to me," I said.

Heather paused. I could tell she was curious as to how I got the girl to talk to me. I needed that curiosity. I needed them to want me to talk to her.

"She told me a lot of things when I was alone with her. Could I get some time alone with her today? I think I could get her to talk again. Maybe I would be able to get her to open up a little."

I looked up at Heather, who seemed very uncomfortable with the situation. "I don't think that's a very good idea. Right now she needs peace and quiet. She needs to forget everything that has happened…"

"I don't see any harm in him talking to her," Ron said, and put a hand on his wife's shoulder.

It made her back off. I got the feeling that he was used to having the last word around here.

Heather nodded. "Well then…go ahead."

"Thank you," I said, heartfelt.

Right now Betsy Sue was my only connection to the man who might have taken my son. I had to get her to tell me more about this strange doctor and where she had been held the past five years in order to find him, and hopefully my son as well. I knew it was a long shot; I knew it was going to take a lot of effort, given how little she had talked about her time in captivity so far. But it was worth a try. It was all I had right now. And time was not on my side.

I turned and looked at Betsy Sue again. "So…could you maybe show me your room? I would love to see it."

30

[MAY 2016]

The room was sparsely decorated and not at all for a child. A bed, a dresser, a walk-in closet, a row of shelves with many books, all thrillers and mysteries or biographies. None of them for children. On the bed lay a deck of cards.

Betsy Sue walked to the bed and sat down. I closed the door behind us. "Was this your room when you were younger?" I asked.

She didn't answer. I wondered if the Hawthornes had simply removed everything that reminded them of their daughter when she disappeared. Would I do that myself once I was forced to realize my child wasn't coming back?

I wasn't sure. But, then again, life has to go on at

some point, right?

"So do you have any of your toys from back then? Maybe a teddy bear?"

Betsy Sue looked at me, and then shook her head. I walked to her and sat down on the bed.

"You like cards?"

Betsy Sue looked up at me with a smile.

"Do you want to play Black JACK?"

She almost yelled my name and it startled me, since it was a lot of sound coming from a girl who hadn't said anything at all while I was there.

I looked into her eyes while wondering what to answer. I hadn't played Black Jack for many years, not since I was in my early twenties. It had been a problem for me back then. I became addicted to it. I couldn't stop. Not till my parents interfered. By then I owed a lot of money. They paid everything and took me home to live with them till I got back on my feet. Cost them a huge part of their savings. I hadn't held a card in my hand since then.

But I couldn't tell Betsy Sue that, and this was her way of reaching out to me. This was an opening; she was actually speaking and communicating with me. How could I say no to that? What harm would one game do?

"Sure."

The girl picked up the cards and started shuffling them in the same way I remembered the dealers did at the casinos. I stared at her, completely baffled at her way of handling the cards so professionally.

"I take it you have played before?" I asked.

She didn't answer and started dealing. I looked at my cards. A five and an eight. "Hit me," I said. She turned a card. The queen of hearts. "Argh."

"Bust. House wins." She collected the cards.

She dealt new cards. I asked for another hit. "Who taught you to play this?" I asked.

"The Doctor," she said.

"Would the Doctor play with you?"

"Sometimes."

"Who else would you play with?" I asked, while she gave me another card. "Hit me again."

She put down another card, leaving me on twenty.

"I stand," I said.

She shrugged and gave herself another card, making her hit precisely twenty-one. "Sometimes I could convince Miss Muffit to play, but she always lost."

"Miss Muffit liked to play too? Who else liked to play?"

"All the girls liked to play," she said. "It could get really boring at the house sometimes." Betsy Sue looked at me. "House won again."

"You're good," I said, making a mental note that there had been several girls, more than just Miss Muffit. It made my heart throb, thinking that this doctor apparently had kidnapped many girls and kept them hidden.

"One more, please. So, who would you say you liked the best of the girls at the house? Who was your best friend?"

"Millie. She was fun to play with."

"Millie, huh? Why was she fun to play with?"

Betsy Sue shrugged, then dealt another round. I asked for a hit again.

"Who else was there with you?" I asked.

"You ask a lot of questions, don't you?" the girl said.

"I'm curious. Did you like it there at the house?"

"I guess. It was my home. It was all I knew. I was born there."

I wrinkled my forehead. "You were what?"

"You need to get those ears checked," she said. "You always ask me to repeat things."

"Okay, you're right. I heard you the first time; I just found it hard to believe. I mean, your parents say you were born at a hospital and that you lived with them for your first five years. Did the Doctor tell you that you were born at the house?"

Betsy Sue shook her head. "No. Rachel told me; she took care of me when I was a baby."

"Aha. Rachel. Is that one of the other girls at the doctor's house?"

Betsy Sue laughed. "No, silly. She used to live there."

"What do you mean? She escaped like you did?"

Betsy Sue shook her head. "No. She can't leave the house."

"So what do you mean that she used to live there?" I asked, annoyed. This was making no sense at all.

"Are you playing cards or what?" Betsy Sue asked.

"Of course, sorry, hit me again." I looked at the card, but didn't really pay attention and asked for another hit. "So what did you mean when you said she *used* to live there?" I repeated.

"She lived in the house till her dad killed her."

Again with the ghost stories! I need answers! Damn it. I need to find my son.

I fought the urge to get mad at Betsy Sue, but held it back. I had to remember what she had been through. Of course she had a hard time dividing reality from fantasy. This doctor had held her hostage for five years. It was vital that I kept her talking now. She was the only one who could lead me to this doctor.

"So, tell me more about the Doctor," I said. "What did he look like?"

Betsy Sue shrugged again. "House wins," she said, and gathered the cards before she added. "Again."

She dealt us new cards and I realized she wasn't going to answer my question.

"What can you tell me about the house you stayed in? Was it a big house?"

Betsy Sue nodded.

"How many of you lived in the house? How many

girls were there when you were going to sleep at night?"

Betsy Sue started counting on her fingers. "Thirteen," she said.

I almost dropped my jaw. Thirteen? Thirteen girls? Could they all have been kidnapped? It was almost too much to believe.

"Is that counting the ghosts as well?" I asked.

"No, silly. Ghosts don't sleep. They don't have to."

"Of course not. Hit me again."

She turned a card and I folded. "Bust again. House wins."

"Do you miss it there?" I asked, as she shuffled the cards again. "Do you miss being at the Doctor's place?"

"I guess," she said.

"So, why did you run away?"

"I told you I wanted to see the ocean."

"But why now? And why didn't you just go back after you had seen the ocean?"

She shrugged and looked at the cards.

"I didn't want to become a ghost myself."

31

[MAY 2016]

I chewed on her last sentence for quite some time, wondering if there was any other way to interpret it other than that the doctor was going to kill her. Was he going to kill the other kids as well? Had he killed this Rachel? Would he kill Tyler?

"How do you even become a ghost?" I asked, my voice trembling slightly at the thought of Tyler in that house with that man. I pushed it back. "I always wondered about that."

"Rachel told me she was killed with a knife," Betsy Sue said. "But the boy at your house died of a fever."

"Yellow fever? Did he tell you that?" I asked, thinking about what our tour guide had told us about the several outbreaks of yellow fever in the town in the eighteen-hundreds that killed thousands of people. How did Betsy Sue know about this, being locked up the past five years? Had the doctor taught her?

"No, he hasn't told me how he died yet. I recognized the yellow color to his skin. I've seen it before. We had one girl in our attic that had died of the same. His name is Billy, by the way. The least you could do is learn his name, now that he is so fond of you."

"All right," I said, chuckling. I liked her imagination. It was quite impressive, but I guessed that it had to be, to keep her alive these many years trapped inside that house with the doctor. Could it really be that he had thirteen girls there with him? Or was that part of her imagination too? It was hard to tell. I sincerely hoped it was just her making up stories. "I'll try and remember that."

"Good. Ghosts like it when you remember their names."

"But you said you didn't want to become a ghost. Why were you afraid of that?" I asked.

"Because it was my turn."

"Your turn? What do you mean?"

She shrugged. "It just was. When the doctor brings you this dress and brushes your hair and sings this song for you, that's when you know that you're going in the chair."

"What chair is that?" I asked.

"The chair on the top floor. Hit or stand?"

"So the doctor makes you sit in a chair? How is that dangerous?"

"Hit or stand?" Betsy Sue said.

"Stand," I said. "The dress that he brings you, is that the one you're wearing right now?"

Betsy Sue didn't answer. I guessed it was. "Do you think you could find the house again, if I drove you around town?" I asked.

Betsy Sue didn't look at me and didn't answer either.

"We could do it just the two of us, if your mom and dad will let us."

Still no answer.

"We can bring Shannon? I'm sure she would love to come," I said, playing on the fact that Betsy Sue loved Shannon and her music.

But she still didn't answer me.

"You see, I really need to find him." I grabbed her arm and tried to make her look up, but she kept staring at the cards in her hands.

"He has taken Tyler."

She gave herself another card. Then she finally looked up at me. Her eyes sparkled in the light from the window. I thought I saw tears in them, but I wasn't sure.

"Player wins."

32

[NOVEMBER 1990]

The blood was everywhere. In her mouth, on her cheeks, and even in her nostrils. Kimberly whined and wiped her face with a towel, then continued to wipe Rosa as well, who was also covered all over her face and dress.

"What is that, Mommy, what is it?" she whined.

"It looks like blood," Kimberly said.

"Why? Why did blood come out of the sink, Mommy, why?"

"I don't know, Rosa. Stand still."

Joseph, who had heard the screams, came up from the basement, a cigar in the side of his mouth. "What the heck are you doing up here?" he asked, chewing on the cigar. "What's with all the noise?"

"There was blood coming out of the sink, Daddy," Rosa wailed. "It sprayed all over us."

Kimberly had the taste still in her mouth and spat in the sink, then grabbed some water and tried to wash her mouth out, but it still remained. Blood had sprayed on all the cabinets as well.

Joseph approached them, looking at them with terror in his eyes. "What on earth…?"

Kimberly's hands were still shivering as she pointed at the sink with the garbage disposal.

"We ran it and seconds later we were covered in it."

The cigar changed position in Joseph's mouth. Now it was hanging from the other side. "I'll be…"

He walked to the disposal and looked down. Blood was all over the sink as well, and the stench coming from it was unbearable. Joseph took off his suit jacket, rolled up the sleeve of his white shirt, and put his hand into the hole. His hand moved around for a bit before he finally pulled it back out, holding the remains of a rat. It was completely shredded to pieces.

Rosa screamed. Kimberly turned around and threw up in the sink next to it.

"That's it," she said when she was done.

Joseph was still holding the animal in his hand, and she felt sick to her stomach just watching it.

"I want out of this house."

Joseph took a baffled look at her. "What? Because

of a rat that crawled into the garbage disposal and died there?"

Kimberly opened the faucet and let the water run so she could wash her mouth again. She gurgled and spat, then gurgled again. "It's not just the rat. It's everything, Joseph. I don't like it here."

Joseph rolled his eyes while the cigar changed position in his mouth again. He took it out and held it in the hand that wasn't holding the rat. Smoke emerged from his mouth when he spoke.

"Not that again? I love it here. So does Rosa, right Rosa?"

The girl didn't answer.

"You can't seriously tell me you want to move out of this wonderful house because of a stupid rat?"

"This house hates me!" Kimberly yelled. "Everything has been going wrong since we moved in here. All these bad things keep happening, and then there's you. You've changed, Joseph. You've changed a lot."

"Me?"

"Yes, you. Since when do you wear a suit? Since when do you smoke cigars or play cards? Who do you even play with down there?"

Joseph shook his head. "What are you talking about? If anyone has changed since we got here, it's you. You keep walking around in the kitchen talking to yourself or to the birds or whoever it is you talk to, and you tell me you hear all these things at night that I don't. Now you say that the house doesn't want us here? What does that even mean? Since when do houses have emotions or opinions? I say you're the one who is changing. For your information, I love it here. This house is awesome and I am staying. I think Rosa is with me, right Rosie?"

The girl nodded. "I like it here, Mom. There are so many hiding places and there's always something to do. I love to play with the birds in the attic. They bring me things if I feed them."

"Guess that settles it, then," Joseph said, and placed the cigar back in the side of his mouth. "Now, if you'll excuse me, I have a rat to get rid of."

33

[MAY 2016]

"**B**etsy Sue has agreed to go for a drive with me around town to see if she can recognize any of the houses, and maybe we can figure out where she was kept."

I looked at Heather and Ron in the living room of their immaculate home. Betsy Sue had followed me downstairs to talk to them.

Heather's eyes stared, terrified, at me.

"No," she said with an air of finality. "She can't do that. It'll be too much for her."

"This could be of great help in the investigation," I said. "We need to find this guy. According to Betsy Sue, he has other children there. Other children who have parents that miss them and want them back. It is vital we find them before they're hurt. You, of all people, should understand."

"Listen," Heather said. "We know about your son. We understand why you would think our daughter could help you, but it's not okay for you to come here and…"

"How do you know about Tyler?" I asked.

Heather looked at Ron. He cleared his throat. "It was on the radio just now."

My heart dropped. Shannon. Our cover had been broken. They knew we were here. And even worse. They knew about Tyler.

"I know it must be hard for you, believe me, I do, probably more than most people," Ron said. "And I understand that you might think that Betsy Sue can somehow help you, but there is no proof that it is the same person who took your little boy as had Adelai… Betsy Sue for all those years. It could just as well be some crazed fan or someone wanting a ransom."

"Betsy Sue promised me she would go for a drive, please…" I said.

"How do we even know she has agreed to it? She hasn't spoken one single word to us, or to you while we were present. How do we know you're not just making all this up?" Heather asked.

"She speaks to me. She really does," I said.

"Say something, Betsy Sue," Ron said. "Talk to Detective Ryder."

The girl stared at them, but no words came out.

"There you have it," Ron said definitively. "She doesn't speak. Not to you or anyone else."

I felt like exploding with rage. But the fact was, they could deny me the right to ever see her again, so I had to hold it back. I had to keep my cool.

Ron put his hand on my shoulder. "I think you should go back to your fiancé. I have a feeling she needs you right now."

"Please…" I said.

"I don't want her going through all this," Heather said. "She's been through enough. Right now we're trying to forget the past around here and figuring out how to be a family again. She doesn't need to keep ripping up the past like that. Besides, the doctor said she can't have too much sunlight. Her eyes and skin need to get used to it. We let you talk to her, didn't we?"

I knew I had lost. I knelt in front of Betsy Sue and looked into her light eyes. "Do you remember anything about the house you were kept in?" I asked. "Anything that could lead me to Tyler? Please?"

"Mr. Ryder!" Ron said. "I need you to leave now."

"Please?"

The girl stared at me like she was deciding what to do. I sensed she wanted to help me, but that she didn't want to speak when her parents were in the room. I wondered why that was. She had told me she spoke to me because she trusted me. Did that mean she didn't trust them?

Betsy Sue leaned over very close to my ear, then whispered:

"The girl screams at night."

34

[MAY 2016]

So far, I had little to go on. I knew he was a doctor, I knew he was holding thirteen girls at his house that I suspected he had kidnapped, even though I found it quite incredible that someone would be able to kidnap that many girls and not be found by the police. I knew he lived and kept the girls in a house here in Savannah, that he had killed some of them, that he played Black Jack—oh, yeah—and that he liked country music and that one of the girls screamed at night.

It sure wasn't much.

I drove around downtown Savannah, looking at every house I passed, wondering if this could be it, if my dear baby Tyler was somewhere behind those walls. I worried that this doctor had him and, at the same time, I worried that he didn't. That I was following the wrong lead and that Tyler had, in fact, been taken by some crazed fan or for a ransom, like Mr. Hawthorne suggested. I couldn't help thinking that the doctor had only taken girls before, never a boy. Why would he take Tyler?

I called Shannon when I left the Hawthornes' house and told her what I knew. She tried hard not to get hysterical. I could tell she was struggling to hold back by the tone of her voice.

"It's all over the news, Jack," she told me. "I don't know how they found out, but they did."

"It's okay," I said. "We knew it might happen, right? We'll get through this too. Together."

I worried that Shannon would start drinking again. She was so fragile and this was tearing at her severely. I couldn't lose her to the bottle once again. I simply couldn't.

"They're saying I have a history of alcohol abuse and debating whether I'm fit to be a mother or not," she said, sounding a lot calmer than I expected her to be in this situation. "They're talking about how it happened with Angela too. But Angela wasn't even with me when she was kidnapped."

"It was completely different back then," I said. "Don't listen to them."

"They don't care. They just want me to look like I can't handle being a mother. Now they're talking about Joe, calling him my abusive ex-husband, and saying how I was accused of murder once, ugh; they're bringing up everything, Jack. My entire story. Everything."

"Turn off the TV, will you?" I said.

"They're setting up outside the house now," she continued. "I see cameras being set up. I don't want to have to go through this once again, Jack. I hate this. Maybe we should just elope to some island far away, and then I promise to never sing again."

I laughed. Not because it was funny. There was nothing funny about this situation. It was more to comfort her and because this entire situation had become completely ludicrous. Here we were, just trying to get married without too much fuss about it, and look at us now.

"Let them tell their stories," I said. "Meanwhile, we focus on getting Tyler back. That's our main focus right now. How are the kids?"

"They're all right. Sarah is with them in the yard. They're scared, Jack. I've been trying to calm them down, to tell them we'll find Tyler, but I get the feeling they don't really believe me much. I'm trying, though. I really am. Thank God for Sarah."

We hung up. I was looking out the window of my rental car, studying another row of old houses, built the typical Southern Savannah-style. How do you hide thirteen girls? According to Betsy Sue, they didn't even go into the yard. She had been deprived of sunlight for years and years.

"The girl screams at night," I mumbled angrily. What

kind of a hint was that? How was that supposed to help me?

My phone rang. I picked it up. It was Detective Bellini. "I have the list of doctors living in the area for you that you asked for. I'm sending it in an email."

35

[MAY 2016]

ittle Miss Muffit looked so pretty in her dress. It was long and pink and had flowers on it, just the way it was supposed to. It wasn't the right dress and it would never be, since Betsy Sue had taken the right dress with her when she ran away. But the doctor had sewn a new one just for little Miss Muffit.

Now she was standing in the big living room while all the girls sat in a circle around her.

Little Miss Muffit was crying, tears rolling across her cheeks. It was a big day for her; the Doctor couldn't blame her for being emotional. The Doctor felt a little emotional too.

Little baby Rikki Rick was in his car seat, watching Miss Muffit getting ready for her next step. The girls were all cheering her on. They knew and understood what was going to happen and why.

The Doctor walked to her and grabbed her hand. "Are you ready?"

Miss Muffit looked up, tears springing from her eyes. "Please," she said. "Please, don't do this to me."

The Doctor grabbed the brush and started to brush Miss Muffit's hair, gently using long strokes. Then Daisy brought her the rose, which she placed in the girl's hair.

"There. Now you look just…perfect."

"Please. I'll be good…"

The Doctor shushed her, then reached out a hand. Miss Muffit looked at it, while the girls all cheered.

"Miss Muffit. Miss Muffit!"

"Come on, then," the Doctor said. "It's time."

Miss Muffit sniffled and wiped away her tears, then grabbed the Doctor's hand in hers.

"Good girl. Say goodbye now."

All the other girls were quiet as she waved goodbye to them. They walked upstairs and stopped by a small door. Miss Muffit gasped when the Doctor put the key in and turned it. The Doctor could feel how the little girl shivered. She held on to her hand tighter, so the girl didn't try and run.

The door opened and the small dark room opened up. Miss Muffit had the same terrified look on her face as the others before her when she spotted the chair. None of the girls were ever allowed in there, yet all the girls knew what was in there, even though they had never seen it with their own eyes.

Now, she saw it. And she knew it was the last thing she would ever see.

Miss Muffit whimpered and tried to pull away, but the Doctor held firmly onto her. Forcefully, the Doctor pulled her into the room and placed her in the chair, where her arms and legs were strapped down.

"Please," Miss Muffit pleaded over and over again. "I'm sorry."

There was a small window next to the chair that she was allowed to look out of, and the Doctor made sure to pull the curtain to the side.

"There you go, my little muffin. You're all settled."

Miss Muffit cried hard now. "Please, let me go. Please."

The Doctor couldn't blame her for her tears. But she knew this was going to happen. They all grew up knowing it.

The Doctor wiped away a tear from her cheek, then bent over and kissed her gently.

"Goodbye, my muffin," she said, feeling a pinch of sadness in her heart. She had really grown to love Miss Muffit.

The Doctor walked to the door and took one last glance at the girl, who was now struggling to get loose, before the door was closed and locked with the key.

The Doctor stood for a few seconds, an ear leaned

against the door, while Miss Muffit's screams finally emerged through the walls.

36

[MAY 2016]

I tried my best. But of course you can't just drive by a house and tell if someone is being held kidnapped there. I looked for signs of toys or girls in the windows, or even houses that seemed to be closed off, but no sign of the thirteen girls or my Tyler anywhere.

Next, I tried the list that Detective Bellini sent me and drove through five addresses of doctors living in the historic downtown area. I rang the doorbell of all five of them. Three of them weren't home, but I spoke to their wives, who hadn't seen my boy or any girls. Two were home. I showed them a picture of my son, asking them if they had seen him. They both answered that they had already seen the picture on the news and that they were terribly sorry they couldn't do more to help.

When the afternoon was approaching its end, I drove to the harbor and parked the car. I walked to the dock where I had found Betsy Sue sitting, dangling her feet over the edge, and sat down.

The shadows on the harbor were growing longer as the sun was about to set behind me. The water in the harbor was calm. A big French tanker was about to dock further down.

I went through everything Betsy Sue had told me in my head, wondering if I had missed something, if there could be anything that I hadn't realized could help me.

I stared at my dangling feet, wondering about Betsy Sue and if it would have been better if I hadn't helped her that evening when I spotted her sitting here.

And that's when I saw it.

I spotted the birds circling the area not far from where I was sitting. It drew my attention because there were so many of them. Hundreds maybe. Hundreds of black ravens. They were making an awful noise, some seemed to be fighting over something. I got up, jumped down on the rocks below me, and avoided the water hitting my feet just because it was low tide. I walked closer and saw some of the birds disappear into the walls, maybe a crack or—as I realized when I got closer—a tunnel.

I stopped at the entrance of it and waved off a couple of ravens that tried to scare me away from whatever it was they had found in there to fight over.

"Shush!" I said and walked inside the tunnel.

It was about three feet wide and about the same height. The rocks underneath me were slippery. There was about an inch of water in the bottom, soaking my shoes. Old bottles, used syringes, and empty wrappers from burgers and pizza told me the place was used only by homeless and others seeking it for shelter. I followed the birds into the damp smelling claustrophobic tunnel and felt my heartbeat quicken the further in I got. I found my phone and used it as flashlight, lighting the ground under my feet as I got closer to where the many birds where gathering.

By the sound of their fighting, and the smell in the tunnel, I had a gut-wrenching feeling inside that this was a little too familiar for a homicide detective. I had seen this type of scene before.

Too many times.

Deep inside the tunnel, I reached an area where all the birds were hanging out and I shone my light on it, holding my sleeve up to cover my mouth and nose. I shooed the birds away and what came to light was even more terrifying than what I had imagined.

Ravens were still picking the meat off the bones, some fighting over pieces in the air. A familiar emptiness in my gut gripped me when I knelt down as I had done so many times before when called out to a homicide investigation. I shone the light on one of the bones. I had been on the job long enough to realize that by the size and length of it, these bones didn't belong to a full grown adult.

37

[MAY 2016]

Shannon couldn't stand it anymore. She couldn't simply sit there in that old wooden house where the entrance was barricaded by reporters, waiting for her son to come back. She knew Jack was doing everything he could to get their boy back, but still she felt like she had to act too. Sitting there in the living room watching the TV crews do their thing had to be the most frustrating thing in the world.

There had to be something she could do. Something.

Shannon got up from the chair with a groan. She walked to the kitchen, where Sarah was fixing dinner for the kids. They all went quiet when she entered.

"Any news?" Sarah asked.

"Did Jack find him?" Angela asked.

Shannon shook her head, walked to the refrigerator, and grabbed a bottle of water. Emily was sitting by the TV, while the kids were eating at the counter. Her plate still sat at the table next to her, untouched.

"I'll be going out for a little while. Do you think you could look after the kids?" she asked. "I don't know when Jack will be back."

"Sure. No problem," Sarah answered, slightly surprised. "But how will you get past them?" Sarah nodded towards the windows. They had pulled the curtains to make sure the photographers didn't take pictures of the children.

Shannon drank from her bottle, then put it down. "I have my ways."

Shannon kissed Angela on the head and smelled her hair, remembering her as a little baby and how much she loved holding her in her arms. The memory overwhelmed her as soon as she started thinking about Tyler. Her stomach was in one big knot from the deprivation, the longing to be able to hold her son again.

"Are you alright, Mommy?" Angela said.

Shannon nodded and kissed her, forcing a smile. "I will be. Soon."

She left the house using the back door into the yard. It was almost dark when she climbed the neighbor's fence and slid into their yard, wearing a hoodie she had borrowed from Sarah.

She walked onto the street on the other side of the

neighboring house, and no one noticed her as she disappeared around the corner.

She reached the Hawthornes' big mansion fifteen minutes later and without being recognized by anyone. The officer at the gate called inside. They agreed to let her come into the driveway. Mr. Hawthorne greeted her there. He didn't seem happy to see her.

"Your fiancé was here earlier," he said. "We've already done what we can for you."

"I know. I was just thinking…I had a connection with Betsy Sue that night we found her. I just really wanted to talk to her. I don't know where else to turn."

Mr. Hawthorne shook his head. "I'm sorry. It's late. My wife isn't feeling well. Betsy Sue needs her rest. I'm sorry about your son, Miss King, but there really isn't much we can do."

Shannon sniffled. "Please?"

"No. I'm sorry. I have to ask you to leave. I don't want anyone to know you're here and end up with the entire press corps parked out here. We've heard what they say about you."

"Is that why you won't let me see your daughter?" Shannon asked, surprised. "Because of the lies they tell about me?"

Mr. Hawthorne didn't answer. He didn't have to.

"I can't believe you. We brought your daughter back to you. My fiancé…and you believe that? Just some stupid lies?"

"Is it a lie, Miss King? Is it all lies? Didn't you lose your daughter? Don't you have a drinking problem?"

Shannon took a few steps back. The resentment in Mr. Hawthorne's eyes felt like arrows to her skin. How could he say such things? Was he right? Were they all right? Was she just a terrible mother?

"I should…" she walked backwards towards the gate.

"I think you'd better."

Shannon turned, put the hoodie up over her head, and left through the gate. As it closed behind her, she felt a tear escape the corner of her eye. She wiped it away. For the first time since she was pregnant with Tyler, she desperately craved a drink.

To hell with all of them.

38

[DECEMBER 1990]

"**B**e careful, my dear."

Kimberly walked fast to keep warm and hardly noticed Mrs. Thomas till she spoke. Kimberly stopped and looked at her, her grocery bag in her arms.

"Excuse me?"

Mrs. Thomas was sitting in her rocking chair on the porch in front of her house, her legs wrapped in a blanket.

"Be very careful," the old lady said, rocking back and forth.

"Of what, exactly?"

The old woman stopped rocking. She stared at

Kimberly. "The room. Don't go in the room upstairs. Evil lurks in there. It's where it happened."

The woman leaned back in her chair and started rocking again.

Kimberly sighed, exhausted. The groceries were heavy in her arms and she was freezing. When they moved to Savannah, she had given all of her heavy coats to one of their neighbors, thinking she was never going to need them again, but last night they had gotten three inches of snow and it was still freezing.

Kimberly wanted to ask more, but decided not to. For all she knew, the old woman was just babbling; she was probably senile as well.

"Have a good day," she said and hurried past Mrs. Thomas's house to get to her own.

Inside again, she put the groceries in the kitchen. Joseph was in the basement, as always. School was out for Christmas break, and ever since the break had started, he had been down there constantly, even sleeping in there. Some nights she had woken up to find the bed empty on his side. What he did down there, she still didn't really know and, frankly, she had stopped caring.

Rosa was in the attic, as she liked to be when she couldn't play outside. Kimberly had decorated the place a little and put a small table and some chairs up there, so she could draw or write, and she had made a reading corner with pillows, so Rosa could catch up on her reading over the break.

Kimberly put the groceries away, but still couldn't shake what the old woman had said. Somehow, she knew exactly what room it was that Mrs. Thomas had talked about. There was a door up on the fourth floor that she had passed on many occasions, but never opened. Was there really a room in there? And, if there was, what was in there? Kimberly had tried to open it once, but it had been locked by a key and she didn't know where to find the key. She had then decided it was probably just a cabinet, since it didn't seem like there was enough room for more behind it.

Kimberly wasn't sure exactly what made her go up the stairs. Curiosity? Stupidity? Fear? She didn't know. But her heart rate skyrocketed as she reached the fourth floor and looked at the door at the end of the hallway.

Why was it again that she shouldn't open it? The old woman never told her. She just said that she shouldn't do it.

Pah, what does she know? Old senile woman.

Kimberly approached the door. She could hear Rosa playing in the attic with those creepy ravens making an awful noise. Kimberly hated those birds. They pooped everywhere and always tried to pull her hair if she approached them. Luckily, they never touched a hair on Rosa's head.

"Don't open the door." Silly old fart.

Kimberly reached out and grabbed the handle, expecting it to be locked like it was the last time she tried. But this time it wasn't. This time, when she turned the handle, the door creaked and opened.

Maybe it was just stuck the last time.

Kimberly gasped, her heart thumping in her chest while she pulled it all the way open.

A chair? Is that it? Is that why the old woman told me to not open the door?

Kimberly broke into loud laughter and walked inside the small room. It had slanted ceilings on both sides which made it hard for her to stand up straight. There was a small window looking into the street and next to it a chair, an old-fashioned wooden chair that looked very uncomfortable to sit in.

"What's so dangerous about that, old woman?" Kimberly laughed. "It's just a chair, for cryin' out loud."

39

[MAY 2016]

called Detective Bellini right away and she arrived a few minutes later with her entire team, including her partner, Detective Nelson. The tunnel was blocked off. I stayed to watch the crime scene techs arrive. I told everything to Bellini while she served me some coffee from her thermos in a white plastic cup.

"It gets to me every time," I said.

"As it should," she said.

I nodded in agreement and sipped the hot coffee. I thought about Shannon. I had tried to call her cell several times to let her know I was going to be late, but she hadn't answered. It worried me.

"There were no tracks in the tunnel," I said.

"What do you mean?" Bellini asked. She had nice eyes. I hadn't noticed before. Blue like mine. Her hair was dark. A rare combination. Her skin had been destroyed by acne when she was younger and left visible scars. Other than that, she was pretty. I wondered what she would look like if she pulled that ponytail out and let her thick hair fall down. The big ring glistened in the light when she moved her finger to her temple to scratch an itch.

"The body of the young girl was laying headfirst in the tunnel," I said, "but there were no signs of her body being dragged across the rocks. If she had crawled in there on her own, there would have been tracks. If she had been dragged in there, there would be some sort of indication of that too. But there was nothing."

Bellini nodded and drank her coffee when a crime scene tech named Sutton came out. Bellini served him some coffee as well.

"So, what do we have?" she asked, after giving the guy a chance to swallow his coffee.

"Female, white, about ten years old, I'd say."

"How long has she been dead?" I asked.

He shrugged. "Maybe a year? Could be more. Could be less. It's hard to tell when there's water present. She's not the only one, though."

I almost lost my coffee on the pavement. "What?"

"There are more bones in there. Older ones," he said with an exhale. "Way older. It's going to take some time to figure out where they came from…how many we're talking about. Right now it's all a mess."

I almost didn't dare to ask, but I had to. "More children?"

The tech nodded and sipped his coffee. "I'm afraid so."

It was easy to tell from the size of the bones. I knew a guy like Sutton could tell just by looking at them.

"I see," I said, feeling sick to my stomach.

"But there are a few full-grown bones as well. I haven't been through them all. They could also belong to a full-grown teenager. It's hard to tell just by looking at them. But what I can say with certainty is that they haven't been in this spot for long; otherwise, the homeless and drug addicts that hang out here would have seen them. Plus, the birds and other animals would have eaten more of them."

"So they were moved?"

"It appears so." He finished his coffee and nodded. "Well, back to work."

I grabbed my phone to see if Shannon had called me back, but she hadn't. It made me worried. What was she doing? She couldn't be sleeping. I knew she would be up, wandering around, worrying about our baby. What was she up to? She was supposed to stay by the phone in case there was news. I didn't like it. I decided to call Sarah.

She picked up right away. "Any news?"

"No. But I'm trying to get a hold of Shannon, is she there?"

"No. She went out."

"She went out? But…but she was supposed to stay at the house and wait for news," I said.

"I think she needed some air."

Air? Oh, my. Please tell me she didn't…

"Are the kids okay?"

"Yes. They're fine. Just getting them ready for bed."

"I'll be right there," I said and hung up, trying hard not to panic. Where the heck was she?

"I think I should be getting back. It's late," I said to Bellini.

40

[MAY 2016]

Come on. Drink it. You know you want to.

Shannon was staring at the bottle inside the brown bag in her hand. She had walked around the corner from the Hawthornes' house and bought it at a small convenience store before it closed for the night. Now she was looking at it, tears running across her cheeks. She had found a bench on the square in front of the Hawthornes' house. A woman walking her small poodle walked around her, pulling her dog closer. Shannon couldn't blame her. She probably looked like a homeless person with the hoodie over her head and bottle in her hand.

See if I care.

She felt so many different and conflicting emotions,

sitting there with the bottle in her hand. Part of her wanted to feel nothing, to not care anymore what anyone thought about her and just get really drunk. The other part knew she wouldn't be able to stop it once she started, and that it would destroy everything she had worked so hard to build. But what did she really have to lose? If they never found Tyler, it would be the end of it anyway. She would never be able to live on without him. Might as well get it over with. Nothing worse than sitting and waiting for your world to crumble and doing nothing about it.

Might as well go out with a bang.

Shannon sobbed and screwed the lid off the bottle. She wiped a few tears away with her sleeve, then lifted the bottle up to salute the house in front of her.

"Here's to you, Hawthorne. For making me realize it was no use anyway, that nothing would ever change."

She lifted the bottle and put it to her mouth, just as she spotted a figure in the Hawthornes' yard climbing over the wall.

"What the heck?" she said and lowered the bottle.

The two officers at the front gate didn't see anything; they were talking and smoking cigarettes. Shannon could see them glowing in the dark. Meanwhile, the figure jumped down from the wall and ran onto the street. As it emerged under the street lamp, Shannon realized it was a child.

Betsy Sue!

Shannon got up, threw the bottle in the trash can

next to her, then followed the girl. Shannon let her run out of sight of the officers, around the corner, and into the bigger boulevard before she closed in on her and grabbed her by the shoulder.

"Where do you think you're going?"

The girl turned with a gasp.

"Caught ya', didn't I?" Shannon asked and pulled down her hoodie so the girl could see her face.

"Shannon King," she whispered.

Shannon pulled the hoodie back on, just to make sure no one else recognized her as well. "Where are you running off to?"

"I...I..." Betsy Sue stopped herself. "Nowhere."

"Well then. If you're not going anywhere, then maybe it would be wise to get you back to the house and your parents, huh?"

Betsy Sue shook her head. "No. Please. I have to help her."

Suddenly, it was getting very interesting. "Help who?"

"Miss Muffit. I have to help her."

Shannon lifted an eyebrow. "You were going back, weren't you? You were trying to go back to that place where you were kept? Why?"

"I have to," she said. "It was a terrible mistake that I left. I need to go back."

Shannon knelt in front of the girl. "Do you mean to tell me you know where it is?"

Betsy Sue shook her head. "No. I don't. I got lost in the tunnels last time I tried."

41

[MAY 2016]

burst through the crowd of reporters, who had apparently decided to spend the night in front of our rental house.

"Jack, how's Shannon?"

"Any news of the baby yet?"

"Is Shannon drinking again?"

"Was she drunk when she lost Tyler?"

"Are you filing for a divorce?"

I stopped and looked at the reporter who had asked the last question. "We're not even married yet," I said. "At least get your facts straight."

"Is that why you're here? To get married? Was that why you came to Savannah? Is the marriage off now;

is it, Jack?"

I continued without answering any more questions and closed the door behind me, the reporters still yelling behind it.

"Are you going to file for full custody of Tyler after this?"

Shannon was standing in the hall when I entered the house. I breathed a deep sigh of relief.

"Where have you been?" I approached her, trying hard to calm down. All the way back in the car, I had been getting myself all worked up, thinking that Shannon had fallen off the wagon again.

"Did you…?"

She shook her head. "But I was about to."

"Phew. You have no idea how relieved I am to hear that." I grabbed her in my arms and held her tight. "You scared me. I was so afraid you had…well, you know."

"Taken a drink. It's okay, Jack. You can say it."

I nodded. I knew she was right. We had taken a few weeks of therapy in the fall together to improve our relationship and talk about the things that were hard to talk about. Like her drinking and my desperate fear that it would happen again, that she would start drinking and leave me. In therapy, I had learned it was all right to ask her directly if she had been drinking or even if she craved a drink. Openness was important, the therapist explained. Shannon was also allowed to tell me if she wanted a drink, and I had to be open towards hearing it and know that it was a big part of her.

It was still hard for me to talk about it.

"Yes. That's what I feared. But you didn't?"

She shook her head again. "I bought the bottle, but then I saw something that made me stop. Come with me," she said, and grabbed my hands in hers.

I followed her upstairs to the bedrooms, where she stopped in front of the room we had temporarily turned into the nursery for Tyler. I didn't understand.

"What…?"

She shushed me and opened the door. Inside on the floor, playing with Tyler's favorite teddy bear, Bobby, sat Betsy Sue.

"What the heck? What is she doing here?" I asked.

Shannon closed the door so Betsy Sue couldn't hear us talking in the hallway.

"I found her. She was running away from the Hawthornes. I spotted her and brought her here."

"You did what? You mean to tell me her parents don't even know she's here?" I asked, startled.

Shannon put a hand on my shoulder to calm me down. "She was running away, Jack. She doesn't want to be with them. Can you blame her? I mean, they didn't even seem happy to get her back. Especially the father. I don't like him."

"Well, I don't either," I said, thinking about how Betsy Sue's room had been so empty, how they had decided to not save any of her things. It was like they didn't expect her to come back, and it had me worried that something was off with them. "But that doesn't give us the right to take their child." I took in a deep breath, trying to calm down my beating heart. It didn't work. Panic soon spread. "They're going to think we kidnapped her," I said. "Oh, my. This is bad, Shannon. We can't keep her here."

I rubbed my chin, thinking about all the consequences this could lead to.

"She can help us find Tyler," Shannon finally said.

I looked into her eyes. I'd had the same thought when I asked her to drive around with me.

"You think?"

Shannon nodded. "She was trying to get back. That's why she left, Jack. Only she can't find her way back. Last time she tried, she got lost, she told me. But I was thinking that if we helped her, then maybe…"

"She could lead us there," I said.

"But she doesn't seem to remember anything when I ask her about it," Shannon said. "She said something about tunnels and getting lost in them, but that's all I could get out of her. I tried to ask more, but now she has shut up like an oyster. I don't know how to get her to talk again."

"I might," I said. "Do you know if there's a deck of cards around here somewhere?"

42

[MAY 2016]

shuffled the cards Shannon had found for me and sat in front of Betsy Sue. "Ready for another round?"

The girl looked up, but she didn't look at me, she seemed to be looking right next to me.

"Billy wants to play too," she said.

"Billy…? Oh, right … Billy, the boy…with the yellow skin, right?"

"Right. Make sure you give him cards too."

I nodded, thinking I better play along if I wanted to get her to talk. I put out cards for both her and Billy. Betsy Sue looked at her cards for a long time.

"Do you think Billy wants another card?" I asked.

Betsy Sue looked in his direction, then shook her

head. "No. He stands."

"And you?"

"Hit me."

I gave her another card. "So, tell me about when you lived with the doctor at the house. What is the first thing you remember?"

Betsy Sue kept looking at her cards. "My four-year-old birthday," she said.

What? That makes no sense!

I decided to play along. Any information we could get out of her would be of help. "So, why do you remember that particular day?"

"Because that's when Miss Muffit arrived," Betsy Sue answered.

"Miss Muffit. You seem to talk a lot about her. How old was she when she came to the house?"

"She was a baby, duh. Just like I was when I got there."

Okay, now it's just getting weird.

"What do you mean you were a baby?" I asked.

"I was a baby. Just like Miss Muffit was a baby, just like Bibby Libby was before me. She took care of me when I was a baby, like I took care of Miss Muffit. It's how it works. Are you going to give me another card or what?"

"Of course," I said, and put down another card, making her bust. "Billy wins," she said.

"Now we haven't seen his cards yet, so we don't

know…" I said and turned Billy's cards. To my astonishment, he had exactly twenty-one. "Wow. You're right."

I gathered the cards and started a new round. "So, when you arrived, there was another girl there," I said. "What happened to her?"

"She is a ghost now," Betsy Sue said and picked up her cards.

"She died?"

Betsy Sue shrugged. "Nothing really dies."

"Was she put in the chair?" I asked, remembering what Betsy Sue had told me back at the Hawthornes' house.

Betsy Sue nodded. "Hit me."

I gave her another card.

"Billy wants one too," she said.

I gave him one as well. I couldn't stop thinking about how it was possible for her to have been so young, to remember her four-year-old birthday when she had been five when she was taken from the Hawthornes. According to them, she had been stolen from a playground one day when they had taken her to Forsyth Park and she had been playing with some kid. Mrs. Hawthorne had turned her back on them for one unforgiving second, she had stated afterwards, and when she looked again, her child was gone. It was every mother's worst nightmare.

I shook the thought and decided that maybe the girl

just got it all mixed up. Maybe the doctor had told her she was a certain age. She probably didn't even know when it was her real birthday. Yes, that had to be it, right?

"What else do you remember from your time at the house?" I asked.

"I remember when it rained outside, all the birds would come to the attic and we would play with them. They brought us gifts."

"The ravens?" I asked.

"Yes. I stand. Billy wants another card."

"Tell me about the tunnels," I said and gave Billy an extra card. "Shannon said you got lost in them? Was that how you escaped? Did you go through a tunnel?"

Betsy Sue nodded, then looked at Billy. "He stands. He has twenty-one again."

I laughed and picked up his cards, only to discover that she was right. I stared at her, wondering how on earth she could have known that. She had to have some special skills when it came to cards.

"How did you find the tunnels?" I asked and gathered the cards again. I started to shuffle them.

"Miss Muffit didn't dare to go down there," she said.

"But you did?"

"Yes."

"Why didn't Miss Muffit dare to go in there?"

"Because of the smell."

"But you didn't care about the smell?" I asked and

gave us all new cards.

"I could smell something else," she said.

"And what was that?"

Betsy Sue looked up. "The ocean. I could smell the ocean."

"How did you know about the ocean?" I asked.

"We had books to read at the house. Only I couldn't read them. I looked at the pictures. But there was one with pictures of the biggest oceans. Bibby Libby taught herself to read a little. She told me about it." Betsy Sue went quiet. I guessed she was sad to think about Bibby Libby, who must have been like a mother, or at least a big sister to her.

"Did Bibby Libby also tell you about the tunnels?"

Betsy Sue nodded. "She showed me where to get into them. There's a door in the kitchen floor, you know. A carpet usually covers it and there's a big heavy chest on top of it, but Bibby Libby found it and showed it to me one day. She said she was going to escape just before she was sent to the chair."

"But she never made it?" I asked.

Betsy Sue shook her head. "Hit me."

I gave her yet another card, while trying to figure out how life had been for such small children, constantly knowing that at some point they were going to die, that they were living on borrowed time.

Quite the burden for such young children.

43

[MAY 2016]

"When I found you, you were sitting down at the dock. There's a tunnel there, did you come through that tunnel?"

Betsy Sue nodded.

"So that's why you smelled the ocean from the house. But when I came to you, you had been out for quite some time and you wanted to go back, am I right?"

Betsy Sue nodded again. "But I couldn't."

"You say you couldn't get back. Why? Did you try to go back through the tunnel?"

"It was blocked. Rocks blocked my way."

"Did you see the body?" I asked. "'Cause I was just in that tunnel earlier tonight and we found a dead body, maybe more than one. Did you see that?"

"Sure."

I was amazed at her indifference to the brutal sight. "Did it scare you?"

"I knew they were down there," she said. "That's where they all go. Bibby Libby was the last one."

So Bibby Libby was the body I found.

"So the tunnels are where the doctor puts the dead bodies when he kills them?" I asked.

"Yes."

Just like they had been used back in the days to hide the many dead people when the yellow fever killed thousands in Savannah. They hid the bodies there to not create panic. Apparently, this doctor had found good use for them again.

"So, you couldn't get back through the tunnel even though you tried, am I right?" I asked.

"That's what I said. Are you going to play or not? Billy needs a card."

"All right," I said and gave Billy a card. He won again, naturally, and Betsy Sue started to yawn.

"I think maybe we should continue our game tomorrow," I said, even though I desperately wanted to keep talking with her. I doubted we would be able to keep her with us, and feared they would come for her in the morning. I wondered if I should call Bellini and tell her we had the child, but then decided not to. It was wrong, but sometimes you do things because you have to, not because they're right. And right now I believed that Betsy Sue was my ticket to finding Tyler and this was our only chance.

There was a sofa that could be folded out to a twin bed in the room that I helped her get into. I tucked her in under the blanket and gave her Tyler's teddy bear to hug.

"Billy wants to know if he can play with us again tomorrow," she said with her eyes half closed.

"Of course he can," I said just before she dozed off. I snuck out and closed the door behind me. Shannon was waiting in the living room.

"So? What did she say?"

"She did escape through that tunnel, like I thought. The one down by the harbor where we found the bodies tonight. But she couldn't get back through it again. Something must have happened," I said.

I grabbed my laptop and started searching for maps of the tunnels of Savannah. Videos of people walking in some of the tunnels came up, so did a lot of webpages writing about it, but there were no maps. According to one webpage, the tunnels remained a mystery even to the residents.

During one of the outbreaks, over five thousand people died due to Yellow Fever. The doctors would take the bodies of people who died into the bottom room in the hospital, then smuggle the bodies into the tunnels late at night and take them to the ship, where they were dumped at sea.

I googled earthquake in Savannah, but found only old stories of earthquakes shaking the city a hundred and twenty-five years ago, and then another in the early nineteen-hundreds.

I scrolled further down, and then found something else. An article from the day before. It told the story of how the restoration of a building in downtown Savannah had led to its collapse on Saturday evening. Neighbors said it sounded and felt like an earthquake. Luckily, no one was in the building at the time, but the collapse had caused a break of the main waterline and flooded a few basements in the neighborhood.

I looked up at Shannon. "It collapsed. The tunnel collapsed," I said. "That's why she couldn't get back."

"What are you talking about?" Shannon asked.

"There was an accident. Saturday night. When the building collapsed, it must have blocked off the tunnel and the water washed out the body from its hiding place in the tunnels. That's why there was water in the tunnel."

"That could explain why she couldn't get back, but how does that help us?" Shannon asked, looking tiredly at me.

"The house that collapsed must be close to the house we're looking for," I said. "It must be in the same neighborhood."

44

[DECEMBER 1990]

Later that evening, they all had dinner in the dining room. Kimberly served roasted duck with parsley potatoes. Joseph came in last. He had left his cigar in the basement, but still reeked of smoke.

"Why are we eating in here?" he asked and stopped at the end of the table. "Is that duck?"

"Sit down, dear," Kimberly said.

"What's going on here?" Joseph asked, puzzled. "You never make duck. We never eat in here."

"Things change. People change," she said. "Now, please, sit down and join your family for dinner."

Joseph sat down. He took some potatoes and some gravy on his plate and Kimberly served him a piece of duck.

"This is really good, Mom," Rosa said and ate from her duck thigh.

"Elbows off the table, dear," Kimberly corrected her.

"What?" Rosa asked.

"Use your manners, dear. No elbows on the table. You know that."

"You never told me that before."

"Well, I am now." Kimberly smiled and poked Rosa's elbow off the table. "Now, guess where I went today?"

"You went to the store," Rosa said. "Twice."

"And I met that nice Mrs. Thomas on my way back the first time," Kimberly said.

"She's not nice," Rosa said skeptically. "She's creepy."

"Whatever. But she told me we had a room upstairs that I had no knowledge of. You know that door that has been locked since we moved in, that we believed was a cabinet? Well, as it turns out, there is a room behind it. Mrs. Thomas told me not to open it, but I did, and I found the cutest little room. I was thinking we could make it my sewing room."

"You opened the door?" Rosa asked, as her jaw dropped.

"Yes, dear. There was nothing but a chair in there."

Rosa dropped her fork. It made a loud noise as it hit the plate. "You do know what that chair was used for, don't you?"

"No. I don't. I don't think I care either."

"I would like to hear it," Joseph said with a grin. He drank from his bourbon that he had brought with him from the basement. His hair was slicked back using gel. It made him look very different.

"All right," Rosa said, while her mother rolled her eyes. "The story goes that this house was built for a general in eighteen sixty-five. Across the street from here, on the other side of the square, lived a young boy that the general's daughter loved to play with. Her father disapproved of their friendship, but the girl kept running across the street to be with him. Legend says that General Milton punished his daughter by putting her in a chair in the room upstairs, placing the chair by the window, and tying her to the chair. She could see her best friend playing outside and she could do nothing but sit and watch.

After days of sitting in such a humiliating position, the little girl died of heat stroke and dehydration. They had no air conditioning back then and the house could get stiflingly hot. It is said that you can still catch a glimpse of the girl up there from time to time, especially at night, where she sits looking out the window."

Kimberly stared at her daughter. Joseph had stopped chewing and was looking at her with his eyes and mouth wide open.

Kimberly was the first to burst into laughter. Joseph soon followed along.

"Where do you hear these stories?" she said, once the laughter had subsided and she had wiped away her tears.

"This one I read in the book I found in the attic," she said, grabbed her plate, and got up from her chair. "May I be excused?"

45

[MAY 2016]

"The girl has been identified."

Detective Bellini called me the next morning while I was in the middle of breakfast with my family and Betsy Sue. The past many hours had passed in a haze of frustration for Shannon and I. The kids were excited to see Betsy Sue again and they were teaching her how to play Minecraft on the iPad. Betsy Sue, who said she had never seen an iPad before, took a quick liking to it, and was soon as involved in the game as the rest of them.

"So, who is she?" I asked and walked out of the kitchen. "Her name is Luanne Johnson. We had her in the database, DNA and everything. She disappeared twelve years ago. She was taken from a house downtown where she was sleeping by an open window. Police believed a homeless mentally ill person had taken her. Someone said they saw a person in a long torn coat and beanie by the window on the day the kid was taken."

"So, she was just an infant?"

"Three months old."

Just like Tyler.

"Case was never solved," Bellini continued. "We have notified the parents. The problem is, where the heck has she been for twelve years?"

"With the doctor," I mumbled, thinking a pattern was beginning to take shape, and it didn't involve any kids being stolen when they were five years old.

"I'm beginning to think your little theory is holding water," Bellini said.

"I think you might want to look into who else has gone missing as infants from Savannah. That might help you with the identification of the other remains we found," I said.

Bellini sighed deeply. "This is getting messier and messier every day. And, get this. Hawthorne called us this morning. Betsy Sue is missing again."

"Really?" I said, wondering if she would fall for my little act. I had never been good at lying.

"I'm guessing she's not at your house," she continued. "Hawthorne suggested she was, but I assured him you would have called me and that she wouldn't be able to get past all the reporters at your door without being seen."

I laughed. It wasn't funny, but I needed to ease up my own tension. I was getting in way too deep here. But I wasn't ready to hand over the girl yet. I had a feeling she could help me today. I had to at least try. For Tyler's sake. "No, that wouldn't be possible."

"All right. I guess I'll be looking for her today. The Hawthornes are pissed. If you ask me, it looked mostly like the girl ran off. There were no signs of intrusion anywhere when I checked the house. They told me Shannon was there last night?"

"She wanted to talk to Betsy Sue. Mr. Hawthorne told her she couldn't. She went home after that," I said. It wasn't a complete lie.

"That's what I figured. He's certain you had something to do with her disappearance, but I think I managed to get him to calm down. I mean, we have to remember, you're the one who brought her back in the first place, right?" she said, chuckling.

It didn't sound like she was amused either. I could tell she wasn't completely convinced I had nothing to do with it. She wanted to believe it. All I needed was for her to give me a little time. Just a little more time. They would get the girl back as soon as I was done.

"All righty, then. Let me know if you hear anything," she said. "We still have the entire force looking for your son as well. We're following a lead from someone who said they believed to have seen a figure run from the parking lot about the time that your son disappeared. I have a good feeling about this one."

"That's great, Detective. You go get my son back."

"I will, Jack. Don't worry. As I said, I have a good feeling about this lead."

I hung up and went back to the kitchen. Shannon looked at me, worry deep set in her eyes. "Who was that?"

"Bellini. We need to hurry."

46

[MAY 2016]

Savannah wasn't exactly showing its most beautiful side. Yesterday's sunshine had disappeared, and now it was raining from a heavy gray sky. I knew there was low pressure in the Atlantic, giving great waves to Cocoa Beach but bad weather up here. I had seen all the pictures on Facebook of my friends enjoying the great swell and started to curse the fact that we'd decided to come all the way up here for the wedding. None of this would have happened had we only stayed home.

Shannon sat next to me, hands in her lap, looking at her fingers, turning her rings like she always did when she was nervous. Betsy Sue was in the back seat being eerily quiet. I wasn't used to children her age being so silent. Mine would have at least asked for a snack by now or told me they were thirsty. Betsy Sue didn't say anything unless we asked her.

"So, do you recognize anything?" I asked, trying to get her to talk. We were driving around the neighborhood that surrounded the house that had collapsed on Saturday. The house itself was blocked off and we started out there, then drove down the street.

The old houses lay like pearls on a string. One more gorgeous and pompous than the next. Many lovely gardens, big trees with lots and lots of Spanish moss. They all looked the same after a little while. Tall, multi-paned windows with dark green shutters, wrought-iron balconies, and broad concrete staircases leading to their entrances. Many had big pots of flowers outside. It was all very pretty, and had the circumstances been different, I'm sure I would have enjoyed it.

But I didn't. I still felt sick to my stomach, missing Tyler so badly, worrying about him and whether he was all right. Was he being fed properly? Up until now, Shannon had breastfed; how was this doctor-person feeding him, if he was at all? It made me so furious to think about.

Betsy Sue didn't answer. She looked out the window at the houses passing by, while I drove slowly down the street, but she didn't seem to recognize anything at all. At least, not yet.

"Maybe she doesn't know what the house looks like from the outside," Shannon said, her voice trembling slightly. "I mean, if she has never been outside. She escaped through a tunnel in the house, so she didn't even see it then."

She had a point. But there had to be something she knew from growing up. She must have looked out the windows, right?

"She'll recognize something," I said. "She has to. Look out now, Betsy Sue. Here are some small shops. Do you know any of them?"

Betsy Sue leaned to the window and looked outside. I slowed down even more and the car behind us started to honk, annoyed, before it finally passed us, the driver telling me I am number one with his finger out the window.

The small shops turned out to be an old-fashioned bookstore, a doll store that sold antique dolls, a small café with a sign telling us they were selling shrimp and grits, and a thrift shop. I looked at Betsy Sue in the rearview mirror to see if she reacted to any of it, and thought I saw her twitch, but I wasn't sure.

"Any of it seem familiar?" I asked again.

The girl shook her head and leaned back down.

"It's okay. It'll come," I said and drove on. The houses got bigger and harder to see from the road, since the big trees out front were covering them up. I slowed down again as we reached more residential areas.

"Anything, Betsy Sue?" I asked again.

Still nothing but a shake of the head. But then something happened.

"Stop," Betsy Sue said.

I hit the brakes and brought the car to an immediate stop. "What is it? Did you see the house?"

The girl pointed.

"I don't understand. Is this the house?" I asked. I looked at the odd one-story house on the lot next to us. It didn't seem big enough to house thirteen girls.

"The birds," Shannon said. "She's pointing at the ravens."

47

[MAY 2016]

The trees in front of the house were packed with ra-vens. Black noisy creatures. Shannon hated birds and really didn't want to have to get out of the car, but for the sake of her son, she did.

The ravens surrounded Betsy Sue as soon as she got out. They were sitting everywhere on her...in her hair, on her shoulders. She laughed and petted them like she knew them.

Shannon shivered and tried to stay her distance from the girl so none of the birds would get in her hair. That had always been her biggest fear...that they would get tangled up in her hair like that time when she was a kid. The thought made her shiver again.

"You think this is the place?" she asked and

approached Jack.

He shrugged. "The girl asked us to stop here, so we might as well check it out. Come, Betsy Sue."

Jack grabbed the iron railing and signaled the girl to walk with him up the stairs to the house. Betsy Sue followed him to the front door, two birds sitting on each of her shoulders and one on top of her head. Shannon stayed a few steps behind.

"Hello?" Jack yelled, while knocking on the front door.

The front porch had big flowerpots that had recently been watered, and everything was very neat and well maintained.

It took a few seconds before the door opened slightly, and a man appeared in the crack.

"What do you want?"

Jack held up a picture of Tyler so the man could see it. "We're looking for this child."

The eyes in the door crack looked at the picture, then spotted Betsy Sue behind Jack, who was still infatuated with the birds. His eyes blinked a few times, then the door opened completely. He was as immaculately dressed as his house looked, his blue T-shirt tucked into his pants.

The man looked at Betsy Sue. "The girl. The ravens like her."

Jack looked at her too. "Yes. She has a way with the birds."

Shannon didn't like the way the man looked at the girl and pulled Jack's sleeve. "Jack, we need to go."

"Not yet," Jack said. "Say, have you seen this girl before?"

The man didn't answer. "Ravens are a bad omen," he said. "They bring death with them. Some people believe that ravens are damned souls or sometimes even Satan himself."

Shannon stared at the man while a wave of shiver ran down her spine. "He doesn't know anything, Jack," she said. "Let's move on."

"Well, I heard they were very smart animals too," Jack said. "Can even learn to say a few words. At least that's what I read. We don't believe in the supernatural, bad omens, and all that."

Speak for yourself, Jack. Geez!

The man groaned while staring at Betsy Sue and the ravens. "Death follows in their trail. They've been here for several days now. I try to keep them out of my back yard with my shotgun, but they always return. It's like when my father died. The days before he fell to his death, the ravens circled his house non-stop."

"So, you haven't seen the boy?" Jack continued, obviously not interested in the man's strange stories. "Do you know if anyone around here might have had a baby recently? Maybe you've seen them walking around with stroller, maybe you've heard a baby cry recently?"

The man shook his head. "It's best you leave now."

"This was a mistake," Shannon said. "We're sorry to

have disturbed you."

Jack handed the man his card just before they left. "Call me if anything comes to mind. Anything, all right?"

The man took the card, then closed the door.

"That was weird," Jack said, as they walked back to the car. "Lots of strange people in this town."

Shannon wanted to get away from the birds quickly. She hurried into the car and closed the door, while Jack talked to Betsy Sue outside before he got in too. Betsy Sue stayed out for a little while longer.

"What's she doing?" Shannon asked.

"Saying goodbye to the birds," Jack said with a scoff.

Shannon stared at the little girl, who seemed to be talking eagerly to the birds before they all took off at once, filling the air with their screams.

Shannon felt chilly when Betsy Sue finally got back in the car and she put on her jacket.

"Now what?" she asked, looking at Jack for answers.

48

[DECEMBER 1990]

"What book?"

Kimberly followed Rosa up to the attic. Rosa went to her reading corner that Kimberly had decorated for her and picked up an old book. She handed it to her mother. "This one. I found it in the corner over there, tucked in behind the rafters."

Kimberly looked at it. She opened it and flipped through a few pages. It was all handwritten. So rare to see anymore.

"Who wrote all this?" Kimberly asked.

Rosa shrugged. "I haven't read much of it. Just the story of the general and his daughter. I flipped through the first pages and fell into the story. There's even a picture of them here, see?"

Rosa pulled out an old photograph and handed it to Kimberly. It was torn and yellow on the edges. It showed the general, sitting proud in a chair, leaning on a cane, behind him stood his wife and daughter. Kimberly stared long at the family, her heart throbbing in her chest.

The general was dressed in a black suit with a bow tie, and in his mouth he had a cigar. His hair was combed back.

He looks just like Joseph!

"Do you mind if I take this book downstairs and read it?" she asked.

Rosa shook her head. "Sure."

Kimberly leaned over and kissed her daughter, then left the attic. She walked into her bedroom and sat on the bed, the book between her shaking hands; she began reading the book, starting with the beginning. The first page told her it was all written by her late Aunt Agnes. Kimberly felt a shiver, thinking of her aunt speaking to her through this book from beyond the grave.

"If you're holding this book, that means you're living in the Blackwood residence. These are the tragic stories that people living in this house have encountered; read them so they won't happen to you. Consider this book a warning."

The first story was the one of the general. It told the tale of how he had built the Blackwood house to suit him and his family after he had retired from the army. It also told how he got involved with con men and gamblers after his retirement and how his wife suffered from the way he changed as soon as they moved into the house.

"She hardly recognized him anymore. He changed the way he dressed, he changed the way he spoke, and he took up smoking, even though he had always sworn he would never touch those things. He drank bourbon and played cards and she hardly saw him anymore. He was always cooped up in the basement, where she had no clue what he was doing. He was no longer the same man she had married."

Kimberly could hardly read the words. She found it hard to breathe. Yet, she turned another page in the book and yet another one. She couldn't believe how much these descriptions resembled her own life. Even how the general's wife believed the house was haunted and was trying to get rid of her. Kimberly read and read and hardly even noticed the footsteps outside her room. When the knock sounded on her door, she screamed, startled.

Joseph opened the door and peeked inside. "What? You look like you've seen a ghost," he said, while chewing on that awful cigar in the corner of his mouth.

Kimberly breathed, her hand resting on her chest, her eyes closed for just a second. "You startled me."

Joseph gave her a lopsided grin and rubbed his chin. "Sorry about that."

"What's going on?" she asked, remembering that Joseph usually never came out of the basement these days, unless it was to eat or to leave the house.

"I have something to show you," he said, still smirking from ear to ear. "Down in the basement."

49

[MAY 2016]

We drove around all afternoon in the neighborhood and knocked on a lot of doors, showing the picture of Tyler, but without luck. To be honest, Betsy Sue was not of any help at all. She didn't recognize anything. I was frustrated when Shannon finally managed to convince me to stop and go home. I threw my jacket on the floor and kicked off my shoes when we entered the house. Abigail and Austin came running down the stairs towards the back entrance that we had used to not be seen by the few reporters that were still camping outside.

"Did you find him? Did you?" Abigail asked and threw herself in my arms.

Looking into her blue eyes made my heart melt.

"You didn't, did you?" she continued.

"Not yet," I said. "But we're not giving up."

"Does that mean Betsy will stay here for one more night?" Abigail asked.

I looked at Shannon, who shrugged.

"I guess so," I said and put Abigail down.

Austin stared at us from a distance. Angela came up behind him. Poor sweet sensitive Austin. He was having a hard time dealing with this. I grabbed him and pulled him close. "We'll find him; I promise you we will," I said, hugging him tight. "Your dad doesn't give up. You know that."

Austin sniffled and nodded. I messed up his hair and sent him along. Angela saw the chance and put her hand in his as they walked back up the stairs.

Abigail grabbed Betsy Sue's hand and pulled her. "Come on. We're playing hide and go seek."

"Do you want something to eat?" I asked Shannon.

She shook her head. "I'm not hungry."

"Neither am I, but we got to eat, right?" I said.

Shannon followed me out to the kitchen where Sarah had left the pot with stew on the stove for us. I grabbed a couple of plates and poured some on them. Shannon and I ate in silence.

"You think we should ask Betsy Sue if she's hungry?" I asked, remembering that she hadn't eaten since this morning either. I couldn't stop worrying that Bellini would stop by and find the girl here. It would get us in a lot of trouble.

"Maybe we should just take her back to her parents," Shannon said. "I'm beginning to think it wasn't such a great idea after all."

I nodded. She was right. "I just have this feeling that if I could get more time with her, then I could get more information…"

"We've been with her all day," Shannon said. "It got us nowhere."

"I just know the house has to be there somewhere," I said. "It has to be in that neighborhood."

"I'm tired," Shannon said, tears in her eyes. "I'm so exhausted, Jack. I need to sleep, but I can't. I need to eat, but I can't. My throat feels swollen when I try and I can't swallow. I want so desperately for this to be over. I am so tired."

I grabbed her and held her for a long time while she rested in my arms. Like me, she couldn't even cry anymore.

"What are we going to do, Jack?" she asked, looking into my eyes again.

I opened my mouth to talk, but no words came out. Not because I couldn't speak, but because I didn't know how to answer her.

For once, I had no idea what to do.

PART THREE:

STAND: To stop asking for more cards.

50

[MAY 2016]

The sound of the bus driving up the street had the Doctor's attention immediately. It happened every day at this hour. The Doctor told the girls to be quiet and put them all in the living room, handing them each a book. Rikki Rick was sleeping in his crib and the Doctor hoped he wouldn't wake up from all the noise from the street.

The Doctor checked all the curtains to make sure they were closed, but not without keeping a constant eye on the baby. The Doctor had hardly slept the past two nights, but it was worth it. It was what had to be done.

"The next house on our tour is very exciting," the Doctor heard the tour guide say over the speakers inside the bus. The passengers took out their cameras and phones and took all their usual pictures.

"I think I saw something," one of them said, her voice trembling in excitement. "I think I got a picture of it, see?"

"What is it?" someone else asked.

The Doctor's eyes rolled behind the curtain. *Always the same.*

"It looks like a girl. Up there in that top window!" she shrieked.

"Yes," the tour guide said. "Many people have seen the little girl in the window. The story goes about this house that it was built by a general back in eighteen-sixty-five."

The Doctor watched while the tour guide once again told the old tale of how the general had put the girl in the chair and listened to them all gasp as they realized the terror of how his daughter died in that chair.

The Doctor shook her head. It was always the same. No one knew the real story, and no one was ever going to.

"It is said that if you keep very still, then you can still hear her scream," the tour guide ended her story.

The entire bus went quiet. "I think I heard it," someone said with a gasp.

"Me too," another said.

The tour guide laughed, obviously satisfied that once again her tour was a great success and that these people would go back to their families and friends and tell them about what they had seen and heard and soon more would come.

"But, as if the sad tale of the general and his daughter isn't enough," the tour guide continued, "there are other mysterious tales surrounding the Blackwood house. In nineteen-fifty-eight, a family from Pompano Beach, Florida, moved in with their four daughters. The general had left the house to his nephew when he died, but knowing its story, the nephew didn't want to live in it and so it was left empty for decades until his own daughter inherited it after his death. The adults went out one evening, and when they returned later, they found three of the girls dead, along with their nanny. Two of them were still inside the house, and one was sprawled on the front porch, as if she was slain while trying to escape. The youngest daughter, age four, was the only one still alive. The sad and senseless murders were never solved. In the nineteen-eighties, the house was briefly rented out and a lot of college students from nearby Savannah College of Art and Design lived there. They heard pounding, heavy pacing, crying and, even more mysterious, a lot of giggling. I once spoke to a local resident who sometimes feels such a negative emotion emanating from the house that she can't even walk past it. In nineteen-ninety, a family of three moved into the house for a time, but they all disappeared while living there."

"So, it's empty now?" a passenger asked.

"Except for the ghosts," the tour guide said cheerfully.

"I mean, who would want to live there, right?"

All the passengers agreed that they certainly wouldn't and spoke among themselves while more pictures were taken. The bus's motor started up again while the tour guide continued:

"You're lucky you got the picture," she said to the woman. "On other tours, I have experienced odd things at exactly this point, in front of this house, like cameras breaking when trying to capture a picture of the girl, several batteries suddenly dying simultaneously, even once a camera went up in smoke right here."

The crowd gasped and giggled nervously, some were trying to decide just how seriously to take these things they'd been told.

Then the driver rang his bell and the bus was off once again. The Doctor watched as it disappeared down the street, then turned to look at the girls. They all seemed so sad, so the Doctor started to sing to drown out Little Miss Muffit's bone-piercing screams from upstairs.

51

[MAY 2016]

I tucked Betsy Sue in the foldout bed in the nursery. Betsy Sue was hugging Tyler's bear, and somehow that made me angry. It was Tyler's bear, not hers. Maybe I was just so frustrated with her after today, I couldn't stand it. Shannon took the other kids and made sure they got to bed. She didn't want to be with Betsy Sue either. Yet, neither of us wanted her to go back to the Hawthornes either. Probably because she was our only hope. Not much of one, but still our only.

"Billy is sad," she said when I had put the covers on her. "He's crying."

I stared at the little girl, trying hard to figure her out. What was she talking about? Why couldn't she just be ordinary and talk to me normally. I decided to play along once again.

"What is he sad about?" I asked.

She shrugged, fumbling with the bear's right ear. "I don't know. He won't tell me."

Was she talking about me here? Was I the one who was sad and she didn't understand why?

"Maybe he's sad because he misses Tyler," I said. "Is that it?"

Betsy Sue looked up at me. "I think so. But I also think he is mad at me."

"Why is that?" I asked.

"Because I was supposed to help."

"Okay. Well maybe you could tell him that I believe you did the best you could. Could you say that to him?" I asked.

She nodded. She was still fumbling with the bear's ear, handling it pretty roughly. I wondered if I should tell her to stop, that I was afraid she might break Bobby. It would destroy Shannon if she did.

Barely had I finished the thought before the ear came off. Betsy Sue held the ear in her hand, then looked up at me. The look in her eyes was strange. She didn't seem sad.

"Oh, no!" I exclaimed and took the bear from her. "Why would you do that?"

Betsy Sue didn't answer. She watched me freaking out over the teddy bear like she was enjoying it. It made me very uncomfortable.

"It happened to Daisy once," she said, her voice eerily calm. "The Doctor fixed her."

I stared at the strange girl, trying to decide if I wanted to yell at her or listen to what she had to say.

"What are you talking about?" I asked.

Betsy Sue turned her head and looked at me, her arms crossed over the comforter, her fingers fumbling with her the edge of her dress, ripping the sleeve.

"Daisy," she said.

"I take it she was one of the girls who lived at the Doctor's house as well?" I asked.

Betsy Sue nodded. "She was my friend. We played a lot together."

"So, what happened to her?"

Betsy Sue looked up, then away from me. "I hurt her."

"What? Why?"

"It was an accident. We were playing and it simply came off. But the Doctor put it back on."

"What came off?" I asked, puzzled.

Betsy Sue turned to look at me again. Her eyes were sparkling. "Her head."

"Her head?" I asked.

"Yes."

I could feel my nostrils flaring in anger. I rose to my feet. "You know what? I am sick of your stories. Ghosts and birds and strange stories of heads falling off. You're not being much help to us. I feel like you're making fools of us. Tomorrow you're going back home to your parents."

52
[DECEMBER 1990]

Joseph led Kimberly down the stairs to the basement. He let her go first down the stairs.

"Where are we going?" she asked and stopped half-way.

Joseph came down after her, and as they reached the last step, he spoke with excitement.

"Close your eyes."

Kimberly wasn't sure she wanted to. Her heart was throbbing in her chest. "Why? Where are you taking me?"

"Just indulge me, will you?" he said, whispering close to her ear.

She obeyed uncomfortably. Joseph gave her a

gentle push down the hallway, a hand on each of her shoulders. His hands felt cold. The basement was cold and soon she shivered.

"Joseph, please tell me…"

"Shhh," he said and she could hear a door open in front of them. "You're gonna loooove it. Just wait."

Kimberly wasn't so sure. Not after reading that book, especially not after seeing the picture of the general and the great resemblance to her husband.

"There's a couple of steps further down," he said.

Kimberly felt the cold iron as he placed her hands on what felt like a railing and she started to walk, wondering where this would lead her to, since there was no lower level than the basement. Was there?

"Okay, you can open your eyes now," he said when they reached the end of the stairs.

Cautiously, Kimberly opened them and blinked a few times to get used to the light. Behind her she saw a long and winding iron staircase. Joseph turned her around. "I found this when I was redecorating the room down here," he said.

Kimberly gasped as she gazed into what looked like a cavern. There were old dusty bottles as far as the eye could see.

"Isn't this amazing?" he asked.

"What is it?" she asked.

"It's bourbon. You know, like other people have wine cellars, this appears to be a bourbon cellar. These bottles are more than fifty years old. And look at this, this table over here," he said and walked away from Kimberly.

"What is that?"

"It's for Black Jack," he said. "I tried to clean everything to make it look nice for you. "It's been down here for a long time. Maybe your aunt's husband created this place or something. Maybe it's even older. Who knows? I think it's awesome. Talk about a man-cave."

"So when did you find out about this place?" Kimberly asked.

"About a month ago," he said.

Kimberly touched one of the bottles and got dust on her finger. "So, why now?" she asked. "Why are you showing this to me now?"

Joseph stared at her, his eyes flaring with madness, she believed. Or maybe she was just imagining things.

He started to laugh. "What? I can't share this with my wife? I wanted you to taste some of the bourbon. Come."

Joseph went to an open bottle on the counter and poured some of its contents into the two glasses next to it. Cards were spread out on the gambling table and two cigars lay smoking in the ashtray.

"Here," he said and handed her the glass. "Taste this. It's really good."

"Who have you been playing with?" Kimberly asked, looking at the green table.

"What's that?"

"There are dealt cards for two players and two cigars in the ashtray."

Joseph looked at it, then laughed again. "Ah, that. Just me being messy, that's all. Now, cheers."

He lifted his glass towards hers and drank. Kimberly never liked strong alcohol much, but this one she emptied on the first try.

"There you go," Joseph said, his voice hoarse, probably from the cigars. "Now have another one."

She drank the second one and soon the room started to spin. Kimberly sat down on a barstool while Joseph poured her another drink. She really didn't want any more; she didn't like how it made her lose control, but somehow she drank it anyway.

"I want to move," she finally said.

"What's that, dearie?" Joseph said, his voice blurry.

"I want to get out of this house. I don't like it here."

"Pah," he said and poured more into her glass. "You just need another one. Here, let me pour you one."

"No, Joseph. I'm serious," she said with a sob. She grabbed his sleeve and looked into his eyes. "We have got to get out of here before something bad happens."

"What could happen?" he said, drinking from his glass again.

"I don't know," she said. "But I'm afraid. Constantly. I'm tired of being afraid. I want you back, Joseph. Ever since we moved in here, you've changed. I don't like it. You're so different."

"Here, have another one," he said and poured more into her glass.

Kimberly drank it and the room spun even faster now. The barstool wouldn't stay still either and she felt like she was falling. She got down from the stool and held onto the bar counter.

"I don't feel so good. I need to…I think I need to get out of here."

"Nonsense. We're just getting started," Joseph said and downed yet another glass.

Kimberly tried to look at him, but he wouldn't sit still. Come to think of it, everything in the cavern was moving. Or was she moving? Kimberly started to laugh.

"What's the axe for, Joseph?" she finally asked and pointed before she slipped and almost fell. She managed to grab ahold of the counter with her other hand.

Joseph laughed. "Here, have another one," he said.

Kimberly could no longer stand on her legs and sat on the floor. The glass was put in her hand and she drank it, even though she tried not to. When she looked up again, the cavern was filled with people. Women in hats and nice dresses and men in suits, all smoking cigars and some sitting at the table, gambling. Joseph laughed and laughed. Music was playing and Joseph pulled her arm to help her get up. He laughed and swung her around and around till she felt nauseated and had to stop.

One of the fancy guests got up from the recliner and let her sit in it. Kimberly laughed and panted to catch her breath, while the room continued to spin and people talked and danced. Soon the noise drowned out every thought Kimberly had in her mind and, seconds later, she dozed off in a sea of dancing stars.

53

[MAY 2016]

"What happened? Why are you so upset?"

Shannon tried hard to get some sleep, but Jack kept tossing around in the bed. He got up and walked back and forth in front of the window. He had been like that ever since he came back from putting Betsy Sue to bed.

"She annoys me, that's what happened," he said. "Telling me all these weird stories of ghosts and whatnot. I can't trust anything she says, can I?"

Shannon sat up in the bed and turned on the nightlight. Jack stood in the middle of the floor wearing only his boxers. She missed the time when she could enjoy looking at him like that, when they were all over each other, and their biggest problem was the preparations for the wedding. Why couldn't she just be allowed to worry about napkins and centerpieces, instead of whether she would ever see her son again or not? It felt so unfair. Finally, she had a little piece of happiness, and then this happened?

God, if you're there, why do you let these things happen?

"She's just a scared little girl who has lived the past five years of her life incarcerated in a house somewhere with a crazed person. She probably needed to make up stories like that to survive, to keep sane."

"She's full of stories all right," Jack said with a snort. "Why can't she just tell us the truth? She knows what's at stake. She knows we're trying to locate our son. Why all the acting? Why all the untrue stories?"

"Maybe they're true to her," Shannon tried. She didn't really want to defend the girl. She was as frustrated as Jack was.

Jack snorted again and sat on the edge of the bed. Shannon curled up, pulling her knees up under her chin, feeling so hopeless, so lonely. Next to her on the pillow lay Bobby, his ear torn off. Jack had brought it in and thrown it angrily on the bed. Shannon had cried when seeing what happened to the bear. Now she felt like crying again. But there were no more tears left. She praised the fact that there was no alcohol in the house.

"Come to bed, Jack. We've hardly slept in days. We both need it. I can hardly see out of my eyes."

Jack rubbed his hair, then got up from the bed again.

He walked to the side of it. "You're right," he groaned and grabbed the corner of the covers.

Shannon turned off the lamp on the nightstand next to her and Jack was just about to crawl under the covers, when he stopped.

"What the...?"

Jack rushed to the window and looked out.

"What is it?" Shannon asked.

"It's her," he said. "Betsy Sue!"

Shannon jumped out of the bed and ran to the window as well. In the yard, she spotted Betsy Sue climbing the fence of the back yard.

"Where the heck is she going now?" Shannon asked, puzzled, while Betsy Sue landed on the pavement and started running onto the street.

"That's a very good question."

Jack grabbed his pants from the floor and put them on.

"What are you doing?" Shannon asked.

He swung a sweater over his head and pulled it down to cover his body. "I'm going after her."

54

[MAY 2016]

caught up with Betsy Sue when she crossed through Forsyth Park. I stayed far enough behind her to not let her know I was following her. She moved fast, but I had no trouble keeping up with her pace.

It seemed like she was following the route we had taken earlier in the day when driving around. She made a couple of turns, then came back to the same street again. It felt like she had memorized the route, even the wrong turns.

Soon we entered the street with the small shops that we had seen earlier in the day. Betsy Sue slowed down as she reached them and then she stopped in front of one of them.

The doll store.

Three dolls were displayed in the window. Betsy Sue put a hand on the glass. I watched her look at the dolls for a few minutes and remembered that I had seen her flinch in the car when we had passed this store. Why, I still didn't know. But I had a feeling I was getting closer to the answer.

Betsy Sue didn't stay long. Suddenly, she walked away from the window, turned on her heel, and started to run. I set off after her as she ran onto the street and turned around the corner of a building. I ran after her, but as I turned around the same corner, she was gone.

Puzzled, I continued down the road till I reached another street corner and looked around it, but there was no sign of the girl.

Where the heck did she go?

I continued down another street, looking around every corner, before I decided to go back where I had seen her last. I walked to the doll store, but there was still no sign of the girl. I had lost her.

Damn it!

I searched for her for about half an hour before I decided I'd better get back.

Shannon was sitting in the living room when I returned. The reporters had taken off and left us alone for the night.

Shannon jumped to her feet when I entered.

"What happened? Where is Betsy Sue?"

"I lost her," I said and closed the door behind me.

"You lost her? How?"

"I don't know. She disappeared suddenly around a corner. I couldn't find her after that," I said, gesticulating wildly. I was very annoyed with myself.

"You think she knew you were there?"

I threw myself on the couch with a deep sigh. "I don't know. I tried my best not to let her, but she might have."

Shannon walked to the window and looked out into the night. "What do you think she was doing anyway? Where was she going?"

I shrugged. "I don't know. She seemed to follow the route we had taken earlier by car. My guess is she did remember something but that she didn't want us to know. Maybe she's trying to get back. I followed her to the doll store. She stopped in front of it and looked at the dolls on display. After that, she disappeared."

"The doll store, huh?" Shannon asked and looked at me.

"There is something about that store. I remember I saw her flinch when she saw it while driving past it. She knows that store."

Shannon looked at me. "Or maybe it was the dolls."

"What do you mean?"

"She said there were thirteen girls at the doctor's house, right?"

"Where are you going with that?"

Shannon approached me. "What if they weren't girls? You know how Betsy Sue has a very vivid imagination.

A lonely girl who talks and plays with birds, talks to ghosts, plays cards with them and thinks they're real. Maybe there are other things she imagined being real while trapped in that house."

I stared at Shannon while a gazillion thoughts went through my mind. She was on to something here. "The head came off! Of course. She told me she accidentally ripped the head off one of the girls and the Doctor put it back on. That makes total sense."

"They're dolls," Shannon said.

"And the doctor's house is filled with them."

55

[MAY 2016]

Trevor Bryden woke in his bed with a start. He sat up in the darkness, panting and sweating. He had been doing that a lot lately. What was it with all these nightmares? They felt like bad omens.

Just like those stupid birds!

Ever since he had seen them around the house just before his dad died, he had hated those black flying rats.

Trevor cleared his throat and got out of bed to get a drink of water. His hands were still trembling from the nightmare when he grabbed his glass and poured water in it from the fridge. Trevor drank while staring out the kitchen window into the small back yard. Light from the street lamps lit up the lawn. Trevor loved his yard and had just planted roses by the fence. Beautiful long rosebushes that were going to cover that ugly wooden fence towards the neighbor's house. The Bryden house wasn't among the biggest around here, but it was the best maintained. That's the way it had always been and that's the way it would continue to be, had Trevor anything to say about it.

He looked out at the bushes and felt satisfied with his choice of flowers. Roses had been his dad's favorites. He had loved the garden as well and taken good care of it when he lived there, before Trevor inherited the house after his death. Trevor was desperately trying to keep the yard the way his father would have liked it. He believed he had managed pretty well.

Trevor finished his water and put the glass on the counter, when he heard the sound.

"CR-R-R-UCK, CR-R-R-UCK, CR-R-R-RUCK."

He lifted his head with a gasp.

The ravens! They're back!

Trevor looked out at the flock of birds that suddenly had arrived and covered most of his back yard. He watched as they landed in his beautiful bushes and started picking at his roses, piercing them with their beaks. The flowers scattered and were nothing but petals, as they slowly fell to the ground one after the other.

"I'll be damned…not the roses!" he exclaimed, then went for his shotgun in the living room.

Trevor grabbed the gun, his nostrils flaring, and his eyes blazing. With angry steps, he walked to the door that he slammed open before he directed the gun at the birds. He was panting loudly while standing on the back porch, aiming at them.

"Get away from the roses, you freaking rats!"

Trevor hoped the birds would move if he made enough noise, and a few of them did take off into the air, but only to come back again, darting towards him, croaking, and screaming.

One grabbed his hair and pulled off a big lock, then took off. Trevor screamed and fired his gun at it, but missed. The other birds became even louder and attacked the roses even more aggressively. Trevor fired the gun at them and a few took off, but only to return seconds later picking at the roses, making the petals fall to the soil.

"My roses," he yelled. "My beautiful roses."

Trevor ran down the steps into the yard, yelling at the birds, waving his arms and the gun desperately to scare them away. Storming through the yard, he somehow knew he would fall, even before he did. He didn't know how he knew. Maybe it had been in one of his dreams.

As he ran across the lawn, he felt his foot hit something and soon after he tumbled to the ground, face first into the pile of fertilizer that he had bought to spread out over the ground and the roses the very next day, to keep them healthy. Just like his father had taught him to.

He had poured it all out on the grass, so it would be easier to spread out the next day. His mouth was filled with the small blue balls and he couldn't breathe. Trevor coughed and lifted his head, then spat out the balls. The birds were circulating above his head.

Trevor spat and spat till the taste went away. He found the gun lying in the grass next to him, then looked up and thought he saw something. Or someone. He couldn't quite figure it out. The birds were screaming above his head as he picked up the gun and aimed it at the figure standing between his beloved rosebushes.

"Who's there?"

Ravens soon swarmed him and he shooed them away. When he turned to look again, the figure in the rosebushes was gone. Thinking it was something he had imagined, Trevor got to his feet. He walked to the bushes and picked up some of the flowers that had been pulled out and landed in the soil.

"Damn birds," he mumbled to himself, looking at the leftover rose petals in his hand.

Trevor tried once again to scare the remaining birds away, but they only took off for a few seconds before they returned. Trevor roared and yelled and swung the gun around in the air before he got ready to shoot once again, when he realized he had run out of ammo.

Grumbling, he walked back through the house and into the kitchen. Being small as he was, he always kept a ladder in the kitchen to be able to reach the top shelves where he kept the stuff he never used much, like the ammo for his gun. Trevor left the gun on the kitchen table, then climbed the ladder and found the packages in his dad's old cookie jar. He grabbed them, then climbed down again, but as he turned to find his gun, it was no longer there.

"What the he…?"

Had he forgotten it outside? Trevor stormed out on the porch and found the gun leaned up against the wall.

Oh, you old fool, he thought to himself and grabbed it. The black ravens were still going at it in the yard. But not for long. Trevor was determined to get rid of them, even if he had to shoot each and every one of them.

Trevor was about to lift the gun into position when he noticed the rocking chair on the porch was moving like someone had just been sitting in it.

What the heck?

He decided it had to be the wind. What else could it be? An animal maybe. Or maybe the wind. Yup, just the wind. Had to be.

Trevor moved on. With the gun lifted, his eye in the viewfinder aiming at the birds, he stepped out on the stairs, but just as he did, he felt a push in his back that made him trip over the first step and tumble down the rest of the stairs, holding onto the gun while he fell. He saw the rock as he approached it and knew in that moment that it was over, that the birds had ended up getting the last word.

Neighbors would later tell each other that it sounded like a watermelon cracking on the pavement when his head split open, but then again, as most people knew, the Savannahians were master storytellers.

56

[MAY 2016]

The three A's woke us up a couple of hours later. Shannon and I had both dozed off in the living room, where Abigail jumped me on the couch.

"Dad. Dad. Wake up. It's morning."

I opened my eyes and looked into hers. I couldn't have asked for a more beautiful sight. I grabbed her and hugged her while tickling her till she begged me to stop. When I let go of her, I saw that Austin and Angela were standing a few steps behind her, holding hands.

Angela let go of him when her mother opened her eyes. "Angie? Baby?"

I signaled for Austin to come closer while I sat up on the couch. "You look tired, Dad," Abigail said. "Where's Betsy Sue? She wasn't in her room."

My eyes met Shannon's. "Tyler's room, sweetie," I corrected her. "It's Tyler's room. Don't forget it."

"Any news about him?" Austin asked cautiously. I grabbed him and pulled him into my lap, then held him tight. It was the only way I could get the boy to hug me these days. It always amazed me how different those twins were.

"Not yet, sweetie, but soon," I said.

"I miss Tyler," Abigail said with a sigh.

"Me too," Austin said. "It was fun not being the youngest for once."

"He'll be back before you know it," I said, swallowing a huge knot in my throat. I was trying hard to be happy for the kids' sake. "Don't you worry."

Sarah made us all breakfast in the kitchen and we ate silently, every one of us in his or her own thoughts. It was a very odd scene for our family, which otherwise was always very noisy.

"Where is Emily?" I finally asked.

Sarah let out a deep sigh. "Sleeping in. As usual. She has been sleeping in a lot lately."

"She's a teenager. Probably needs it," I said with a shrug.

"You know, she might be sad as well," Sarah said, looking at me. "You know, with everything that's going on."

My eyes met those of Sarah. How did this woman, who was supposed to be Shannon's PA, how had she suddenly become our babysitter and now therapist?

"I'll talk to her," I said.

"By the way, don't forget your parents are arriving today," Sarah continued. "And your mother and sister are arriving tomorrow," she said, addressed to Shannon.

I nodded. I hadn't forgotten. I had talked to them the day before. They were completely freaking out over the fact that Tyler was missing and decided to come earlier than planned. I told them there really wasn't much they could do, but they wouldn't listen. I had to admit that I was looking forward to having them here with us. They could be a big help with the kids. Get Sarah off the hook for a little while.

"They have rented a condo a few blocks from here," I said, addressed to Shannon. "The kids could go and spend the night with them tonight."

Shannon didn't say anything. She looked out the window, where rain was pounding again. I knew she wasn't exactly looking forward to seeing her mother again. They didn't quite get along. Why she had invited her to the wedding in the first place, I didn't understand, but she said something about it being the right thing to do. I, for one, wasn't looking forward to meeting her, not after the stories Shannon had told me.

I wiped my mouth on the napkin and looked at Shannon. We had planned to go to the doll store today. I felt convinced the place had some significance in Tyler's whereabouts. It was a clue and I was clinging to it.

Sarah promised to look after the kids for the morning, and Shannon and I grabbed our raincoats and put them on.

"At least there will be no reporters waiting for us in this weather," I said.

But I was too early in my assumption because when we opened the door, a camera clicked and a reporter stormed towards us.

"Was Shannon drunk when she lost Baby Tyler?" the reporter asked me. "Is she off the wagon again?"

I refused to answer and pushed the woman away. Behind her appeared a very familiar face. It was Detective Bellini, wearing a raincoat and holding an umbrella. Her face told me this wasn't a friendly visit. Two officers on each side flanked her. I approached her.

"Detective Ryder?"

"Detective Bellini?"

"We need you to come down to the station."

"Why?" I asked, my heart starting to throb. *What's going on here? Have they news about Tyler? Has something happened to him? Oh, my God, no.*

"We need to question you about the death of Trevor Bryden."

57

[MAY 2016]

The Doctor decided to have a party. All the girls were lined up in the living room, dressed in their nicest dresses, their hair brushed and put up with bows. They were giggling and laughing and the Doctor was spinning around, Millie between her hands.

"She's back! She's back!"

The Doctor looked at Betsy Sue, who was sitting at the end of the table, staring back gloomily. The Doctor had put on her favorite song by Shannon King, *My beautiful Baby Doll*. The Doctor had read somewhere that Shannon King had written this song to her son after giving birth and found it appropriate for this celebration.

It was the GPS watch that had alerted the Doctor

that Betsy Sue was in the area in the middle of the night. The Doctor had stopped tracking her once she saw the Hawthornes come to Shannon King's house. The Doctor knew then that it was no use to try and get her back. At least for now.

But then, in the middle of the night, as Rikki Rick woke up to get his bottle, the Doctor looked at the phone and the app was open from the last time it had been used for tracking Betsy Sue. A notification revealed that the girl was on the move.

And boy was she ever on the move.

"Smile, Betsy Sue," the Doctor said cheerfully.

The girl squirmed in her seat, trying to get her arms loose. She was sobbing behind the duct tape and tears were rolling across her face.

"Ah, come on, Betsy Sue. Don't cry. Now we're all together again. Isn't it great? Look at all your little friends. They're so happy to have you back."

The Doctor had put Rikki Rick in his stroller, then run into the night, following the map in the app. She had spotted the girl running down the street and grabbed her as she turned a corner. The girl had fought bravely, but she was still no match for the Doctor. She had gotten stronger though, and that worried the Doctor. As the girls grew up, there would come a time when they grew bigger and maybe even stronger than the Doctor.

Now the Doctor had brought a second chair up to the room upstairs, and as soon as the party was over, the Doctor grabbed Betsy Sue, swung her over her shoulder, and carried her up to the fourth floor.

The Doctor found the key in her pocket and unlocked the door. As it was opened, Miss Muffit's brown eyes stared fearfully at them both.

"Let me go," she said, almost hissing, her voice hoarse from all the screaming. Her eyes were big and frightful and her cheeks sunken. "Let me go!"

"Sorry," the Doctor said with a tilted head.

The Doctor approached the girl and stroked her head gently. The girl groaned and fought to get loose from the straps. Her arms were bloody from fighting them.

"It's for your own good. You know that, right?"

The Doctor grabbed Betsy Sue, who was kicking and screaming behind the tape, then put her down in the chair next to Miss Muffit. The Doctor then strapped her legs to the legs of the chair and tied her arms behind her back. Then the Doctor knelt in front of the girl.

"I'm so glad you came back. Now everything is as it should be."

The Doctor grabbed the duct tape and pulled it off, letting Betsy Sue's screams fill the air.

"Help! Help!"

The Doctor caressed the girl's cheeks with gentle strokes. How the Doctor had loved those girls, watching them grow up.

"It's time."

The Doctor rose and walked to the door.

"NOOOOO!" Betsy Sue screamed, as the door was shut and the key turned in the lock.

58
[DECEMBER 1990]

She woke up on the couch. Kimberly opened her eyes, blinked a few times, and then sat up. She was in her living room.

How did I get here?

Kimberly rubbed her forehead. She had a headache and felt strange, but it didn't feel like a hangover.

"The cavern!" she exclaimed and rose to her feet. She looked around. Everything looked normal. Where were all the people? Were they still down there drinking and partying?

And where is Joseph?

Kimberly walked down to the basement and knocked on the door to Joseph's room. She opened it, but didn't find anyone there. She walked to the end of the room where she believed the iron staircase had been, but couldn't find it. Was there a door somewhere that she had to open first?

Kimberly looked around for secret doorknobs and lifted the carpet to see if it was in the floor. But she couldn't find anything.

"That's odd," she said. "I could have sworn it was right here."

She remembered that she had had her eyes closed when he guided her there, so maybe it was just somewhere else? In one of the other rooms maybe?

Kimberly started looking. She went through the laundry room, the pantry, and the storage room, but found nothing. She listened carefully to see if she could hear anyone, but it was all very quiet.

Puzzled, Kimberly walked up the stairs back into the kitchen. She looked at the clock. It was late in the afternoon. Had she slept all day? And where was Rosa?

Oh, my God. The axe! He had an axe down there!

Kimberly ran up the flight of stairs, till she reached second floor and stormed inside Rosa's room, her heart pounding in her chest, expecting to find her daughter sprawled on the bed, chopped to pieces.

But she found no such thing.

The room was empty, so Kimberly continued to the attic where Rosa loved to hang out. She wasn't there either. The birds weren't even there.

He's done something to her, hasn't he? Like the dad in those awful stories. He's gone mad. The house has made him crazy. I knew it would. I just knew it! Why didn't I listen to my instinct? Why didn't I listen? Oh, my!

"Rosa? Rosa?" she called out.

But the house remained eerily silent.

The room. The small room with the chair!

Kimberly stormed down from the attic and opened the door to the small closet room, but the chair was empty. Relieved, she breathed deeply and held a hand to her chest. But the image of the axe still remained in her mind and kept reminding her that Joseph was up to something. Something bad.

Kimberly ran down the stairs, frantically calling out her daughter's name, but continued to receive no answer. As she reached the bottom of the stairs, the front door suddenly opened and Joseph stepped inside.

Kimberly threw herself at him. "What have you done to her, you bastard! What have you done?"

Joseph looked at her, startled, then pushed her away. "What are you talking about?"

As she stumbled backwards, Kimberly spotted Rosa. She was standing behind her father, a bag in her hand.

She lifted the bag. "We bought peaches. We know how much you love the Savannah peaches."

59

[MAY 2016]

"Do you recognize this man in the picture?"

They had taken me into an interrogation room. Detective Bellini and Detective Nelson were sitting across the table from me, looking at me the way I suppose I usually looked at criminals.

I didn't know what was going on, and had never heard the name Trevor Bryden before. I kept telling them that, but they didn't believe me. I didn't like the way they wouldn't answer my questions or even speak to me while driving there in their car. We were colleagues, for crying out loud. What was going on here? And how was it related to Tyler? I didn't understand anything.

Now they placed a picture in front of me and asked me to look at it. That was when I realized I did know the man.

"Is that him?" I asked.

"You tell me, Detective," Bellini said.

"But, I don't know. I don't know that man's name."

"But have you seen him before?"

"Yes. I saw him yesterday."

"Where?" Detective Nelson asked.

They had offered me coffee and so far I hadn't even tasted it. I was so shocked about this strange turn of events. I tried a sip, but could hardly swallow it. My throat was in a thousand knots and my stomach too. I kept wondering how long they would keep me here. Shannon had to be completely out of it.

"At his house," I said. "Shannon and I went to his house yesterday, asking if he had seen Tyler. We showed him a picture of our son and asked if he had seen him. Just like we did to a lot of other houses."

"So you do know him," Bellini said, annoyingly conclusive. It felt like she was twisting my words. "And you were with him yesterday."

"I wouldn't say I know him or was with him, but I did talk to him very briefly yesterday afternoon, yes."

Detective Nelson leaned over and pushed another photo towards me. I looked at it, then felt sick to my stomach. It was the same guy again, only this time, his head was cracked open and I swear I could see parts of his brain.

"Where were you last night between eleven p.m. and two a.m.?" Detective Nelson said.

"I was in my bed. With my fiancé."

"And she'll testify to that?"

"Of course. We were awake a lot because…well, you know we haven't slept much since Tyler disappeared."

"And you didn't leave the house at all within this timeframe?" Bellini asked.

I stared at her, biting my lip. There was no way I could tell her the truth. Then I would have to tell her about Betsy Sue and how we kept her at the house without telling them. If I left out Betsy Sue, then it would be strange for me to leave the house. Either way, I wouldn't come out good. I could, of course, lie, but I didn't know if they had a witness who might have seen me leave the house or maybe on the street. They still hadn't told me why they were questioning me.

I decided it was better to leave out a part than to lie completely.

"I went for a walk," I said. "I couldn't sleep; I kept thinking about Tyler and worrying about him, so I went out for a little while. I walked around in the neighborhood. Only for like half an hour."

Nelson wrote it down, then looked up at me. "What time was that?"

I sighed. I didn't know. I didn't exactly look at the clock when I spotted Betsy Sue sneaking out. There was no time.

"I want to say around midnight, but I'm not sure," I said.

Bellini looked at me. She smiled sarcastically. "I thought that usually people who suffer from insomnia know exactly what time it is, because they keep looking at the clock. But I could be mistaken."

"I didn't look at the clock," I repeated, aggravated with the suspicious tone to her voice. I knew she had to be like this; I knew what it was like to sit at her end of the table, but still. We were colleagues. We should be helping each other instead. "Could you at least tell me why you're even questioning me here?"

The two detectives looked at each other, then Bellini nodded. Nelson looked down at his papers. He tapped his finger to his lips, pausing. Finally, he said:

"Trevor Bryden fell to his death last night between eleven p.m. and two in the morning. His head hit a rock and he died from his injuries."

"So what? If he fell, then what's there to talk about?" I asked.

"We have reason to believe he was pushed, or rather kicked," Bellini remarked darkly. "A muddy footprint on the back of his T-shirt. You know how much it has been raining the past couple of days. Muddy dirt kind of sticks to the shoes."

"What does that have to do with me?"

"We found your card in his hand."

"Well, clearly it was placed there by someone," I said. "I wouldn't be so stupid as to leave my card with him, in his hand after I murdered him, now would I?"

Bellini looked up at me. "Maybe you didn't see it.

Maybe he had it in his hand because he had just called you or spoken to you."

"That's ridiculous," I said. I was beginning to understand how people felt sitting across from me during interrogation. I felt like they had already decided that I had killed this guy, that no matter what I said it was of no use, it wouldn't change their minds. It was scary, to put it mildly.

"We need your shoes," Nelson said. He sat back in his chair, smug and confident.

"You do realize my son is missing, right?" I asked, annoyed with the waste of everyone's time.

"Your shoes, please."

"Why aren't you out there looking for him instead of wasting our time with all this nonsense? I don't get it."

"Your shoes," Bellini said.

I stared from one to the other, wondering if they ever used their common sense when solving cases. I usually had a lot of respect for my colleagues, but this was ludicrous. And so incredibly frustrating because it was my son who was missing and no one seemed to care anymore.

"Shoes, please, Detective," Bellini repeated with more authority.

I pulled off both my shoes and put them on the table with an aggressive movement. "Here. Keep them."

60

[MAY 2016]

"Hi there. Can I help you with anything?"

Shannon looked at the hundreds of beautiful old dolls on the shelves through her sunglasses. On the sign outside it said Carol's Doll Shop. Shannon wondered if the woman in front of her was Carol or just someone working there.

"Are you looking for anything in particular?"

Shannon shook her head and held on to her hat. She knew it must have seemed odd that she was wearing a hat and sunglasses inside, but she couldn't risk being recognized.

"Not really. Mostly looking."

"Well, let me know if you have any questions," the

woman said with her deep Southern accent. "Just holler if you need me. I'm Carol, by the way."

"I will. Thank you."

Shannon hadn't really thought about what she was actually looking for in the shop. All she knew was that Jack believed this shop had to be connected somehow to the person who kidnapped Tyler and Betsy Sue. After looking at the woman behind the counter, Shannon wasn't so sure anymore. It could, after all, just be that Betsy Sue liked the dolls she saw and that was why she stopped in front of the shop.

"Say, haven't I seen you somewhere before?" Carol asked, looking up from behind the counter.

Shannon blushed and turned away. "I don't think so."

"Haven't you been on TV or somethin'?"

Shannon shook her head and walked towards a doll. She looked at the dress and felt the fabric. "That's a nice one right there," Carol said. "Fabric is gorgeous, don't ya' think?"

"It feels very nice."

"Now I know where I've seen you before!" Carol suddenly exclaimed.

Get out of here now, Shannon! Before the press finds you here!

Carol looked at her, all excited, but then it was like she remembered something and she stopped herself. "No, that can't be." She looked at Shannon. "She's a lot older. But you sure look like her, though. I mean, I can't see your eyes and all, but the chin and mouth and that nose. They're just like hers. Well, don't you mind me. I'm just babbling along here. Tell me what you need, sweetheart. A new doll? A brand new outfit? We just got a new summer collection. It's *be-au-ti-ful*, I tell you. And let me know if you ever have a doll that needs repairing. We have a great doctor who even makes house calls, so you don't have to go anywhere with your precious doll."

Shannon stared at Carol. Without noticing it, she slid off her sunglasses. "Did you say doll *doctor*?"

"Yes, oh, my gosh, you really do look just like her. It's striking. Only younger, of course."

Shannon shook her head. Usually, it was the other way around. Usually, people said she looked younger in the pictures and videos they saw of her than in real life. This woman was strange. Shannon decided to not care.

"Do you have an address for this doll doctor?" she asked.

"Nope. But I do have her number. You want it, sweetheart?"

"Yes, please."

Carol took out her phone and started looking through her contacts. "We've used this lady for years and years," she said. "She's the best around. Haven't seen a doll she couldn't fix yet. Ah, here she is. I'll write it down for you on a piece of paper."

Carol wrote the numbers down, then handed the

slip to Shannon with a smile. "I tell you, even your eyes. It's scary how much you look like her."

"Thank you so much," Shannon said. She left the store, holding the number in her hand, smiling for the first time in many days.

61

[DECEMBER 1990]

"What are you talking about? What cavern?"

Joseph stared at Kimberly. They were sitting in the kitchen eating peaches and drinking sweetened tea. The peaches were delicious. Soft and ripe and every bite was like an explosion. Yet, Kimberly couldn't quite enjoy them or her family's company. The many questions kept bothering her.

"You took me to the basement, remember? Last night? You told me to close my eyes, then dragged me down some iron stairs into this cave, this small place where you had all the bourbon and a gambling table and then…then we drank a lot and got drunk and then you had a bunch of people over."

Joseph looked at Kimberly with a grin. The same

grin she remembered he had worn in the basement. "I don't know what you're talking about."

"Mom, are you alright?" Rosa asked, her face smothered in peach-juice. "You seem a little…odd today. You were sleeping on the couch all morning. Maybe you dreamt it all?"

"No," Kimberly said. "It wasn't a dream. It happened. I'm sure. You were there too, earlier, before we went into the basement. You gave me the book, remember?"

Rosa looked at her, then shook her head. "What book?"

"The book you found in the attic," she said, looking from one to the other across the table.

"I don't know what you're talking about."

"Are you kidding me?" Kimberly asked. Her voice was shivering. She couldn't stand this. They had to be joking. It happened. It really did. "Joseph, you heard her talk about the book at the dinner table as well. Tell her."

"I…I don't remember anything about a book," he said.

"Come on, Joseph. Last night. She was talking about the general and telling the story of how he put his daughter in that awful chair upstairs. Don't you remember? We ate in the formal dining room. We had roasted duck!"

"I remember the duck," Joseph said.

Rosa laughed. "Me too."

"I think Rosa is right," Joseph said. "You must have dreamt it. There's no cavern under the basement containing old bourbon bottles. Believe me, I would know. And we didn't have guests over last night. We never have company anymore. Not since we moved."

Kimberly felt dizzy. What was all this? Why were they denying these things? Could they be right? Did she just dream it all? The book? The cavern, the bourbon, the cigars, and the guests?

She felt so confused.

"Are you all right, Mommy?"

Kimberly shook her head. "I'm not sure. I feel like strange things are happening to me. This house. This place. I don't know…maybe I'm…Joseph," she said, looking at her husband for comfort. He touched his hair that was still combed back on his head. At least he wasn't smoking now, but he did smell an awful lot like old cigars.

"I have to say, you have been acting weird lately. I heard you yesterday upstairs talking to yourself sitting in that small room with the chair. And this morning when I came up from the basement you were sleeping on the couch. You slept all the way through breakfast and lunch. We were worried about you, but thought you needed it and let you sleep."

Kimberly looked at her daughter, then at her husband. She didn't know what to say to them. Her mind kept wandering down to that cavern and all the guests. What was she supposed to believe? She grabbed her hair and closed her eyes. She pulled her hair to make sure she was actually awake this time. It hurt like crazy and she let it go.

"Moom? You're scaring me," Rosa said.

Kimberly opened her eyes. The words felt like they emerged in slow-motion as she spoke:

"I think I need to lie down."

62

[MAY 2016]

The Doctor watched Shannon King as she stood at the bus stop across the street from the doll store. She watched as Shannon walked out of the store, grabbed her phone in her purse, and walked around the corner to make a call.

Just as expected, the Doctor's phone soon rang in her purse and she picked it up. "Yes?"

"Hello, I have a doll that needs repairing. I was told you could do that?" she heard Shannon say on the other end. The Doctor watched her across the street as she leaned against the brick wall of the store.

So, you found me after all, dear Shannon. Well, it was bound to happen at some point, wasn't it?

The Doctor had seen Shannon walk into the doll

store from inside the house and knew she was getting closer. It was okay, really. The only thing that bothered her was the fact that Shannon thought she was so stupid as to fall for her little show.

"I do, yes."

"Great. Carol's Doll Store referred me to you. When can you take a look at it? If you give me the address, I can come to your place right away. I'm downtown anyway. I could just stop by?"

Nice try, Shannon. Nice try.

"That was very nice of them," the doctor said. "I make house calls, if you like."

"I heard that, but since I'm downtown anyway and have the doll with me, I was thinking I might as well just stop by."

"All righty, then. You just come on by, dear."

"Right away?"

"Yes. That would make things a lot easier. I actually live right across the street from Carol's little shop. It's number 237."

"All right. See you in a few."

Sure will, Shannon dear. Can't wait!

The Doctor hung up, then started to walk back towards the house. She hurried up the stairs and let herself in. She arranged the dolls in position in the hallway.

"We're expecting nice company, girls," she said and corrected Millie's hair. "Now, you all be on your best behavior, you hear me? It's your favorite singer."

The Doctor turned up the music, playing Shannon's newest album, before she checked on Rikki Rick, who was still sleeping in his crib. She closed the door, then listened to make sure she couldn't hear the two girls upstairs. She kept them drugged during the day. Their screams were only for the night. To keep people away.

She walked to the entrance, where she spotted Shannon as she stopped outside the fence and looked up at the house. She seemed puzzled, like she felt like she was in the wrong place, then shrugged and walked up the stairs while looking behind her a few times.

She rang the doorbell and the Doctor pulled the door open, smiling from ear to ear. Shannon King stared, baffled, at her; her jaw dropped.

"You? I know you! What on earth are you doing here?"

"Well, I live here, dear Shannon."

"But…but the tour guide told us that the house was abandoned," she said. "When we took the tour. What are…what the heck is going on here, Kimberly?"

"Don't believe everything those guides tell you. It's all just old stories and fairytales. I'll tell you all about it, dear *niece*. As soon as you come on inside. Come, come."

Shannon didn't move. "I don't know. Maybe I should wait for Jack. Wait…was that what the lady meant, that Carol lady when she said I looked like…she was talking about you, wasn't she?"

"I have no idea what you're talking about, dearie, but do come on inside and we'll talk about it."

Kimberly reached out and grabbed Shannon's arm, but she pulled it away. "I think I need to…"

"COME IN!" Kimberly yelled, annoyed. This small charade was taking way too long. The neighbors would see them and blow her cover. Staying in an assumed haunted house was excellent for keeping curious people away. For years, they had thought the house was empty. There was no need to tell them it wasn't.

Shannon shook her head. "I think I'll have to…" she said and walked a few steps down the stairs. But something made her stop. A sound so sweet Kimberly couldn't have staged it better herself.

The sound of Rikki Rick crying.

6 3

[MAY 2016]

"What was that?"

Shannon stared at her aunt and took another step towards her. She had recognized her face from pictures that her mother had showed her when she was a child. Only this face was a lot older, probably in her fifties or maybe even more.

She heard the sound again, through her own music playing in the background. Shannon gasped. She would recognize that cry anywhere.

"Tyler!"

Without thinking further about it, Shannon pushed Aunt Kimberly to the side and stormed in. Inside, she was met by an inferno of ugly dolls staring back at her with their creepy dead eyes.

"Where is he?" she yelled, while Aunt Kimberly closed the door behind her and locked it.

"Well, go on," she said. "He's right in there. Second door on the left."

Shannon ran to the door and pushed it open. There he was. Lying in an old wooden crib, crying his little heart out. Never had his crying sounded more heavenly to her. Tears sprung to her eyes as she ran to him and picked him up in her arms. Holding him close was the best feeling she'd ever had.

"I'm never letting go of you again, my dear baby boy," she whispered and kissed him over and over again, tears rolling across her cheeks. "Oh, Tyler, oh, dear Tyler, how I have missed you."

Kimberly came up behind her. "I bet you missed him a lot, huh?"

Shannon sniffled, then looked at her aunt. "Why? Why did you take him? Why would you do such a terrible thing?"

Kimberly smiled. "For his own good. And for yours, dearie." She moved her neck from side to side with a crack of her joints.

Shannon scoffed. "What do you mean? How can stealing a child from his mother ever be the best for anyone?"

Kimberly exhaled. "There is so much you don't understand, Shannon. You're still so very young."

Shannon felt her heart racing in her chest as anger rose in her and replaced the joy of finally being with her son again. "You're sick. Mom always said you went mad when you lost your child. That was why we never saw you. She said you were dangerous."

Kimberly smiled again. "Well, your mom always did run with half the truth, now didn't she? I kept your son perfectly safe."

"What about the children, the girls? What about Betsy Sue? You stole her from her mother when she was just five years old. Who does that?"

Kimberly shook her head. She pursed her lips. "Again, with only half of the truth. Betsy Sue was just an infant when I brought her here. So were Miss Muffit, Bibby Libby, and Rikki Rick. All grew up in this house perfectly protected."

"Until you killed them. Betsy Sue told us you tied a girl to the chair and let her sit there till she died? They found the bones in the tunnels."

"Yes, Bibby had to go, I'm afraid. She was getting too dangerous," Kimberly said, shifting in her seat.

"What the heck do you mean?" Shannon snapped, feeling suddenly very tired. Her aunt was creeping her out. She just wanted to leave with Tyler now.

"When we first moved here, I thought it was the house," she continued. "We inherited this house from my aunt, who had lived here with her husband and four girls. Only, three of them were killed one night. Stories were also told about the general who built the house, who…"

"Let his daughter die of thirst in the chair," Shannon

said. "The tour guide told us the story. Why didn't I make the connection before, when Betsy Sue told Jack about the chair?"

"Yes. At first I believed the house turned people evil, like Joseph, my late husband. The changes were visible. He started to dress and act like the general, like in the pictures I had seen in that book that my daughter… well, that doesn't matter. But soon I realized it wasn't the house. What did all these people have in common? We were all related, the house being handed down through generations, and the killings happened every time someone moved into the house, except when some students lived here in the eighties. It took me a while to get to the conclusion, but at some point, I realized that it wasn't the house. It had nothing to do with the house and everything to do with us, with our family, our genes."

Shannon exhaled. What was all this? Kimberly was blocking the door, so she couldn't just walk out. Did she really have to stand there and listen to all this craziness?

"Listen," she said. "I need to get back to…"

"NO! You are a part of this, just as much as I am," Kimberly yelled. "It's in your DNA as well. And in the boy's. Do you think I didn't read about how you killed that man? They let you get away with it, but you did kill him."

What the heck?

"It was self-defense; besides, it was my ex-husband who killed him. Not me." Shannon took a step backwards. The look in Kimberly's eyes was that of a madman.

Kimberly walked close to Shannon, pointing her long crooked finger at her. "You have it too, and you know it. The murder gene. It's in your blood."

64

[DECEMBER 1990]

Was she really the one going insane here, Kimberly wondered, while lying on the couch in the living room. Rosa had gone back into the attic, while Joseph was hiding in the basement, as always.

Didn't it happen? Was there really no cavern and no guests? Or was Joseph messing with her? Was he pretending it didn't happen just to make her believe she was losing it? Was it all just a part of a sick game he was playing?

The general killed his daughter. Aunt Agnes' husband killed those three girls. Even though they say they're just rumors. He did it, didn't he? There is always some truth to every rumor. That's what they say, isn't it?

"He's tricking me into believing I'm going mad,"

she mumbled to herself, while staring at a raven on the branch outside the window. "He did all those things, didn't he? He let the raven into the kitchen; he put the rat in the sink, didn't he? He could have. Could he somehow have planted the fleas between the planks?"

Kimberly got up, the blanket tucked around her shoulders, while thinking back over the past months. A theory was slowly shaping in her mind, and she was getting more and more determined that she was right. It was like all the pieces finally came together. He was trying to drive her insane. The only thing she didn't have an answer for was why? Why would he do this to her?

Kimberly felt sadness overwhelm her. She had loved him so dearly through all these years. But lately, the love had started to fade away. She didn't like what he had become; she didn't care for the way he dressed or how he acted. He simply wasn't himself anymore.

"It's time we have a talk," she said and walked towards the basement.

They had always been able to talk and sort things out. Before they had Rosa, they would sometimes talk all night. Even after Rosa came along, they were good at it. They would always just sit down, have a cup of coffee, and talk. Why wasn't it like that anymore? Why was she suddenly afraid of her own husband?

Kimberly took the eight steps down to the basement, then walked towards the door to Joseph's room. The door was ajar.

That's odd. Joseph always closes the door.

Kimberly walked closer, then pushed it open and peeked inside. "Joseph?"

No answer. Kimberly walked inside and took a few steps towards the couches he had put in to make it more of a man-cave.

At first, she couldn't see his body because it was blocked by the back of the couch, but as she walked closer, she spotted it, lying on the carpet between the two couches where a coffee table would have been had a woman decorated the room.

Kimberly gasped and froze. Then she walked to him and knelt beside him. Blood was on the floor. It had run from the wound in his head where the axe had hit him. It was still sitting there, making him look like someone in a terrible horror movie. The blood on his face reminded Kimberly of the tomato soup she had made a couple of days before.

"Joseph?"

Kimberly grabbed his hand, but it was lifeless in hers. "Joseph, wake up," she said. "Don't toy with me. You know how much I hate blood."

But Joseph wasn't moving. There was no pulse in his wrist when she tried to feel it.

Slowly, the realization sank in. Kimberly started to sob. Then she felt the salty tears hit her upper lip. The blood had left a pool around him and when she kneeled, she had placed her hands and knees in it. Then she rubbed it on her face when wiping away her tears.

"Who did this?" she asked and tried to wipe away the blood from her hands onto her skirt. She was crying hard as she backed up towards the stairs and fumbled up to the kitchen.

"Who would do such a horrible thing?" she kept repeating to herself, when she heard the ravens in the attic. They were making an awful noise, sounding almost as if they were crying.

"Rose," she said to herself, then grabbed a kitchen knife.

65

[MAY 2016]

They kept me waiting in the interrogation room for hours on end. I felt so frustrated and angry with them for making such a big deal of this, even though I tried to convince myself that they were only doing their job.

It was just such a freaking waste of my time and I could have been out there looking for Tyler. Didn't they know how much every minute counted?

Finally, Bellini entered the room. "You can go, Ryder."

"So, it didn't match?" I asked and grabbed my jacket.

"The footprint didn't," she said.

I smiled. "Don't want to say told you so, but I kind of did."

"The dirt on your shoes did match, though," she continued with a skeptical look.

I sighed. They weren't going to let this go, were they? "Which is only natural when I told you I was at his house yesterday," I said.

Bellini handed me my phone back. There were several unanswered calls.

"We'll be in touch," Bellini said and held the door for me.

I walked outside and went through my calls. My parents had called me from Cocoa Beach, letting me know they were leaving town now. Then Sarah had left a message telling me my parents had called and told her they were leaving town now and asking me when I believed I would be back, since the kids were asking. The next message was from Shannon. I listened to it, standing in front of the police station on the street, eyes open and jaw dropped. When I had heard it to the end, I listened to it one more time to make sure I had heard everything right.

The doctor is a woman? She's a doll doctor? But, how does that...Betsy Sue told me it was a man; I don't get it...or did she? Maybe she just didn't correct me? But why wouldn't she tell me the truth? Doesn't she want us to find her? Is she protecting this woman? Does she have like a Stockholm syndrome or something going on?

I called Shannon back, but she didn't pick up. Then I called Sarah and asked if Shannon had come back.

"No. We haven't heard from her all day," she said.

I looked at the time. It was almost five in the afternoon. What had she been doing for all these hours? Something wasn't right.

I tried to call her again and left a message, telling her I was done at the police station and asked for her to call me back when she heard it, then I hung up and called Sarah back again and told her I wanted her to call me as soon as she heard from Shannon.

"Is something wrong?" she asked. "Did something happen to Shannon?"

"I hope not," I said, while waving at a taxi. It drove right past me. I cursed, but didn't say it out loud. Anxiety was beginning to rise within me. "Just stay with the kids and make sure they don't sense that anything is wrong, all right? I don't want them to be more worried than they already are."

"Of course not. Don't worry about them. They've been playing all afternoon in the yard. They say they miss Betsy Sue and, of course, they keep asking if you know anything about Tyler. I had a long talk with Austin earlier because he started to cry out of the blue. He said he was afraid he'd never seen his little brother again. He was sad that he never even got to play with him and he was looking so much forward to it, because all the girls wanted was to hold hands. I told him that Tyler would come back and that he would be playing with him soon."

"Good," I said, feeling a pinch in my heart. I wasn't sure I could go on much longer without knowing where to find my child. I wondered where Shannon was. Had she decided to call this doll doctor on her own? In the voicemail, she only said she had gotten the number from the store, so that's where I was going to start.

I hung up on Sarah, when finally a taxi responded to my waving. I decided not to take it.

66

[MAY 2016]

Shannon could hear her phone vibrate on the counter where Kimberly had put it, but she couldn't pick it up. Kimberly had asked—no, demanded—that she sit in a chair by the kitchen table and have some coffee. When Shannon had refused and told her she wanted to leave, she had pulled a knife. She had stabbed Shannon's arm with it so she almost dropped Tyler.

Now she was sitting in the chair, Tyler in her good arm; she wasn't going to let go of him again. She was looking at her arm where the blood was soaking her white shirt and her bracelets.

Meanwhile, Kimberly was making coffee, humming along, taking out cookies from the cabinet, the knife placed on the counter next to her. The phone vibrated again and again, and Shannon had a feeling it had to be Jack. Hopefully, they had let him go. Shannon had been terrified when they had taken him away. All they said was that he was needed for questioning about the death of some guy. They had seemed so serious and it had frightened Shannon. She hoped they just needed his help on some police work connected to the case, but she wasn't so sure.

Kimberly looked at her like she wanted something from her.

"I'm sorry, what?" Shannon asked.

"I asked, do you take milk or sugar?"

Shannon felt confused. Her arm was hurting badly. "I told you. I don't want coffee. I think I need to go to the emergency room with my arm. I need stitches."

"Pah. Stitches, *smitches*. You're fine. Don't you know it's impolite to say no when someone offers you coffee?"

"I don't care, Kimberly. Just let me go, will you?"

Kimberly turned on her heel, then tilted her head to the side. "I am sorry. No. Can. Do. You're staying here with me. You and your boy."

Shannon sighed and looked down at Tyler. He was so peaceful in her arms, sleeping through everything. She smiled when his mouth twitched in his sleep. It was tough to hold him with just one arm, but she didn't care. She wasn't letting go of him anymore. Never again.

"What do you want from me?" Shannon asked, exhausted. She was constantly watching the knife on the counter, wondering if she would make it if she went for it. But, then again, looking at her bleeding, hurting arm, she knew that Kimberly wouldn't hesitate for even one minute to hurt her again. "Has it anything to do with Mother? 'Cause I feel like you should take it up with her instead, then."

"Your mother...I will deal with later," Kimberly said and poured the finished coffee into two cups. She turned with a big smile, the cups in her hands. "I take it you want it black then."

Kimberly placed the coffee on the table in front of Shannon, then went back for the knife and sat down across the table from her. She sipped from her cup, her eyes flickering back and forth, when suddenly noises started to emerge from upstairs. It sounded like vague screams.

Shannon felt a chill run down her spine. "What was that?"

Kimberly shook her head and drank her coffee. "That's just the girls." She looked at her watch. "They usually wake up at this time. I slip them something so they can sleep during the day. At night, they can scream all they want to. Screaming during the day will attract attention, whereas at night, well people will just chalk it up to that fact that the house is haunted."

Shannon stared at her aunt while she was slurping her coffee. How could she just sit there all calm and cool when there were children screaming upstairs, sounding like they were screaming for their lives. She almost seemed like she was enjoying their screams, like it made her feel happy.

Shannon felt sick to her stomach. The screams were getting louder and louder and she couldn't stand the sound. "Why are they screaming like that? What are you doing to those girls?"

Kimberly leaned in towards me. "Oh, don't let their innocent looks or screams fool you. They are pure evil. I am only doing this world a favor keeping them here." She sat back in her chair, cool and collected, smacking her lips like she was thirsty.

"So, you're telling me they are the ones who have this gene? What was it you called it? A murder gene?"

"Yes. You're getting it, Shannon. You always were the smart one among your sisters. Nevertheless, you have it in you as well. And, therefore, I cannot let you leave this house ever again."

Shannon stared at her deranged aunt, wondering how she had gotten herself into this mess, and especially how she was going to get out of it. The screams were intensifying now and it gave Shannon goosebumps. "So what, you're telling me I am related to these girls that you kidnap?"

"Yes, exactly. They're all children of distant cousins. Like the Hawthornes. Heather is your mother's cousin."

Shannon leaned back in her chair. She hadn't touched her coffee and wasn't planning on it. So Betsy Sue was family? Was she here? Shannon wondered if one of the screaming girls was her. It made her feel differently about the girl. She had to somehow get up there and help her.

67

[DECEMBER 1990]

"Rosa?"

Kimberly yelled up the stairs while she ran, taking two steps at a time, the knife tightly squeezed in her hand.

"Rosa? Where are you, girl?"

Images of Joseph in the pool of his own blood wouldn't leave her mind. Her heart was racing in her chest as she approached Rosa's room. She opened the door cautiously, holding the knife in front of her.

"Rosa?"

Rosa wasn't in her room. Kimberly walked inside and looked around. The bed was neatly made, but something was wrong with the dolls on the shelf.

Kimberly walked towards them. Rosa had always loved these antique dolls that she had inherited from Kimberly, who had gotten them from her mother. Rosa especially loved the one with long blond curly hair and blue eyes that looked mostly like Rosa herself. That was her favorite. But what had happened to her?

Who would do such a thing?

The doll's head was lying in her lap. Ripped off. The one next to it had lost an arm. All the dolls had been completely destroyed. Some were even painted with red lipstick smeared all over their faces, making them look like Kimberly with all the blood on her face. Kimberly gasped and took the favorite doll down.

"Betsy Sue," she cried, remembering the many wonderful times she had played with that doll as a child. It had been her favorite too. Kimberly sobbed and tried to remove the red lipstick from the doll's face, by spit washing it, using her sleeve to wipe it. But she only made it worse. She tried to put the head back on, but it needed to be sewn. Luckily, Kimberly knew exactly how to do it. She had been making a good sum of money fixing dolls for other people, mostly collectors. It was a craft her own father had taught her growing up.

Kimberly heard footsteps coming from the attic and the birds were still making an awful noise.

"Those damn birds," she groaned. Was Rosa up there with them?

Kimberly climbed the stairs to the attic, knife between her teeth, and opened the hatch. A bird darted down towards her with a loud scream and pulled a lock of her hair out. Kimberly screamed, grabbed the knife in her hand and swung it in the air.

"Get away from me, you bastards. You creepy bastards! I hate you!"

The bird flew away and Kimberly crawled into the attic. "Rosa?"

She spotted the girl in her reading corner, sitting with her back turned towards Kimberly, reading something.

She looks fine.

"Rosa?"

Kimberly approached her daughter and looked over her shoulder, when she realized exactly what she was reading.

"It does exist," she gasped. "You lied to me!"

The girl finally looked up. Kimberly reached down and grabbed the book, remembering how she had been reading all about the general and was about to read her Aunt Agnes' own story when Joseph had disturbed her.

"You told me there was no book," she said angrily to her daughter. "Why did you say that?"

Rosa exhaled. "I thought the book made you sick. You were so out of it after reading it; I believed it was better if you never saw it again. Dad agreed we'd better not let you read it anymore."

Kimberly shook her head, while desperately flipping the pages to get to where she had stopped. "I don't believe you," she said, holding the knife towards her daughter.

She looked her in the eyes. Rosa seemed eerily calm. "What did you do to your father?" she asked, panting heavily as she spoke. "What did you do to him?"

Rosa shook her head. *Was that a smirk?*

Kimberly pointed the knife at the girl. "What did you do to your father?"

"I don't know what you're talking about," she finally said.

"You did it, didn't you? You killed him, didn't you?"

Now Rosa reacted. "I what? No! What…is Dad…?"

"Don't give me that. I know you did it, Rosa. Just like I have always wondered about Rick. You were in his room the night he died. Why were you in your brother's room, Rosa? What were you doing there?"

Rosa took a step backwards while looking at the knife in front of her. Now she started to cry. "Mom. I…I didn't do anything; you have to believe me. Please, Mom. I think…I think you're losing it."

"I'm not falling for that again, you little monster. I am not! You've tricked me for all these years with your innocent eyes. I'm not falling for your tricks anymore. I know you killed him. I know you killed the both of them!"

"But…but…Mom? Please? I didn't do anything!"

Kimberly shook her head. Images of her baby in the crib, lying lifeless, not responding to her CPR, not breathing, no pulse, were coming back to her. For so many years she had blocked them out, trying to forget and move on, but now they were back.

The knife in Kimberly's hand was shaking heavily when she made the decision. She wished that there was another way out, but there wasn't.

It had to be done.

Kimberly grabbed Rosa's hand and pulled it hard… so hard that Rosa screamed.

"You're coming with me," Kimberly said, ignoring her daughter's bone-piercing screams.

"Stop, Mommy! Stop! You're hurting me!"

Kimberly pulled her down the stairs, to the fourth floor, and then dragged her across the wooden floors in the hallway towards the door at the end of it.

"NO! Mommy!"

She opened the door with the key in the new lock she had told Joseph to put in months ago, then pulled the girl into the room and placed her in the chair. She tied her down, using a rope that was already in the room, still ignoring the girl's helpless pleading.

When she was done and the girl could no longer move, she wiped her sweaty and bloody face with the edge of her shirt, which was ruined anyway, and then looked down at Rosa, who was crying hard. She knelt and looked into the girl's eyes. "This hurts me as much as it does you," she said, wiping a lock of hair away from her face. She put it behind her ear, but it kept falling back into her face. "Believe me, sweetheart. But this is the only way. This is what must be done. Do you understand that? I have to do this. To protect you from yourself."

"But…Mommy, please…"

Kimberly looked into her beloved daughter's eyes once again and knew it would be the last time. She walked to the door and hesitated for just one second before she walked out. Rosa was squirming in the chair, her pleading eyes looking at her mother for help. Kimberly looked away, closed the door, and locked it by key.

Before she left, she put a hand on the door and whispered:

"I'm sorry, baby."

68

[MAY 2016]

"Why do you keep them up there? Why do you put them in that chair?"

Shannon had to try and keep her temper down. The girl's screams were getting louder and louder and more and more insistent. She had a hard time coping with it and with the fact that the mad woman in front of her was in fact her own family, her flesh and blood.

Kimberly finished her coffee, pretending like she couldn't hear a thing, then looked at Shannon. She cleared her throat as if she wanted to make sure Shannon was listening. Shannon's plan was to keep her talking while she figured out how to get all of them out of there.

"I don't get it," she continued. "If you're going to kill them anyway? Why not kill them right away?"

"Oh, but I'm no monster," Kimberly said. "I keep them with me; they grow up here with me until they reach a certain age and I see traits in them come to life. Until then, we have a great time here. But, at some point, they start to change. It can be as early as six years of age as it was for Little Miss Muffit or maybe not until they are around ten, like Betsy Sue. I observe them closely, especially when they play with the dolls; if the dolls tend to get hurt a lot, if limbs are being torn off, then I know it's about time for them to go in the chair. It's all for their own—and for the rest of the world's protection."

"So you keep them up there, tied to a chair, to prevent them from what…killing someone? Is that what you think they'll do?"

"Oh, I know they will."

"But they die up there!"

"Oh, no. I feed them and give them water. But I have to keep them strapped down. I see the shift in their eyes. It doesn't happen overnight, you know. It comes gradually. When it's time, it's time. There is nothing much I can do about it. As I said. It's also for their own protection. But once they're strapped down, I keep them fed and provided for. I am no monster."

"But Bibby Libby died. They found her remains in that tunnel just the other day," Shannon argued. She knew the woman in front of her was mad, and her answers wouldn't make much sense, but she had to keep her talking.

"Bibby, I had to kill. Just like Rosa. Once they mess up, once they overstep the line and kill, I have to get rid of them. I tell them that when they're younger. I tell them they have the gene in them, that they are predisposed to be killers, and if they do it, they will be killed themselves."

"Who did Bibby kill?"

"Old Bryden. The man who lived across the street from us. She developed the traits so fast, it was too late once I realized it. She had snuck out through the tunnels in the kitchen and had escaped. I came too late. He was already dead when I got there. Hit his head on a rock in the back yard. She made it look like an accident, the clever girl, but it wasn't. I was the only one who knew it wasn't. Last night, Betsy Sue killed his son. Kicked him in the back so he'd fall to his death. Again, I came too late, but I caught her as she tried to escape the place. I placed your husband's, sorry *your fiancé's* card in his hand, to keep the police looking in the other direction, if you catch my drift. Anyway. That's when I grabbed her and brought her back. She's too dangerous to have running loose. All these girls are. That's why the ravens like them so much, you know. Because they smell like death. All these little girls do."

"So now you have to kill her, is that it?" Shannon asked, wondering if Kimberly really couldn't hear how crazy it all sounded.

"Yes. I got the idea from a book my aunt wrote. See, it was while reading it that I realized the general didn't punish his daughter for playing with the wrong boy. No, I researched it. Old newspaper articles at the library told me the boy died. He fell from a rooftop. So that's when I realized why the general punished her. He had to. He must have realized that she had pushed the boy down from their roof." She paused for effect, it seemed, then continued. "I went through the same thing myself. My daughter Rosa. I had to punish her, you must understand this, I had to do it. Once I realized she had killed her baby brother and her father. Now, I couldn't kill her myself. I didn't have the heart to, just like the general couldn't kill his own daughter, so I simply left her there. I didn't go up there till a week later when she had been quiet for at least a day."

Shannon could hardly breathe. The gruesomeness of her stories was too much to cope with. Shannon wanted to scream and run, but knew that her aunt was crazy enough to kill her if she did.

"So, who do you have up there now?"

"Right now I have Miss Muffit up there with Betsy Sue. The worst part is the smell, you know from when they defecate themselves. It's quite a mess. Now Betsy Sue hasn't been fed or had a drink since I brought her back; she's being punished for what she did to the younger Mr. Bryden, whereas Miss Muffit, I am still feeding. I only noticed her being very rough with the dolls, ripping off an arm the other day, but there is still hope for her. Alas, probably not for long." Kimberly smacked her lips and looked into Shannon's eyes with a smile.

"More coffee?"

69

[MAY 2016]

Shannon sipped her coffee using her bleeding arm. It hurt like crazy to even move it. Yet she managed to grab the handle of the cup with the inscription, *I may look like a doll, but I'm not a toy*—on top of a picture of a doll with big blue eyes. Shannon could hardly lift it and the cup was shaking heavily as she tried to reach her mouth. Shannon didn't dare not to drink her coffee and make Kimberly upset.

She managed to get one sip in and fought long to swallow it, before she could finally put the cup back on the table. Luckily, Tyler was still asleep and didn't seem to notice any of what was going on. Shannon was getting more and more nervous after listening to Kimberly and realizing just how crazy she really was.

Kimberly gulped down more coffee. She emptied cup after cup. Shannon noticed her lips were getting brown and dry. Every time the cup left her mouth, Kimberly wet them with her tongue, and then smacked them again.

"Heather never killed anyone, so there's a hole in your little theory right there," Shannon said. "With the whole gene thing."

Who am I kidding? Trying to argue with her? Trying to reason with her?

Kimberly looked at Shannon, then smiled. "She didn't, did she?"

"No. And neither did my mom. She never killed anyone either."

"She didn't, did she?"

"Stop saying that!" Shannon snapped.

Kimberly leaned back in her chair. "I'm just saying: how do you know?"

Because I know, you crazy freak!

"Plus it was my aunt Agnes's husband who killed those three girls and the nanny – not Aunt Agnes," Shannon said.

"Really? And just how do you know that it was him? As far as I know the murders were never solved."

Shannon sighed. She was so tired and had no more strength to argue.

"So, what do you think?" Kimberly asked after a few minutes of silence between them. She was drumming her fingers impatiently on the table. The sound was driving Shannon nuts.

Shannon looked at her, confused. "What do you mean?"

Kimberly tilted her head and smiled. "I'm trying here, Shannon. I'm trying to involve you."

"I...I don't think I understand."

Kimberly sighed, then rolled her eyes. "What do you think I should do with you two?"

Shannon stared at her aunt, scrutinizing her eyes, wondering what she would say if she simply said *Let us go*?

"I just want to go home," Shannon said. "I have a daughter. I am engaged to be married. We're supposed to be married this Saturday, as a matter of fact."

"Tsk, tsk. And you didn't even think about inviting your old aunt, now did you?" Kimberly said.

"I...I didn't know where to find you," Shannon said. "I didn't even know you lived right here."

"Nice try," Kimberly said. "No, I know my family doesn't want me. I know they all believe I've gone mad. But they'll know I'm telling the truth. Some day the world outside will understand."

"So what are you going to do with us?" Shannon asked, trying to get the talk away from once again digging into her aunt's crazy theories.

"I knew they never would understand why I killed Rosa," she said, ignoring Shannon's attempt to turn the conversation. "That's why I put her in the tunnels after she had gone quiet. Her and her dad. I had to keep them away and pretend we had all left so no one would wonder where we were. I closed off the house and used only the back entrance when going out. My dolls and I were safe here for a little while. Until I realized that this murder gene would only spread. I read lots and lots of articles about it, and it is real. I'm not making this up, Shannon. Murderers are born with a gene that makes them more likely to kill. Scientists from the Karolinska Institute in Sweden have conducted tests on prisoners. They found that the majority of violent criminals carried the same genes. It's true. It was published in the journal of *Molecular Psychiatry*, and they concluded that violent criminals have a particular set of genes, but these genes were not carried by petty criminals. So now you understand why I had to react, right? People in our family were still having children and there was no telling what they would end up like. Would they develop the gene? Would they become murderers themselves? I knew no one would ever believe me. Still, I had to protect people, protect everyone from ending up like my poor Rick and poor Joseph. No one should suffer the way I have. NO ONE!"

Kimberly hit her fist on the table as she said—well, more like yelled—the last words out in the kitchen. "So, yes, I took their babies. I observed the girls as they grew up and hoped and prayed that they wouldn't develop into monsters, but so far they all have. The world should know I only did it to protect them."

Shannon didn't know quite what to say. Kimberly's yelling scared her. It woke up Tyler, who had started to fuss. Shannon tried to calm him down by moving her arm carefully up and down.

Kimberly looked at him with a gentle smile. "And now you have given me a boy," she said. "He looks just like my baby Rick. We used to call him Rikki Rick. Did you know that? And now he has finally come back to me."

70

[MAY 2016]

Kimberly was holding the knife in her hand. She was staring at Shannon and Tyler, while the tip of the knife was tapping rhythmically on the table. No one had spoken for five minutes or maybe even more. Shannon tried to keep still and not say anything to offend Kimberly, to not set her off. She let her eyes run around the kitchen, looking for a way out. All the windows had bars on them; Kimberly was blocking the door to the hallway; there was no way she could get past her. But maybe there was something else she could do. Her eyes landed on the chest leaned up against the wall to the right of her. She remembered what Jack had told her after talking to Betsy Sue. An idea shaped rapidly in her head.

But what about the girls upstairs? You can't just leave them?

She'd have to come back later for them. With the police. As long as she managed to get Tyler out with her. It was risky and she knew she risked the girl's lives. It certainly wasn't an easy decision. But if she didn't do something, they might all end up dead.

"But Shannon, I hope you'll one day forgive me for doing this to you," Kimberly said. "But you two are too dangerous to have roaming about out there. I will have to kill you. And it's such a shame, because I really do enjoy your music. You are my favorite singer of all time. Did you know that? Well, you are. I play your music for the girls all the time. It really is too bad. But don't worry. I will take good care of little Rikki Rick here. We can only hope he'll be the one to break the evil cycle, break the curse lingering upon our family, am I right?" she ended her sentence with a loud laugh.

Shannon felt like punching her in the face, but the knife in her hand scared her. She had already stabbed Shannon's arm and she was terrified she would hurt Tyler if she tried anything. She had to think it all through.

"So, what do you say, Shannon? You've been so quiet the past few minutes." Kimberly smacked her lips again.

Shannon licked her own dry lips. "I say I would like that second cup of coffee after all."

Kimberly lit up. "Well, what do you know? I can't deny a dying woman her last wish, now can I? I'll have to make some more then."

With the knife in her hand, she got up and walked to the kettle, still so close to the door that Shannon wouldn't make it if she tried to run for it. Kimberly boiled the water, while Shannon put her plan together, drops of sweat running from her forehead. Kimberly whistled as she prepared the cup for Shannon and put it on the table in front of her. Shannon looked at it.

"But it's empty," she said.

Kimberly laughed. "I have been among killers for so very long, my dear. Don't you think I know how they think? How they see every little item as a weapon? You were planning on throwing the coffee in my face, weren't you? And then making a run for it. Tsk. Tsk. Do you really think I am that STUPID?" With the last word, Kimberly raised the knife high in the air and let it fall on Shannon's hand, the one on the already hurt arm, pinning it to the table.

Shannon screamed in pain.

"There. Now you're not going anywhere," Kimberly said and sat down. She grabbed herself a new cup of coffee and sipped it, slurping every sip like it was soup. Shannon was crying now. "Please. Just let me go," she said.

"Sorry. No can do."

Kimberly looked into her steaming coffee cup, while Shannon reached under the table and with one leg, managed to kick the leg of Kimberly's chair so she tipped over, the hot coffee spilling in her face.

Now it was Kimberly's turn to scream.

Meanwhile, Shannon had to react fast. She put Tyler onto her lap, grabbed the handle of the knife with her good hand, and pulled it out of her wound with a loud scream worthy of an Amazon Warrior Woman.

Now she was the one with the power. Somehow, she managed to get Tyler up in her hurt arm so she could swing the knife in front of her, threatening Kimberly, who was slowly getting back on her feet now, her face red and burning.

"You bastard. I knew you'd try and kill me. You're a murderer, Shannon! Just like the rest of them."

Shannon had an almost manic look in her eyes as she stared at Kimberly, her nostrils flaring.

"Yes. Yes, I am a murderer. You better stay away from me, Kimberly, or I will make sure to show you exactly what this murder gene is capable of."

71

[MAY 2016]

"Don't be stupid, Shannon," Kimberly said. "You can't get out of here. The door is locked and I have the key. Give me the knife."

"Get back!" Shannon yelled. Her bleeding hand was hurting like crazy, but she still managed to hold on to Tyler by clutching him close to her torso. Blood was dripping rapidly onto the floor. Shannon was getting dizzy from the loss of blood and the room soon started to spin.

Shannon tried hard to stay conscious, but had to close her eyes again and again to not fall. She swung the knife at Kimberly, hoping it would scare her, but soon she didn't know what was up and what was down anymore. Seconds later, the floor came towards her face and she wondered why she didn't even feel it as it smacked her cheek.

Then everything went black.

When Shannon came to, she was awakened by a loud noise. Voices, loud voices yelling, Kimberly screaming. A baby crying.

Tyler!

Shannon blinked her eyes several times to better be able to see, and as her vision slowly came back, she realized Kimberly was fighting someone, and that someone seemed to be winning. They were throwing punches at each other, kicking and screaming, but mostly Kimberly was flying through the air.

Tyler. Where is Tyler? I can hear him crying!

Shannon spotted him on the floor. He was lying on his back, crying helplessly, but otherwise he seemed unharmed. She dragged herself to him, using her good hand and pulled him close to her, using her body to protect him, while she turned to watch the two women fight. Kimberly now grabbed a chair and swung it at the other woman. It broke on her back and the woman fell to the ground with a thump.

Kimberly stood above her triumphantly with the knife in her hand, lifting it high in the air, ready to let it fall, when Shannon managed to get up on her good arm, grab a coffee cup with a doll image that had fallen to the floor and swing it at her. It hit Kimberly right in the head. She froze, the knife in mid-air, then her eyes rolled back in her head and she fell, stiff like a tree, to the ground.

"Gotcha!"

The woman got up, checked on the knocked out Kimberly, then came towards Shannon. Her face seemed familiar, but Shannon didn't know where from. She was extremely strong for someone who looked like she could be in her sixties.

"Are you okay?"

The woman lifted Tyler up from the floor and handed him to Shannon, so she could hold him with her good arm. Then she grabbed a dishtowel, ripped it apart, and wrapped Shannon's hand in it, then used the other part for her arm. "We need to get you to the hospital," she said.

"Thank you," Shannon said.

"Oh, by the way, I'm Melanie Vann," she said.

Shannon blinked again. "Vann? As in Agnes Vann?"

"Here, let me help you get up," Melanie said, and put her arm around Shannon's back and helped her get up on a chair. "Yes, Agnes was my mother."

"So you were the last child? The one who survived?" Shannon asked.

Melanie nodded. "Yes. I guess you've heard the story like most people around here. My sisters were all killed in this house many years ago. I was only four when it happened. Never saw a thing. Sound asleep upstairs. I told my mother I didn't want the house when she died. No wonder, huh? Never could stand it. I haven't thought about it for years, not until they called me a week or so ago from City Hall and told me the house was abandoned and had been for a long time. They had tried hard to track me down for years and they wanted to know what I wanted to do with it. It was still in Kimberly's name, but no one had heard from her for years. I told them to tear the thing down. Nothing but bad things have happened here. Still, I wanted to come and see it for myself, you know face my demons and see if there was anything worth saving. Maybe get some closure. I flew in late this afternoon and wanted to come here right away. Get it over with. I didn't know there would be anyone here. I heard screaming when walking down the street. The front door was locked, so I had to break down the back entrance. I'm sure glad I did. That woman was about to stab you when you were out cold."

"Thank you," Shannon said. "I'm sure glad you came by."

"Say, aren't you Shannon King?" she asked. "The singer?"

"Yes."

"I believe we're related then. My mother always told me we were. She's your mother's aunt, I believe? I think so. It's far out, but as I always say, family is family, am I correct?"

72

[MAY 2016]

Shannon slowly felt better. Melanie poured her some water, which she drank till the dizziness went away. When she put the glass down, she suddenly remembered the girls upstairs. They hadn't been screaming for a long time now and it was all eerily quiet from up there.

"The girls!" Shannon exclaimed.

"What was that?" Melanie asked.

She was holding Tyler so Shannon could drink and rest, tickling his tummy and toes. Now she was looking up.

"She's keeping two girls up there, in a small room, locked up and strapped to chairs. We have to get them out of there."

Melanie looked, startled, at me. "What kind of a sick monster is this woman?" She handed Tyler back to me.

"Don't get me started. I'll explain everything a little later, but now we need to get them out of this awful house."

"Naturally," Melanie said. "I'll go up there and help them out. You stay here and rest."

"There's supposed to be this small room up…"

"On the fourth floor," Melanie said. "I know exactly which one it is. We used to play up in that room until one of our neighbors told us what had happened up there. Awful story."

Shannon moaned, still feeling the pain. "Kimberly has the key, I think. Try her pockets."

Melanie went through Kimberly's pockets and found a bundle of keys. "This ought to be it," she said. "You're in no shape to go anywhere. You wait here, dear, and I'll get the girls. Now keep an eye on her. If she moves, you scream! Here's the knife in case you need it."

"I'll call the police," Shannon said, and looked for her phone while Melanie left her.

With Tyler clutched in her good arm, she searched the counter, but when she found it, she realized that Kimberly had smashed it. It was shattered into pieces on the counter. And there didn't seem to be any landline around. Shannon would have to wait till Melanie came back down with the girls.

Shannon sat down with a deep sigh, holding Tyler close to her heart. "We'll be out of here soon, baby.

Don't you worry. Mommy's going to get you home with Daddy and your siblings real soon. Real soon. Mommy will never let go of you again. No, she won't."

Shannon looked at her beautiful boy and felt such happiness again, such joy to be with him again. *Everything was going to be alright now*, she thought, with a feeling of serenity and happiness.

She was so wrapped up in her relief, so much that she forgot to keep an eye on Kimberly and didn't see it when she rose to her feet, grabbed a chair, and swung it at Shannon. Shannon was knocked backwards to the floor, while Tyler went flying. Shannon screamed and Kimberly grabbed the boy mid-air, then stood above her, her foot pressed against her chest, holding her down.

"Now, my dear Shannon. Say goodbye to your baby. You won't see him again," she said, pressing her high heel into Shannon's chest. She reached over and pulled out a drawer with the other hand, while Shannon tried hard to get up, but couldn't. Kimberly pulled out a corkscrew. She hardly looked at it before she leaned down towards Shannon and stabbed the corkscrew into her stomach. Then, without even blinking, she pulled it out through Shannon's flesh before she stabbed it into her stomach once again.

73

[MAY 2016]

Kimberly stormed out of the kitchen and into the living room. She made it to the front door when she realized she didn't have her keys and the top lock needed one. Kimberly cursed when she heard a car door shut outside and looked out. Five police cars had driven up onto the street and parked in front of her house. Out of one of them stepped Shannon's fiancé, flanked by two detectives. They were pointing and talking about the house, running towards the stairs.

Kimberly let go of the curtain and stepped backwards. She turned and ran back into the hallway, towards the back door, when she spotted officers in the back yard as well. Two of them were approaching the door.

Now what?

The baby still tucked in her arms, Kimberly turned on her heel and stormed back into the kitchen, where Shannon was lying lifeless on the floor, blood gushing from her wounds. Kimberly stepped on her to get past her, then walked to the chest and pulled it to the side, using only one arm. Meanwhile, she heard the front door being knocked in and voices filling the living room. She also heard voices from upstairs, then steps and cheerful yelling and knew the girls were loose.

Kimberly pulled the hatch open, grabbed a flashlight from a drawer, took off her high heels and left them on the kitchen floor before she—with the baby in her arms—carefully climbed the steps into the darkness, closing the hatch behind her.

As soon as it was closed, she heard voices in the kitchen; she even believed she heard Jack scream Shannon's name out, then ask for someone to call for an ambulance.

That should keep him busy till I get out of here.

Kimberly put her feet in the water and walked, her head bent so she wouldn't hit the ceiling, flashlight in her other hand, slowly through the tunnel. She had only been down there to get rid of the bodies. First Joseph, then Rosa, and finally Bibby Libby. She had dragged them as far in as she had thought necessary so the smell wouldn't reach her house. She knew a good part of the tunnel, but had never walked all the way through. She knew it was connected to the ocean at the other end, but she also figured it was a long walk before she got to it, since she didn't live very close to the harbor.

But she knew that Bibby Libby and Betsy Sue had escaped through the tunnels and, if they could do it, then so could she. It couldn't be that difficult, now could it?

The tunnels were cold and damp, and soon she was freezing. Every now and then her flashlight hit a rat and she shrieked, remembering the time the rat had crawled into the garbage disposal and she had been covered in its blood. Oh, how silly she had been back then, thinking it was the house, thinking the house was trying to drive her insane. How could a house do that? It wasn't like it was alive. She didn't believe in all those old stories, especially the ones about it housing ghosts. But she had used the old stories for the girls. So they didn't feel so lonely growing up. She had told the girls about the ghosts living in the attic, but told them they were their friends that they could play with them, and even that they ate with them when they gathered at the dinner table. Like the dolls she had made the girls believe were real. In that way, when they asked to go outside and find friends to play with, she could tell them there was no need to. She could always make up new ghosts.

Kimberly knocked her head on the ceiling and cursed. The tunnel seemed to get smaller down here and she had to crouch even more. Her head was bleeding, she realized, when touching it with a finger.

How long is this tunnel anyway?

Kimberly snarled and shone the light in front of her, when suddenly she heard a sound coming from behind her. She gasped and turned to look. She couldn't see anything, but could clearly hear the sound of steps in the watery tunnel.

They were gaining on her.

74

[MAY 2016]

could see her flashlight ahead of me and I could hear Tyler crying, while carefully walking on the wet floor beneath me. I had no flashlight and my eyes had a hard time trying to acclimate to the darkness. It was hard to breathe in the heavy musty smell of moldy water. I lowered my head cautiously, to not hurt it on the lower ceilings.

I tried to judge how far ahead she was, but it was impossible. All I could see was her light far down the tunnel.

I tried to run, but the floor was slippery, and I didn't want to risk falling and hurting myself. I was getting my son back, no matter what.

My heart was still racing rapidly in my chest, heaving

up and down with my deep ragged breaths. I couldn't escape the image of Shannon lying on the kitchen floor, blood gushing from her stomach. It haunted me and I was desperate to get this woman for what she had done.

I had asked Bellini to call for the ambulance and she had told me she would stay with Shannon and go with her to the hospital, while I went to get my son. I kept wondering if I should have stayed with her instead, but how could I? My child, my baby was in this tunnel being abducted once again, and this time I had to stop it. I had a chance once I realized the woman had escaped through the tunnel. It wasn't hard to guess, since her shoes were on the floor next to the hatch.

After going back to the police station, I had followed Shannon's trail to track her down, along with Bellini and Nelson. The lady at the doll store had given me the number for Kimberly Milligan, the doll doctor. It was easy from there for the detectives to track her phone to her house, even though Bellini and Nelson kept telling me the house was abandoned and that no one had lived there since the nineties.

I was closing in on Kimberly, slowly but steadily. I didn't know if she knew I was behind her or not, and I didn't care. I was going to get her no matter what. I tried to run a little again, and for a little while it worked, but then the tunnel got narrower and I banged my head on the ceiling. I screamed in pain and felt my forehead. I couldn't see it, but it was definitely warm blood I could feel.

I knew my scream blew my cover, and I sensed she

accelerated. The light in front of me started to move faster, almost flickering.

She was running.

I sped up as well. Holding a hand to my hurting head, I ran through the water, my head lowered, my back bent, thinking only of my son and getting him back home with me.

If it's the last thing I ever do.

I was faster than her, or maybe I was just more driven by my fear of losing my son once again, but soon I was gaining on her even more. Running, sometimes slipping and falling, I could soon see the back of her and hear my son's crying very loudly.

"Stop," I yelled. "Give me my son back!"

The woman continued, her feet splashing in the water. I was panting, breathing heavily, my heart pounding in my chest.

Almost there, almost there!

She could have been no more than a hundred feet in front of me, when she suddenly stopped. The light stopped moving, her back stood still.

Why has she stopped?

As I approached her, I realized why. The road was blocked. Big rocks had fallen and made the road impassable.

Of course. This is where the tunnel had collapsed when the building did. Ha! You're not going any further, my friend.

With the prospect of actually getting to her, I slowed down a little to make sure I didn't slip again, thinking there was no way she could get out of this, but of course I reached that conclusion too quickly. When I was almost there, I raised my gun towards her, since I didn't know if she was armed or not.

"Hand over my son!" I yelled. "Hand him over now."

But, as I came closer, I soon realized there wasn't just one tunnel. The tunnels were connected underground, and soon the woman turned to look at me, then lit up her own face with her flashlight, showing a big smile, before she took off running to her right down another tunnel.

Oh, no!

Desperately, I started to run again, but as I reached the blocked part of the tunnel and tried to turn, I slipped and fell face-first into the water. I managed to hold the gun out of the water, with the result that my face fell all the way in. The water tasted so gross I almost threw up. I rose to my feet, only to see the woman's flashlight disappear further down the tunnel.

"Stooop!" I screamed, then raised my gun and fired it in anger. I fired three shots, knowing I would never be able to hit her from this distance. The gun made a loud noise that echoed into the tunnels and the sound was overwhelming.

When it stopped, I was left in the greasy wet tunnel all alone, panting, breathing angrily, when suddenly everything was drowned out by another sound. A much louder sound than what my gun had provided. It sounded like a train.

The tunnel and the ground underneath me shook like an earthquake and I fell to my knees, holding my ears.

When it finally stopped, I rose to my feet and realized the flashlight had disappeared. Meanwhile, a cloud of dust emerged towards me and blew me to the ground once again.

When I managed to get up, I realized to my terror what had happened. The tunnel had collapsed! The tunnel that the woman had disappeared into with my baby had collapsed, probably from the loud noise of my gun going off.

"NOOO!" I screamed, and ran through the dust cloud towards where I had seen the light disappear, but when I reached it, there was nothing but rocks and debris.

"TYLER!!"

75

[MAY 2016]

was digging with my bare hands. Removing rocks, digging through dirt. A crew of firefighters had joined me from inside the tunnel and some from above the ground, where they told me the floor had collapsed inside of a house, in the basement of another house that was being renovated.

Please God, please God.

There was dust and dirt everywhere. In my eyes, in my mouth, and nostrils. I coughed and spat, but never stopped digging.

"Please, my son is in there, please," I pleaded. "Please, find him!"

The firefighters next to me removed rock after rock, while I scrabbled frantically through the rubble, but still no sign of either the woman or my son. Hope was oozing out of me slowly, and I was beginning to cry. It felt like so much time had gone by now, since the tunnel collapsed. Was there even the slightest chance that either of them could be alive at this point?

I didn't dare to ask or even think about it. I didn't know if Shannon was alive or not. I wasn't going to lose the both of them in the same day. I simply refused to.

I dug my fingers into the dirt once again and scraped small rocks and soil away, while the firefighters removed the bigger bricks and rocks. They were working incredibly hard. I felt a hand on my shoulder coming from behind and turned to see Detective Nelson. He was the one who had called for the firefighters and had helped me dig until they arrived. He had a flashlight in his hand and in the sparse light from it I could see his face was covered in brown dirt.

"It's been two hours," he said.

"My son is in there. Under all that rubble."

"I know. But I think that maybe…well, you know the chances aren't very good for survival after this long."

I shook my head in disbelief. I wasn't going to give up. If I had to dig all night, then that's what I would have to do.

"I'm sorry," I said, "but I have to get back to digging. Every second counts."

I fell to my knees again and dug my fingers into the dirt, while tears rolled across my face.

He's not dead. He's not dead.

I dug till I reached a big pile of bricks that I started to remove one after the other, the flashlight the firefighters had given me between my teeth. When I removed one at the bottom, I spotted something. A small finger was sticking out.

My heart dropped.

"Hey! I got something!" I yelled, then frantically dug and removed the bricks. Two firefighters joined me and we removed brick after brick till more of what I recognized as my son's arm stuck out.

Oh, my God, oh, my God, please, please let him be...

I barely finished the thought before two of his tiny fingers moved. "He moved!" I almost screamed. "He moved his fingers!"

Crying heavily and breathing raggedly, I removed more bricks and stones until I, from under the rubble, heard faint cries.

"It's him. It's Tyler; he's alive!" I screamed.

Seconds later, we removed the last of the rubble and I was able to pull out my baby boy from the debris. He was crying hard and the sound echoed in the tunnels, but it was the sweetest sound I had ever heard.

"He's alive! My baby boy is alive!"

PART FOUR:

SURRENDER: To surrender is to abandon your hand, while recovering half of your initial bet.

76

[MAY 2016]

Shannon suffered severe damage to one of her kidneys as the corkscrew went through her, and she was in intensive care, fighting for her life for two days before the doctor finally told me she was stable.

My parents, Shannon's mother and her sister Kristi, and all our kids were with me when he came out to tell us. Cheer and joy took over in the small room at the hospital, and I sunk to a chair, relieved.

They had examined Tyler, but as a miracle, he had suffered no injury from being buried under the rubble. Not even a scratch. It was amazing.

They had dug out the Doctor, aka Kimberly Milligan, but they weren't able to save her. I felt bad about that; I wanted her to go to trial; I wanted her to receive her punishment for all the pain she had caused my family.

"Now maybe you could do with a coffee, huh son?" My mother asked and sat next to me. "You haven't eaten or drunk anything for two whole days. I have an energy bar in my purse if you like?"

I smiled for the first time and nodded. So glad my mom never changed. "I would love that, thank you."

My mother gave me the bar, then went for coffee from the vending machine. She brought back the cup and several bags of chips and chocolate bars.

"I wish they would put healthier stuff in those things," she said. "It is, after all, a hospital. Wait, I think I also have an apple in my purse."

"I'll start with this," I said and took a bite of the bar. I looked down at Tyler, who was sleeping heavily in his cot. I couldn't believe all the things he had gone through and how well he slept even after all of it. I envied him. I hadn't slept in forever.

"You can see her now," the doctor came out and said.

I grabbed Tyler in his cot, got ahold of the kids and parents, and we followed the doctor into Shannon's room. I peeked inside first. My eyes met Shannon's and she smiled feebly. I turned and looked at the kids.

"No screaming, okay? Nice and quiet."

Austin and Abigail didn't listen, as usual, and stormed in there screaming and yelling. "Shannon!!"

They threw themselves at her and she laughed, even though I could tell she was in great pain. Angela walked in with me, holding my hand. She had been so nervous, so scared, and I had tried the best I could to comfort her along the way.

"Go on," I said. "Go to her."

Shannon reached out her heavily bandaged hand and started to sob. "Baby girl."

Angela approached her and hugged her carefully, while I told my kids to get down from the bed and sit in chairs. Angela and Shannon spoke for a little while and hugged a lot. When they were done, I grabbed Tyler from the seat and put him on top of Shannon. She held him the best she could, tears streaming from her eyes.

"My baby boy."

"And he's perfectly fine," I said. "Not a scratch on his head."

"That's amazing."

Tyler didn't even wake up. He kept sleeping on his mother's chest, while she played with his fingers, laughing, crying, and kissing him all over. When I could tell she was getting tired, I removed the baby and put him back in his cot.

Of course, that woke him up and he started to cry. "I know, baby boy. I want Mommy too, but Mommy needs her rest."

"Let me take him," my mother said. I handed her the boy. Meanwhile, Shannon's mom and sister spoke to her.

I spotted Emily standing by the door, as if she was

deciding whether to come in or not. Shannon saw her and signaled for her to come closer.

"Are you going to be well?" she asked. "Like, will you be able to play guitar and sing again?"

"I don't know yet," Shannon said with an exhale. I could tell this was all a little much for her. She was getting tired. "Right now, I'm just happy to be alive."

"And we're just happy you're alive too," I said and approached her with a kiss to her forehead. "Now we'll leave you alone so you can get some sleep."

77

[MAY 2016]

I spent the rest of the afternoon at the house. After two days in the hospital, the kids needed to get out of there and just play in the yard. My mom cooked us a big dinner, which we ate together, no one speaking much except for the children.

After dinner, I was sitting in the darkness of the living room when Sarah brought me a beer.

"You're an angel, do you know that?"

"I do," she said and sat in a recliner next to me, a beer in her hand. "I'm just glad Shannon is better. I really love working for her and for your family."

I looked at her and laughed lightly. "Even with all the craziness?"

"Even with all that, yes."

I sipped my beer. It hit the spot. Just what I needed right now.

"So, what were you thinking about alone in here in the darkness, Jack?" Sarah asked. "If you don't mind me asking."

"I don't. I was actually thinking about Betsy Sue and all the strange conversations I had with her. I still can't quite figure out what parts of what she told me were true and what was a lie. Maybe it doesn't matter. She's back with her parents and so is Miss Muffit. Or should I say Adelaide and Chandelle, which are, after all, their real names. We shouldn't use those silly doll names that the crazy lady gave them when she kidnapped them." I shook my head and drank again before I continued. "Chandelle's mother lost her six years ago at the hospital when she took her in because the girl had a fever. In the middle of the night, the girl simply vanished from her crib. It gives me the chills even thinking about it. What a nightmare. On top of it all, everyone thought she had hurt the baby somehow. The police interrogated her again and again. Even her own friends and family believed she had done something awful to her own kid. It was mostly based on rumors about her being depressed and overwhelmed by becoming a mother. No one believed a child could just vanish from the hospital. Susan Murray, Chandelle's mother, was publically humiliated on top of losing her child. People wrote graffiti on her house walls, calling her a child killer and everything. They came up to her in the street and yelled it to her face. They threw dolls and used diapers in her front yard. Can you imagine going through that?"

"Not even going to try," Sarah said. She paused. "So they're both back with their parents again?"

I nodded, put the bottle to my lips, then drank.

"That's good, then. Everyone is happy," Sarah said.

"Yeah, I guess," I said and drank again.

"You're not quite satisfied with the outcome?" she asked.

I sighed. "I don't know. Maybe I'm just being paranoid, but something doesn't quite add up."

"And what's that?"

"Every time I spoke to Betsy Sue, or Adelaide, she talked like she had been at the doll doctor's house a lot longer than possible. She remembered birthdays way before her fifth year, which was when she was kidnapped, according to her parents. And it seemed like they hardly knew each other when she came back. They had kept nothing of her stuff, like they didn't expect her to come back."

"People grieve differently."

"Yes, I know, but still. It was like they...like it wasn't their child at all, but that's just crazy, right? I mean the DNA test showed that Betsy Sue was, in fact, Adelaide. DNA tests can't be wrong."

Sarah shrugged. "Unless she has a twin, I don't see how."

I turned my head and stared at Sarah. "Oh, my God," I said. "You're right."

"What?"

I got up from my chair, grabbed my phone, and dialed a number.

"What? What did I say?" Sarah yelled after me.

78

[MAY 2016]

"My apologies for disturbing you this late," Bellini said.

I was standing next to her in the Hawthornes' driveway. "May we come in? There are a few things we need to clarify."

"What's he doing here?" Ron Hawthorne asked and nodded at me.

"I'm the guy with the questions," I said, and walked past him inside the house. I knew I was supposed to wait for him to tell me it was all right to come in, since we didn't have a warrant, but I was simply too agitated.

"Do come in," Ron finally said, and Bellini followed me. We walked into the living room, where Heather Hawthorne got up from her chair, a magazine dangling from her hand. She stared at us, startled.

"Detectives. What's going on? And at this hour?"

"It's not even ten o'clock," I said and sat down.

The Hawthornes exchanged a glance.

"Please, sit down," I said. "This won't take long."

Heather could no longer disguise her nervousness. The magazine in her hand was shaking when she put it down and approached us. They both sat down.

"We've been in contact with the hospital," I said. "And they told us something very interesting."

"Oh. And what might that be?" Heather asked.

"They told us you gave birth to not one child in 2006, but *two* children," I said.

Ron Hawthorne grabbed his wife's hand in her lap. "Yes. That is true. There were twins, but one of them died. Please don't rip up this old story. It was very traumatic, especially for my wife. You must understand…" His angry mask cracked and we saw the raw pain from the loss of his child.

"I do understand. A nurse named Kimberly Milligan, who worked at the hospital back then, led you to believe that one of your children died. How this could happen, Detective Bellini and her crew will have to investigate further. But what happened was that Kimberly Milligan took the child and raised it as her own." I paused to observe their reaction. I could tell I was on the right track. "But you already know that, don't you? How else would you explain suddenly getting your child back when you thought she was dead?"

"Excuse me?" Heather asked. Her face clouded over and she bit down hard on her lip. "Why…you…"

She received a look from her husband.

"It's over, Heather," he said. "They know." He sat back, looking rattled.

Heather protested once more before her shoulders finally settled down. She bowed her head and her hair fell forward, covering her face.

"All right," she said and nodded. "But you must know it was self-defense."

"Maybe you should tell us the story from the beginning," Bellini said.

Heather inhaled deeply and looked quickly at her husband before she started. "We loved Adelaide dearly. You must know that. We really did. She was a very quiet child. She could spend hours and even days in her room, playing with her dolls. We never had any trouble with her. Not until she turned five years old, and one night my husband and I were sleeping in our bed, when I woke up to find Adelaide standing at the end of it. What are you doing up? I asked her. Did you have a bad dream? Adelaide never sleepwalked or had bad dreams, so it was quite the mystery to me that she would all of a sudden get out of bed in the middle of the night. And that was when I saw it." Heather stopped to cry. She was a very good actress. Yet, I didn't buy it.

"What did you see, Mrs. Hawthorne?" Bellini asked. She was better at the sympathetic role than I.

"My husband's handgun. She was holding it in her hand, and when I asked her why she had her father's gun, she didn't answer. I woke up my husband, who started to scold her and tell her to hand it over. But she didn't. Instead, she lifted it, pointed it at Ron, and fired. She missed, but Ron threw himself at her and they fought for a long time, while I could do nothing but watch. Finally, my husband got the gun from her, but she was screaming so terribly and fighting him, scratching him on his face. I was afraid he would hurt her. She got up and ran, and I ran after her, wanting to grab her, but instead I...I...tripped her. I made her fall and she fell down the stairs, ending up face-first into one of our big antique vases; she hit her head on it and broke her skull open. I screamed and screamed as I watched the blood run out from her little...head."

Heather stopped again and clasped her mouth while crying. Her husband took over:

"We knew no one would ever believe us, so we decided to bury her in the yard. She's still out there. By the big oak."

"And then you made up the story of her being kidnapped while you were at the park," I said.

"Yes."

Ron Hawthorne looked at his wife. "But then our little girl came back all of a sudden. We believed it was the Universe—or whoever is in charge—that was giving us a second chance. We didn't know where she came from; we never even talked about it. I guess we both knew somewhere deep down that she had to be the twin we lost so many years ago."

I looked at Bellini. I didn't believe one bit of their story, except for the part where they killed their daughter.

"You must believe us," Heather said. "It was a terrible accident."

"I really don't," I said. "I don't believe a little girl would try and kill her own parents unless they had done something really bad to her. Either that or you came up with the story of it all being self-defense to protect yourselves. Either way we look at this, you two come out as bad guys. I've heard enough."

"Me too," Bellini said and got up.

Heather was crying helplessly. Her husband wanted to console her, but somehow, he hesitated.

"I have to ask the both of you to come with me to the station," Bellini said. "You're under arrest for the murder of Adelaide Hawthorne."

79

[MAY 2016]

Shannon was well enough the next day for Bellini to get her story and take her statement for the report. Meanwhile, I waited outside her room, walking back and forth, worrying that she would get too overwhelmed, too tired, that it was all too much for her. Needless to say, I drank a whole lot of coffee until the mid-afternoon, when Bellini finally came out. Her face was red and it looked like she had been crying a little, but I could be wrong. Bellini wasn't the type who showed emotion publicly.

"Quite the story, huh?" I asked, coffee still in my hand.

"Can't say I've ever heard anything like it," she said with a deep sigh. "But it's all going in the report now, so we can get the case closed as soon as possible. Can't wait to put it away for good. Between you and me, the whole story of Kimberly Milligan makes me feel really creeped out, though. She lost a child, you know. Right before they moved here, she lost a baby boy. Sudden Infant Death Syndrome, they concluded. But I guess that set her off. She lost touch with reality. She believed her daughter had killed the baby and that she was going to kill her, so she killed her herself. And we believe she killed her husband too in 1990. Put their bodies in the tunnels thinking no one would ever find them. Then for years, she worked as a nurse and saw one baby after another come into the world. I guess that's how she got the idea. Stole the first child from the hospital in 2004, Luanne Johnson or Libby Bibby."

"Bibby Libby," I corrected her. We started to walk down the hallway.

"Whatever it was she called her. She stole Betsy Sue or Adelaide in 2006, and then Chandelle, better known as Miss Muffit in 2010. It was then that Kimberly Milligan disappeared from the face of the earth, quit her job, and started to work as the doll repair doctor instead. Shannon told me the girls were all related. That she had the idea that she had to protect the world from these children or something. Probably just what she told herself to justify that she was stealing children. Anyway, my guess is she took them to replace the children she had lost. The tragic story of a woman driven mad by great sorrow. It's really sad, I guess."

"Sure is tragic," I said, thinking of Bibby Libby, who

had to die. Luckily, we had managed to help the two others before it was too late.

"I am working on finding evidence enough to pin her up on the murder of Trevor Bryden and his father as well, but I haven't found anything yet. Could be good to close those two cases as well. I've found an old claim from back in 1990 where she argued with the older Bryden. Apparently, he reported her daughter Rosa for killing his cat, but could never prove she had done it. It had its head cut off. He found it on his doorstep one morning when he went to get the newspaper. That's as far as I've gotten."

"What's going to happen to Betsy Sue?" I asked, as we reached the lobby.

Bellini stopped. "I wanted to talk to you about that. She is awfully fond of you and Shannon...and she *is* related to your fiancé...I mentioned it briefly to Shannon while I was in there, but..."

I nodded. I knew where she was going, but I couldn't make this kind of decision on my own. "We need to talk about it," I said.

Bellini's hand landed on my shoulder. "You're a good man, Jack. And an even better father."

"Thanks," I said and emptied my coffee cup.

Bellini looked at her watch. "Guess I know what I'll be doing the next several weeks, huh? Listen, I have a briefing in half an hour. I'll call you later."

She waved at me while she walked out the sliding doors leading to the parking lot. I watched her disappear, then threw away my plastic cup and hurried upstairs and into Shannon's room. She was still awake when I entered.

"Hi there," I said and approached her.

"Hi," she said, her eyes half closed in exhaustion. She smiled. "Did Bellini talk to you about Betsy Sue?"

I nodded and grabbed her good hand in mine. "We don't have to make any decisions till you feel better," I said. "She's at a foster home right now."

"I want her," Shannon said.

I smiled. "I do too."

Shannon laughed for the first time and it hurt. She made a grimace of pain, but was still cheerful. Her big eyes looked up at me, as beautiful as ever. "Will you marry me, Jack?" she asked.

"I thought we already settled that," I said. "You know, back when I proposed to you, remember?"

"No," she said. "I mean I want to marry you."

"And I want to marry you too, Shannon. As soon as you're better and everything has fallen back into place again."

She grabbed my arm with her good hand. I looked into her eyes. She was serious. "No. I want to marry you now. Right here. Right here at the hospital."

"Shannon...I..."

"No, Jack. It's perfect. Can't you see? Everyone is here already. Even our pastor is still in town. Let's do this!"

"Shannon…you're not well…let's wait…"

"No! You're not listening to me. I want to marry you right here. Right now. Call everyone and have them come here. I almost died in that house, and all I could think of while losing consciousness was the fact that I came so close, but never got to marry the man I love. I want it now, Jack. I need this."

80

[MAY 2016]

We had to wait till the next day before we could do it, naturally, but we set it all up really fast. I told our family to be ready, and the hospital was all in for it. Even Pastor Daniel thought it was a great idea. That evening, right before bedtime, everything was ready, and I guess I was going to get married.

I had put the three A's to bed and told them Betsy Sue was going to come live with us soon. Abigail thought we should find a new name for her, one that started with A like theirs did, so she would feel more welcome.

I kissed all three of them, then checked on Tyler, who was sleeping heavily after his last bottle. He had started to sleep through the night lately and that sure made everything a lot easier. Not that I minded having to get up for him. Not after almost losing him.

I walked to Emily's room and knocked on the door. A weak "Come in," sounded from behind the door and I opened it.

Her face lit up when she saw me.

"Dad?"

"Hey there. I wondered if you were up for some *Tonight Show* with your old man. You know, like in the good old days?"

She didn't answer, but nodded instead, and I could tell she was very happy that I asked.

"I feel like we haven't seen each other at all on this trip," I said, and closed the door behind me while she turned on the TV.

We sat on her bed and watched Jimmy Fallon as the intro ran over the screen the usual way. We even found ourselves humming along, then burst into laughter because we both did it. It felt good to be with Emily again. I had missed her and I knew she had missed me as well. It was just so hard to have time for everyone in my life lately. I had decided to get better at it.

"Listen," I said, while the music still played. "I know this is a hard time for you, but I promise you it'll get better. I haven't had much time to spend with you since the baby came, or even since Shannon and Angela came into our lives. I want you to know I am sorry about that and I promise to make it up to you."

Emily swallowed hard. I could tell she was emotional, but tried hard not to be. *This must have been hard on her as well*, I thought to myself. *Always having to be the strongest.*

She turned her head away. As she moved, I could see her collarbone poking out and part of her bony shoulder. It made my heart jump. Had she lost even more weight? Or was it status quo? No matter what, she was too thin; it wasn't healthy. I decided I needed to have someone professional talk to her when we got back. Shannon was right. She wasn't well and needed help. So far, I had believed it was going to pass on its own, that she would soon be eating ice cream with me again and pancakes in the middle of the night like we used to when it was just the two of us. But now I realized it wasn't changing; it wasn't getting better. This time I was going to do it. No more talk.

Jimmy Fallon came on and started his monologue. I sighed and leaned back on Emily's bed, my head on her pillow. She lay down next to me, tucked herself close to me and, as usual, I fell asleep during the monologue, thinking it was good that some things always remained the same.

81

[MAY 2016]

"We're going to make you the perfect bride," Sarah said.

She was holding Shannon's dress on a hanger. Shannon had barely finished her breakfast in the hospital bed when Sarah had stormed inside, flanked by the tailor, a hairdresser, and a make-up artist.

Now they were debating how to put on the dress with all the tubes, drips, and bandages. Shannon was far from ready to get out of her bed yet. She could still barely move.

"I can open it on the side, then we slide it on," the tailor said.

"But they need to be able to change the bandages," Shannon said. "They do that three times a day."

"So we do it right after they change them next time," Sarah said. "The wedding is at two o'clock. I have arranged everything with Pastor Daniel. The nurses agreed to roll your bed to the hospital's chapel and up the aisle. We have two girls as flower girls, Angela and Abigail, while Austin will be with his dad, and he has the ring. Remind me I have to call them and make sure he has the ring. And your brother-in law, Jimmy, will give you away. Did I leave anything out?"

"I think you got it," Shannon said, feeling tired already. Seeing the stressed out face on Sarah made her think that maybe Jack had been right. Maybe it was too early. Right now, she really wanted a nap.

"All right, then," Sarah said. "Let's get her ready."

Hands were all over her face and hair. They were pulling her up so they could wash her hair, then arrange it nicely and put flowers in it. Meanwhile, the make-up artist did her work with brushes and sponges, and soon Shannon was sweating behind all that glitter and concealer. It made her feel very uncomfortable.

Once the bandages had been changed, they pulled and pushed and slid the dress on her, Shannon crying out several times in pain, the nurses trying hard to prevent the tubes from falling out.

It was a lot of hassle, a lot more than Shannon had imagined, but when she saw the final result, she realized it had all been worth it. Sarah held a mirror to her face.

Shannon gasped and felt tears spring to her eyes.

"I don't think there has even been a bride more

beautiful than you," she said.

"Wow," Shannon said. She looked up at Sarah, her lips shaping a heartfelt "Thank you."

"My pleasure."

Sarah walked to the door and opened it. In trotted Angela and Abigail in their pink dresses, baskets of flower petals in their hands. Shannon couldn't cry because of the make-up, but it was hard not to.

"You two look so pretty," she said, and kissed them as they approached her in the bed.

"You do too, Mommy," Angela said.

"Yeah. You can hardly tell that you almost died," Abigail said with a shrug. "Except for the bed and all the drips, heh."

Shannon couldn't help laughing. Sarah grabbed her hand. "You ready?"

"You tell me," Shannon said.

"I think you are. I say you're more than ready. I just checked and everyone is set and ready in the chapel as well." She turned to look at the girls. "All right, girls. You're up next."

The two girls exchanged a glance, then opened the door and walked hand in hand down the hallway. Two nurses grabbed Shannon's bed and started to roll it after them. Shannon entered the hallway with a nervous tickle in her stomach. She could hear the wedding march playing in the chapel at the end of the hallway. As the girls reached the entrance, they started throwing flower petals. Kristi's husband Jimmy was waiting for Shannon and, as she came closer, he grabbed her hand.

"You ready?"

Shannon nodded and Jimmy handed her the bridal bouquet. He nodded at the nurses and they started to push. Slowly, Shannon rolled up the aisle, while the spectators turned to look at her.

This has got to be the weirdest wedding ever.

82
[MAY 2016]

My legs were shaking. I watched as Shannon was rolled down the aisle and couldn't hold back my tears. Even in her sickbed, she looked so beautiful, stunning even. I couldn't believe I was so lucky.

Next to me stood Austin in his small suit, looking all grown up and serious. Pastor Daniel was on the other side of me, ready to perform the ceremony.

Shannon looked tired, but so very, very happy. Emily stood with my mother and father and on the other side stood Shannon's mother and sister. A small crowd of nurses and doctors stayed in the background to watch.

I spotted Bellini and Nelson in the crowd. Bellini smiled and nodded approvingly. They were both nicely dressed up for the occasion.

Melanie Vann was there too, sitting by herself. Shannon had insisted on inviting her. It was only natural, I thought. The two of them had talked a lot since Melanie saved Shannon's life, and Melanie had visited Shannon every day in the hospital.

Shannon's eyes met mine as she approached me, the young girls dancing and throwing petals on the floor in front of her. It was all a little odd, but also very beautiful in its own strange way. The girls looked so happy. They had really grown to love each other. I wondered for a second if bringing Betsy Sue in would change that. I hoped and prayed they would be able to get along. Betsy Sue was, after all, very different from the rest of them.

I heard Tyler's small cry and turned instantly to look at him. My mother took him up from his cot and jumped him lightly up and down, then when that didn't work, she rocked him back and forth till he finally calmed down.

Shannon was disturbed by his cry as well. She looked in his direction, then back at me, and I smiled from ear to ear. She smiled back and relaxed. Tyler was in good hands. She knew he was.

Finally, Shannon's bed was rolled all the way up to me and I grabbed her hand in mine.

"Hi," I whispered.

"Hi."

We faced Pastor Daniel, who cleared his throat, then started the ceremony.

"Dearly beloved. We're gathered here today to join this man and this woman in holy matrimony."

I felt such a deep sensation of love for Shannon as he spoke the words to us. I couldn't stop looking at her. She was so gorgeous, and I was a very lucky man. It wasn't the kind of wedding I wanted to give her, and it bothered me slightly, since I believed she deserved better than to be tied to a hospital bed on her wedding day, but I kept pushing the thought away. This was what Shannon wanted and when everything came down to it, it didn't matter. Our love for one another was what was important.

Daniel turned to face me, then said:

"Jack, if you'll repeat after me. I, Jack Ryder…"

"I, Jack Ryder…"

"Take you, Shannon King…"

"Take you, Shannon King…"

"…to be my wife, to have and to hold…"

"To be my wife, to have and to hold…"

"From this day forward…"

"From this day forward…"

"For better or for worse, for richer, for poorer, in sickness and in health, to love and to cherish, till death do us part."

I took in a deep breath to say the last part, but as the first word left my mouth, something happened. A noise coming from behind us immediately stopped everything. The plump sound of a body falling to the ground. I turned to see what it was and spotted Emily, lying lifeless on the tiles.

"Emily!" my mother shrieked, her voice echoing eerily in the chapel.

Without thinking, I turned and jumped towards her. I grabbed her shoulders, but she felt limp in my hands. I put a finger to her throat. "There's no pulse!" I yelled. "Oh, my God! Please. Someone help her!"

83

[MAY 2016]

"Her organs gave out."

The doctor stood in front me in the waiting room where we were all sitting, waiting for news about Emily. Shannon had been taken back to her room to get some rest, even though she said she wanted to be with us. The doctor told her she needed to think about her condition.

"Her body couldn't take anymore," he continued.

Couldn't take anymore. What is he saying?

"How long has she suffered from an eating disorder? She is severely emaciated," he said.

"I...I knew she...I mean she...is she...? Will she be all right, Doctor?"

"She's not in the clear yet, but so far we have managed to get her heart beating again, yes. The next couple of days will show if she'll pull through. When someone starves herself like this, at some point, her body starts to eat of itself, so to speak. It starts to eat from her own organs. And once that process has begun, it doesn't take much longer before the heart can't endure anymore. It's been running on overtime for several months."

I felt like screaming. I covered my face with both my hands. How could this have happened? How did I not see it? How did I not act?

After finishing up with the doctor, I walked to my mother and sat down crying, my head on her shoulder.

"How could I have let this happen, Mom? How did I not stop it?"

"We all saw it, Jack. The blame is as much ours as it is yours. We saw what she was doing to herself, but we didn't do anything about it."

"But she is my daughter; she is *my* responsibility, Mom. I'm the one who should have gotten her help. I'm the one who should have reacted. I kept thinking it was going to pass, that she was going to get better soon. I kept asking her how she was and she told me she was fine. And then what? She was about to kill herself? Why?"

My mother stroked my face the way she always did when I was a child. "You must not blame yourself, Jack. We need to look ahead now and not back. Emily needs us more than ever."

"What am I going to do if she dies? I've had her with me since she was six years old. I promised Lisa; I promised her, Mom. I looked into her eyes as she was dying and told her I would take care of her daughter."

"We don't know what will happen, Jack. You have to keep your cool. The young ones need you too. They need you to be strong. So does Shannon."

Shannon. She told me something was wrong with Emily. She told me to do something about it. Why didn't I listen?

I walked out of the waiting room and found Shannon in her bed. She wasn't asleep, but had her eyes closed. She opened them when I entered.

"Jack," she whispered. "How is she?"

I sat next to her bed in a chair and grabbed her hand. "They still don't know. They got her heart beating, but don't know if it has the strength to keep on, to keep her alive." I looked into her eyes as tears sprung up. I bit my lip in anger. "I failed her, Shannon. I failed Emily and her mother Lisa. I promised I would take care of her. She died in my arms, Shannon. She looked at me and begged me to take care of Emily. I failed her. I failed Emily and I failed you, Shannon. Look at you. I couldn't protect you. Because of me and my job you're in this bed, you almost died. Same for Tyler. All the bad things in our lives happen because of me."

"That's not true, Jack, and you know it. Kimberly took Tyler because of me. Because of our family. It had nothing to do with you. Me getting hurt had nothing to do with you. I went in there alone because I thought I could save Tyler on my own. It wasn't your fault. You saved all of us."

I shook my head, crying. "I cause you nothing but trouble. You and the kids. I can't offer you security. You deserve better than this."

She grabbed my chin and lifted my head. "I'm a celebrity, Jack. I'm used to being a target. I'm used to insecurity. My life comes with huge risks too. But do we really want a risk-free life?"

I shook my head and wiped my tears away on my sleeve. I pulled away.

"Don't you give up on us, Jack! We're great together. We're good at taking risks together, Jack."

I could see tears in her eyes as well and it made my heart bleed to have to do what I did next.

"Don't you dare walk out on me, Jack!"

She was breathing through her tears.

"I'm sorry. I can't…"

"No, Jack, no, don't…"

"I can't marry you."

I couldn't say anymore. I couldn't take anymore. No more being the strong one, no more taking care of everyone. I simply had to get away.

So I left.

I ran down the hallway, took the stairs to the lobby, and ran onto the street.

84

[MAY 2016]

grabbed a taxi and told the driver to just start driving. I just wanted to get away, and didn't know where I was going. I asked him to drive me to the harbor, but didn't want to get out when we got there.

"So, where to now?" he asked.

I knew when I said it that it wasn't the smartest thing to do, given the vulnerable state I was in, but I also knew that earlier in my life it had provided comfort and made me forget when things got bad. I wasn't a heavy drinker, so that was out of the question, but this provided some of the same relief for me.

It made me forget.

"Do you know where a man can get a good card game?"

The driver looked in his rearview mirror and his eyes met mine. I knew drivers like him always had a finger on the pulse and knew exactly where to find one, but I wasn't sure he would give the information to me. Guys like him could smell a cop from very far away.

"I think I know the right one for you," he said and started the car. He drove me to a building, then dropped me off at the back entrance.

"The password is Black Jack," he said out the window, as I paid him an extra bill for his help.

I got in only with a few suspicious looks, then sat at the table, a couple of guys on each side of me. We nodded politely, but exchanged no other glances or pleasantries. This was our refuge; this was our hideout, and we didn't want to know anything about each other.

I was dealt my cards and placed my bet. My phone vibrated in my pocket and, as I picked it up, I saw it was Shannon. I stared at it for a few seconds, then decided to hang up. I silenced the phone and put it back in my pocket.

"Hit," I said, and the dealer gave me another card.

"Bust," the dealer said and removed my cards and my money.

Someone brought me a drink, bourbon, and I drank it while losing a few times more, before I started to win. Three rounds in a row soon made me excited and I bet more money.

Hours later, I was getting drunk and had lost a lot of money. Yet, I still believed I could get my winning streak back, so I continued, not caring if I lost everything. I had forgotten the world outside this room and that made me feel good.

Until around one in the morning, when someone entered the room and sat down next to me. I didn't turn to look at first, not until she placed her bid and I saw her ring.

I sighed and finished my drink. Seconds later, a new one was planted in front of me. "How'd you find me?"

"Being in law enforcement has it perks. You know that," Bellini answered.

"You tracked my phone? I knew I should have shut it off."

"Well, maybe you wanted me to find you."

"Very funny," I said.

"So, Black Jack, huh? What have we got?" Bellini asked.

"A ten and a five and a guy who feels lost."

"Well, do you feel lucky today?" Bellini asked.

"Not really."

"I do." She looked to the dealer. "Hit him again."

A card landed in front of me.

"A five. See, I told you. You are lucky," Bellini said. "He stands."

I exhaled and leaned back. "Listen. It's nice of you to come down here and all, but I'm not in the mood for all this."

Bellini nodded. "Okay then, let me be frank with you. You listen to me, Ryder. You have a good thing there at that hospital. A very good thing indeed. Don't throw it away."

"They're better off without me; believe me."

"Don't be one of those guys, Jack. Pity will get you nowhere. You have to choose in life, my mother always said. You can be pitiful or powerful; you can't be both. Stop feeling sorry for yourself. It's really unsexy, Jack."

I looked at Bellini. The corner of her mouth ticked upward in a fleeting movement you couldn't really call a smile. There was a flicker of an eyebrow that might have been approval.

"What?" she asked.

"You think I'm sexy, don't you?"

"Oh, get over yourself, will you?" she said, appraising me coolly. She exhaled and threw a peanut my way. I looked into my half empty drink. I didn't even like bourbon that much. I lifted my head. Bellini got off the stool and threw me a glare.

"So, what's it gonna be, Ryder?"

85

[MAY 2016]

The hospital room was so empty and so dark, Shannon could hardly take it. She hated lying there all alone in her bed, not being able to even go to the bathroom on her own, not knowing where her beloved Jack was or what he was up to.

How could you do this to me, Jack? How could you leave me like this? After all we've been through?

All night, since he left, she had been crying, soaking her pillow, but now she had no more tears left in her. She stared at the black window, at the city, and cursed Savannah.

Why did we even have to come here?

She knew it wasn't the city's fault that everything had turned out this badly, but she couldn't stop thinking that if they had only stayed in Cocoa Beach and decided to get married on a surfboard like Jack wanted, then things would have been so much different.

If only…there is always an if only…

She looked at the phone again, but still no message from him. It was almost two o'clock in the morning now. Where could he be? If it had been her, she would have gone to a bar and gotten drunk, but that wasn't really Jack's thing. He liked a beer or two, but he didn't like to get drunk.

The night was long and Shannon knew there was no way she was going to get any sleep. Yet she tried again and again to close her eyes and forget everything, maybe just dream away for just a few hours, but it was no use.

Shannon heard a noise and opened her eyes when she realized the door was being opened.

It was Jack.

She held her breath. He was sneaking in, holding the bridal bouquet in his hand, Pastor Daniel and Detective Bellini following in his trail. They probably thought she was asleep.

"Jack?" Shannon said, tears in her eyes again. "You came back!"

Jack grabbed her hand in his and they looked into each other's eyes. Pastor Daniel turned on a lamp on her small table. That was when she realized he was dressed up.

"What's going on, Jack?"

"We're getting married," he said. "Just the two of us, right here right now. Detective Bellini will be our witness. No wedding dress, no music, no flower girls, no cake, well maybe we'll find cake somewhere afterwards, but right now it's just the two of us and our love and devotion for each other, and this bridal bouquet, of course. I found it in the chapel. Do you want to marry me, Shannon? Right here and now?"

Shannon sobbed. "Yes. Yes, Jack."

He turned and looked at Pastor Daniel, who lifted his Bible. "All right. I believe it was your turn, Shannon. Repeat after me. I, Shannon King..."

"I, Shannon King..."

It was a struggle for Shannon to say the words without crying, but she managed to get through them and, seconds later, Pastor Daniel finally said the words they had longed to hear:

"By virtue of the authority vested in me under the laws of the State of Georgia, it is with the greatest pleasure that I now pronounce you husband and wife." Daniel looked at Jack.

"You may kiss the bride."

86

[JUNE 2016]

Emily was standing by the window when we entered her room. She was dressed, her arms crossed over her chest, her back turned to us.

I walked up to her, Tyler sleeping in the sling on my chest. Shannon was walking carefully behind me. It had been three weeks now and she had just gotten rid of the wheelchair a few days ago. Luckily, nothing had been destroyed when the corkscrew went into her stomach. She had been very lucky. Her hand was in a bandage and they still didn't know if she would be able to play the guitar again. Shannon was certain she would.

"Hi there, beautiful. You ready to go?"

Emily didn't turn to look at us. She hadn't spoken much since the incident, and it worried me a lot, even though the doctor told us it was normal behavior.

I, for one, couldn't wait to get back to Cocoa Beach. Shannon, Tyler, Emily, and I had stayed in Savannah, while Sarah and my parents had taken the three A's back to Cocoa Beach to finish up the school year. Due to her condition, Emily had been allowed to stay away till the next school year. Luckily, she was a very good student and had great grades, so the school believed she would be fine with missing a couple of weeks.

"Or do you want to stay a little longer?" I joked.

Emily turned, but didn't look at me. She grabbed a plastic bag with her things in it. The hospital had to feed her through a tube for all three weeks she was in here, since she still refused to eat. Now she had finally gained enough weight to leave. She was out of immediate danger, but the struggle was far from over.

"Do you want us to take the flowers with us?" Shannon asked. "Some of them are still very pretty."

Emily looked at them. "I don't understand why people sent me flowers," she said with a scoff. "You'd think I was dead or something."

"Well, you almost did die," I said. Her eyes met mine. "You do realize that, don't you?"

Emily looked down and away from me, then turned and approached the door.

"You have to understand how serious this is," I continued.

I felt so frustrated. I had no idea how to make her better, how to fix her, when she refused to even see how bad her condition was. The doctor told me that when she was this skinny, her brain didn't work like it used to; without the proper fuel, it kind of went in circles, he told me, only focusing on one thing, to lose more weight even though she knew deep down that it could be fatal. She didn't care. All she could think about was how she believed that losing even just one more pound would make her happier.

It was devastating.

So far, all we could do for her was to get her fed, get her to gain weight, so she would stop controlling herself and so her brain would start to work properly, along with the rest of her organs.

"Are we going home or what?" she asked, her hand on the door handle.

I sighed. "Well, sweetie. We are, but you're not."

"What's that supposed to mean?" she let go of the handle.

Shannon and I exchanged a glance. "Well, the doctor helped us find a nice place for you. It's in Orlando, so I'll be able to visit as often as they'll let me. We're taking you there right away. It's a recovering place for young girls with eating disorders like you. They have psychologists to help you and doctors who will monitor your weight gain."

Emily shrieked. "You can't do that to me. Dad! I'm not going to some place where crazy girls are whining about food."

"Well, you have to," I said.

"But…I don't want to, Dad. I don't want to get fat!"

Shannon put her hand on Emily's shoulder. "They're not going to make you…"

"Let go of me. You're not my mother!"

Shannon backed up. My heart throbbed. I tried to stay calm. I knew Emily wasn't herself; she was sick and needed us to be in charge.

"This is the way it's going to be," I said and grabbed Emily by the arm. "You're getting well; do you hear me? Whatever it takes. We love you and want to see you live a normal teenage life. This is the way it's going to be; there's nothing you can say or do to make us change our minds. You'll stay at the place all summer and, if you show improvement, if you start to eat and gain weight, then you'll be back with us by the end of summer, but if not, you'll have to stay. That's it, and there is no discussing it. Now, let's get to the car."

Emily pulled her arm out of my grip with a loud groan. "I hate you!" She turned and walked out of the room. Shannon and I followed. She put her hand in mine and squeezed it. We knew this was going to be rough, but it was the only way. Emily had survived, but she wasn't out of danger yet. It was going to take months of recovering, maybe even years, the doctor had told us.

But if anyone could do it, it was us.

No one spoke in the car on the way back to the house, where Detective Bellini was waiting on the porch. I got out. Next to her stood Betsy Sue. Shannon came out of the car as well and walked up to us.

"You ready?" Shannon asked, addressed to Betsy Sue.

The girl looked up at Detective Bellini, who nodded. "She's all yours now."

I reached out my hand and Betsy Sue grabbed it. In her other hand, she was holding a deck of cards.

"I guess player wins this one, huh?" I asked.

Betsy Sue stared at me, then shook her head. "No. House always wins."

I laughed. "We'll see about that."

"Take care, Ryder," Bellini said. "Look me up if you ever come back to Savannah."

"Yeah, that might be a while," I said with a grin.

I thanked Bellini and gave her a hug, then walked down the stairs with Betsy Sue and Shannon. We got in the car, Betsy Sue in the back with Emily, and Tyler between them. Tyler was awake now and hugging Bobby, whose ear Shannon had sewn back on.

I rolled down the window and waved at Bellini, who waved back, and as I put the car in drive, Betsy Sue suddenly yelled from the back seat.

"Wait!"

I stopped and looked at her in the rearview mirror. "What?"

"We forgot Billy!"

I looked at Shannon. "Billy?"

"We can't leave Billy," she said. "He'll be lonely. Can

he come with us, please?"

My eyes met Shannon's, who shrugged with a wry smile. "An extra kid *and* a ghost?"

"Please?"

"The more the merrier, right?" I said with a shrug, "Why not? Bring him onboard."

EPILOGUE

BUST: Having a total over twenty-one, resulting in an automatic loss.

[JUNE 2016]

Susan Murray stared at her child. For six years, Chandelle had been gone, since the night she disappeared from the hospital when they took her in because she was sick. Six whole years where she had wondered every day what happened to her baby, looked at every child she saw on the street, wondering if that was her girl and what she would look like now.

Now she was looking at her. Finally, she was actually looking at her.

A deranged woman had stolen her from the hospital six years ago, they told her, because she had lost her own child. She had given her a new name and raised her inside of her house, never letting her out. Chandelle's skin was so fair and her eyes so sensitive, she could hardly stand to be outside.

All of that didn't matter. What mattered was the fact that she was back. Finally, their family was complete again.

"You want another one, Chandelle?" Susan asked, referring to the ice cream the girl was eating.

Chandelle didn't react. She didn't respond to the name yet, only to that awful name, Miss Muffit, that the crazed lady had given her.

They had talked about the woman being so mad she actually believed Chandelle had a certain gene that made her want to kill, and that the woman believed she needed to protect the world against her.

Never had Susan heard anything so strange. The newspapers had written about it too and how the famous singer Shannon King had been involved. Susan knew she was related to Shannon King and was forever grateful to her for bringing her daughter back to them. She never had the chance to thank her in person and now she had heard that she had left town and gone back to Cocoa Beach with her husband and children. They had even taken the other girl from the house with them, they said. There was something about an older daughter who belonged to her husband, she believed, who had gotten sick as well, but now she was better. An eating disorder, according to the newspapers that also wrote that she was going to be checked into an eating disorder treatment facility, but Susan didn't know if it was true. You never knew what to believe. The girl had looked very skinny in photos, though, but again, they always wrote stuff like that. The media were ruthless. Susan had gone through it herself when they had lost Chandelle that night at the hospital. The speculations had been many and awful. Telling the public that the police believed she had somehow hurt her own child and made it look like she disappeared. How could they think that?

Chandelle didn't answer. She jumped down from the chair without a word and ran upstairs. Susan felt a pinch in her heart. She wanted so badly to talk to her, to get to know her, but she didn't seem very interested in them. Not her or her husband Bob. It had been three weeks now since she got back, and she still hardly spoke to either of them.

"It's going to take a lot of time," their doctor had told them. "You have to be very patient."

Still, Susan thought she was a very odd kid. Always talking to herself in her room, and when Susan asked her who she was talking to, she would name some ghost that she believed lived in their house. The doctor told them to let her be, that it was okay to have imaginary friends. It would end eventually. Susan shouldn't worry so much.

But she did. She couldn't help herself. She worried how much damage had been done to their daughter.

She worried that she would never bond with her or even get to know her. And, most of all, she worried that she was slightly afraid of her.

Later that night, Susan and Bob were in bed and Susan told her husband about her concerns.

"I'm not sure I like her very much," she said. "Am I a terrible mother for saying that?"

Bob looked at her. "I don't know. We have to give her time. But, I have to admit, it feels weird that another person has raised your child. She looks like us physically, but it's hard for me to think of her as my child."

Susan nodded. She knew what he meant. But, after all, it had been only three weeks. She had been gone for six years. They just had to be a lot more patient.

Susan turned off the light and they went to sleep. At night, she dreamt of Chandelle, like so many times before, but when she woke up panting and sweating— also like so many nights before, the nightmare wasn't over.

At the end of the bed, she spotted Chandelle, a gun in her hand, pointed directly at her.

"Chandelle?"

As the gun went off and the bullet pierced through her body, all Susan Murray could think about was how the newspapers were going to blame it all on her again. Or maybe this time on guns and make it political.

Because no one would ever think a little girl could be *that* evil.

THE END

DEAR READER,

Thank you for purchasing *Black Jack* (Jack Ryder #4). This was a fun book to write. I was on a trip to Savannah recently to attend a wedding and that was when the idea took form. The ravens, the Spanish moss, the beautiful but slightly scary old houses, and of course all the stories. If you have never been to Savannah, you should go.

As always, a lot of what I write about is actually true. At least parts of it. There are tunnels under Savannah and, as far as I have been told, they were used to shanghai sailors to ships and to get rid of bodies during the Yellow Fever epidemic. All houses in Savannah worth anything are haunted, especially if you ask the tour guides. The story of the general is one of the stories they tell, and so is the one about the three girls being murdered in that very same house while the parents were out to dinner one night. When they came back, three of the girls were dead, the fourth had survived. A tour guide I spoke to told me that tourists often take pictures of the house, and when they look at the pictures afterwards, they find the image of a little girl sitting in one of the windows. It is said that it is the general's daughter.

I got the idea for a house driving people insane (or at least that's what they think is happening) when we moved into our new house recently. There were so many strange things going on and so many sounds waking me up at night, roaches on the toilet seat, bugs flying into my hair, and strange smells in the kitchen, that I at some point thought, *Boy this house doesn't want us here, does it?*

My friend told us how they had once experienced the part about the fleas. Nope, I didn't make that up either. Her two daughters had screamed from the living room of their house and she had run in there to see their legs covered in fleas that had been living underneath the planks. It creeped me out when she told me, so I thought it would creep you out as well. You're welcome.

Oh, and then there is the theory of the murder gene. It is actually real. Scientists believe they have found out that killers share a gene that others don't. Read more about it here:

http://www.mirror.co.uk/news/technology-science/
science/killers-born-murder-gene-scientists-4528684

The thought is kind of terrifying to me. My guess is that people who have the gene either become killers or writers, right?

Anyway, it has been my pleasure to write this book. I hope you'll leave a review if it is in any way possible for you.

Take care,

Willow

CONNECT WITH WILLOW ONLINE AND YOU WILL BE THE FIRST TO KNOW ABOUT NEW RELEASES:

Sign up here: http://eepurl.com/wcGej

IF YOU WANT TO BE THE FIRST TO KNOW ABOUT BARGAINS AND FREE EBOOKS FROM WILLOW ROSE, THEN

Sign up here: http://eepurl.com/bE5t4z

I promise not to share your email with anyone else, and I won't clutter your inbox (I'll only contact you when a new book is out or when I have a special bargain/free eBook).

THE FOLLOWING IS AN EXCERPT FROM
WILLOW ROSE'S BESTSELLING MYSTERY NOVEL

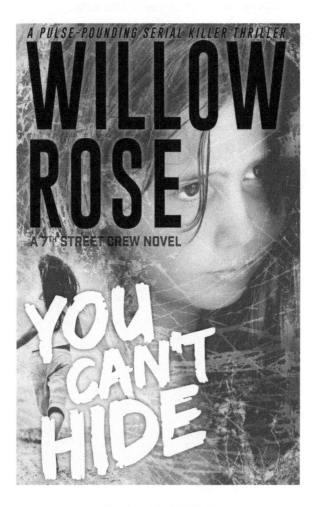

A PULSE-POUNDING SERIAL KILLER THRILLER

WILLOW ROSE

A 7ᵀᴴ STREET CREW NOVEL

YOU CAN'T HIDE

YOU CAN'T HIDE
SEVENTH STREET CREW #3

PROLOGUE
OCTOBER 2015

SHE'S NOT RUNNING, but it is close. Maria Verlinden rushes through the aisles, leaving behind the sections with towels and bathroom accessories. She hopes to be able to get through Target's dreaded toy department without Tara acting up. She doesn't have time to look at toys today. As a single mother with only one income, she can't afford to buy her toys every time they shop. Today is about getting her some new shoes, that's all. Quick in and quick out. Without spending money on anything unnecessary.

"Moom, can I get a toy?"

Maria sighs. She looks at her nine-year-old daughter as they walk past the many teddy bears staring back at them with big cute black eyes, begging Maria to buy them.

"You know Mommy can't afford it today. You need new shoes, remember? The school won't let you wear flip-flops. You have to wear sneakers."

"But, Moom, I really want a Monster High doll. Ally has one."

"Not today, honey. I am sorry…"

"But, Moom!"

Maria pulls Tara's arm a little too hard as she tries to get past the toys and into the clothing department.

"You're hurting me, Mom!"

"I'm sorry, baby. We just need to hurry. Mommy has to go to work."

Maria feels exhausted, thinking about going into the office today. Selling office supplies over the phone has to be the worst job on the planet. But she needs the money. And it sure beats working at Wal-Mart like she used to. Tara will spend the rest of the day with a neighbor who is out of work and who takes care of her when Maria has to work and they're off from school. Today is a teachers' workday so there is no school. Maria hates having to ask her neighbor for help, but what else can she do? She can't wait for Tara to be old enough to stay home alone. Maria has got to work.

"Here it is," she says and stops.

Tara is whining. She is complaining about not being able to have a toy. Maria fights the urge to yell at her. How can she be so ungrateful? She is getting new shoes, after all. Can't she be excited about that at least? Doesn't she know how much Maria has to work and save to be able to afford these shoes?

Maria has promised herself to stop yelling so much at Tara. She wants to be better about it. But the pressure of not having any money and living in a bad neighborhood at the age of almost thirty, with a nine-year-old, is getting to her. She hates her life. Worst of all, she sees no way out of it. It's not like she'll meet someone when she has a kid and as long as she lives in that awful place. She feels so stuck. She loves her daughter, but there are days she wonders how her life would have turned out had she gotten that abortion her parents told her to get, before they cut her off. But how could she? It was a baby, for crying out loud. You don't just kill a baby just because the father doesn't want it.

"This baby will destroy your life, Maria," her mother said the day she also told her to get the abortion or they would disown her. Their daughter being a single mother was apparently too much for them, too much of a disgrace. "The kid will be a bastard," they said.

Maria had no idea beforehand that her parents would react like this. But she decided to keep the child anyway, even though it would never know its father or grandparents. After all, it wasn't Tara's fault.

Maria looks at her daughter as she touches a pair of very sparkly shoes. Maria can't help smiling. Yes, Tara is annoying at times, and yes it has been hard, but she loves her; she is the love of her life. How a beautiful little girl like that could cause so much commotion was beyond her comprehension. Maria would give her the world if she could afford it.

"Can I have these, Mommy?"

Maria looks at the price. It's a little more than what she can afford. "Let's see what else there is," she says.

"Okay, Mommy, but I really like these. Ally has a pair like them."

"Good for Ally. Now, how about these over here?" Maria picks up a pair of shoes and shows them to Tara when she spots a man at the end of the aisle touching a pair of shoes but not picking them up. He spots Tara and makes a face at her. Tara laughs. "That man is funny," she says.

Maria grabs Tara's hand in hers and pulls her closer. "Do you want to try these?"

"They're ugly, Mom."

"All right. How about those over there?" Maria asks, still looking at the man who hasn't taken his eyes off of Tara. Something about him fills Maria with unease. She pulls Tara even closer. Tara looks at him again and he makes another funny face. Tara bursts into laughter. The man smiles. Maria eases up slightly. Maybe she is just being paranoid. Maria picks up another pair of shoes and shows them to Tara.

"How about these?"

"Okay. I'll try them on."

Tara grabs the shoes and sits down on the bench. She takes off her flip-flops. Maria keeps an eye on the man. He seems to be circling them, looking at shoes, but not picking any of them up. She doesn't like the way he is looking at Tara.

"Hurry up, Tara," Maria says. "I have to go to the office. They only allowed me to be an hour late today."

"I don't like these, Mommy. They're too tight on my toes."

"Then try another size," she grumbles, and pulls out a box with the same shoes in another size.

The man is still circling them, making faces at Tara whenever he gets her attention. Maria starts to wonder if there is anyone else nearby, in case he tries to steal her purse. It's very early and she hasn't seen anyone else in the store except for the cashiers at the entrance.

"Do you need help with that?" the man suddenly says to Tara.

Maria turns and sees him kneeling in front of the girl and helping her with the shoe. Maria stops breathing. She doesn't like him being this close to her daughter. But, then again, he is just being nice. Maybe he is just a lonely man. She looks at his basket; he hasn't put anything in it.

That's odd, she thinks, but then shakes the thought again. *Maybe he's just here to buy a pair of shoes just like you. You don't have anything in your basket either.*

Maria laughs at herself. The man smiles at her, then at Tara, as the shoe slides right on.

"There you are. It fits perfect. Just like *Cinderella*."

Tara giggles. She doesn't like *Cinderella*, she is more of a *Frozen*-girl, but she is being polite. The man gets up.

"I think we have a winner, *Mom*," he says, addressed to Maria.

"I want these," Tara says and looks proudly up at Maria.

Maria smiles, relieved. She looks at her watch. Only ten minutes till she needs to be at the office. She can't make it in time, but if they move fast then maybe she won't be too late, not so late they'll fire her. They did that last week to one of the other girls. She didn't show up and the next day they had simply given the job to someone else. They didn't even tell her, so when she finally did show up, she found someone else at her desk and had to leave. There are plenty of other girls out there who want Maria's job. They never hesitate to tell them that.

"Thank you so much," she says to the man.

"No problem, *Mom*," he says, and nods.

She knows it is silly, but for some reason she holds her purse tight to her body as she passes him. She kneels in front of her daughter and takes off the shoes that she puts back in the box.

"All right. Let's get moving," she says to Tara. Tara gets up and they start to walk. Tara turns and waves at the man as they disappear down the aisle. He makes another funny face and Tara burst into a light giggle.

As they reach the check-out and give the shoes to

the cashier, Maria spots the man walking towards the exit quickly. She notices that he didn't buy anything.

At least he's gone, she thinks to herself with a light shiver when she hands the cashier the money for the shoes.

OCTOBER 2015

TARA WANTS TO WEAR the shoes right after they have paid for them, and Maria lets her put them on before they leave the store. Tara laughs happily and runs circles around Maria as they walk towards the parking lot.

"Look at how fast I can run!" Tara yells.

"You are very fast," Maria says, and looks at her watch again. Just five more minutes. Her office is all the way in Melbourne. There is no way she'll make it in time. She'll be at least half an hour late. Maria sighs. She'll have to stay half an hour longer this afternoon to make up for it. Well, at least Tara is happy. She is jumping and running around giggling.

They approach the car and Maria grabs her keys and unlocks it. Tara jumps inside and Maria hurries to her door and opens it, when someone sneaks around her vehicle. It is him again. The same man that stared at them inside the store.

Maria gasps in shock.

"I'm sorry," the man says. "I didn't mean to startle you."

Maria places a hand on her chest. Her heart is beating fast. "It's okay," she says. "I am just…in a hurry."

"I was just wondering if you could help me," the man says, and moves a step closer.

Maria wonders if she should just jump inside the car and drive off. The man stares at her. Tara is yelling from inside the car.

"Come on, Mommy!"

"I really don't have any time," she says, and is about to get inside of her car.

"It'll only be one second. You see, my wife is in that car over there and she's not well. The car won't start and…"

Maria looks at the man. She feels confused, conflicted. Normally she would always help, but this time…there is something odd about this guy. She turns her head to look at the car he pointed at, but can't see anyone inside of it. Tara is yelling again.

"There's no one in the car," Maria says.

When she turns her head, the man is right in front of her. He pushes her inside the car. Maria screams.

"What are you doing?"

"Mommy?" Tara says.

The man is strong, and even though she fights him, she can't get up. "Help! Someone heeelp!"

She tries to kick him, but can't. She manages to scratch him on his arm with her nails while panic spreads inside of her. She has to get him off her. She has to get away from here, now.

"Lie still, bitch," he yells, and slaps her across the face.

Tara screams when she sees him hitting her mother. "Get out of the car, Tara," Maria yells. "Get out and run for help!"

Tara yells something, but Maria doesn't hear what it is. She just keeps screaming at the child to run for help inside Target. Maria regains more of her strength and manages to punch the attacker in the stomach, when she hears the car door open and Tara scream for help.

That's it, that's my girl.

But the attacker punches Maria in the face and she loses consciousness for a few important minutes. When she opens her eyes, Tara's screams have changed character and sound more panicked and helpless. Maria manages to look outside and sees her daughter in the arms of the man, who is carrying her over his shoulder back towards the car.

"No!"

"Oh, yes," the man says, as he throws Tara in the back of the car and slams the door shut. He approaches Maria and leans over her.

"The deal was for the both of you, *Maria*."

OCTOBER 2015

TARA?

Maria opens her eyes. She can still taste the fumes from the white cloth that was held against her mouth until she gave up the fight. It makes her want to throw up. She is panicking. She blinks her eyes. Tara is here. Tara is right next to her on the bed. What a relief.

Tara seems to be asleep. Maybe she too is knocked out. Maria has a headache. Probably from the fumes.

We've got to get out of here.

Maria gets up from the bed. She leans over her daughter and can hear her breathing. It fills her with relief again. The girl is alive, sleeping heavily, but alive. Maria walks to the window and realizes she is in a house somewhere. The view is spectacular, but she's got to be at least forty feet up. Beneath her are a tennis court and a lap-pool. She grabs the handle to the sliding door and tries to open it. It is locked and you need a key to open it.

Maria looks around the room. It is sparsely decorated with a queen bed and a dresser. Nothing on the walls. Nothing on the floors. Just while tiles. She looks at the door to the room and walks to it. She grabs the handle but—as suspected—it is locked as well.

Maria sighs and walks back to the bed. She can't see her purse anywhere, so she doesn't have her phone. Tara is breathing heavily. Maria leans over her and kisses her on the lips. She can't begin to say how happy she is that she is still alive and still here with her.

But, now what?

Where the hell are we? Are we at that awful man's place? What does he want with us?

Tara starts to slowly wake up as well. She is smacking her lips, probably thirsty. Maria realizes there is a small bathroom attached to the room and she goes in there to get some water from the tap. She finds a plastic cup and fills it. She wets Tara's lips with water. Soon Tara blinks her eyes and opens them to look at her mother.

"Mom?" she says sleepily.

Maria feels like crying, but she holds it back. "It's okay, baby. I got you some water."

Tara sits up and Maria lets her drink from the cup. When she is done, Maria drinks some as well. It tastes like chlorine, but it's better than nothing. She finishes the cup.

"Where are we, Mommy?"

"I don't know, baby."

"I wanna go home now."

"Me too. But we got to wait till the man lets us out, all right?" Maria can hear her own voice shivering as she speaks. She is terrified by what the man wants from them, but she is also determined to get out of here, alive and with her daughter in her arms. No matter what.

"What do you mean, Mommy? Has the man kidnapped us?"

"I...I don't know."

Tara is about to cry. Maria wants to cry as well, but she doesn't allow herself to. She grabs her daughter in her arms and holds her tight.

"It'll be all right, baby. Mommy will get us home; don't you worry, baby. Don't you worry."

OCTOBER 2015

THERE IS A SOUND behind the door. The handle is moving, and a key is put in the lock. Maria gasps and grabs Tara. She pulls her close to her while staring at the door handle.

Who is behind that door? Is it the guy from Target? What does this person want with us? Will he kill us? Will he take Tara from me?

Maria swallows her desire to scream, as the door slowly opens. A face appears. He is big. His hair thick for his age. She has seen him before, she thinks. He reminds Maria of some actor, but she can't remember which one. The way he looks at them makes her very uncomfortable. He is wearing a suit that looks very expensive to Maria. The kind of suit her dad's clients would wear when they came to his office at the law firm.

The man places both hands on his sides and smiles. He walks towards Tara and strokes her cheek gently, with slow yet firm movements. Tara becomes stiff in her arms and Maria tries to pull her away from him.

"Look at you two," the man says. "Even prettier in real life than in the pictures. I have been looking forward to seeing you both."

"Mommy!" Tara says and throws her arms around Maria's neck.

"Where are we?" Maria says, snorting in anger. "Why are we here?"

Maria notices that the door to the room is still left open. She wonders if she can make a run for it.

The man shakes his head. "Tsk, tsk. Now don't you worry your pretty little heads with that. You're finally here, and boy how we are going to have fun together."

"I wanna go home, Mommy!" Tara says, while clinging to her mother's neck.

"Now, don't say that," the man says. "This is your new home. You will stay here with me until I get tired of you. As long as you do what I say, I will keep you alive, huh?" He touches the tip of her nose. He smiles and tilts his head. "Now, let's see what I have here." He puts a hand in his pocket and pulls out a red lollipop. He hands it to Tara. She doesn't want to take it and turns her head away while clinging tightly to her mother.

"Please, sir," Maria says. Please, just let us go."

The man sighs. "Now, that is the only thing I can't do. See, I paid good money for the two of you and I can't get that money back if I let you go. So…well…" he shrugs and pushes the lollipop at Tara. "Here."

She shakes her head. Maria doesn't like the expression in the man's eyes when she rejects him. Anger is building and it scares her. She has seen it before in one of her earlier boyfriends.

"Take the lollipop, Tara," she says.

"But, Mooom! You always say…"

"I know what I say; just take it. Do as I tell you to."

Tara sniffles and looks at the man. He places his hand on her back and caresses it gently. Maria can't stand the way he is touching her. She feels like screaming at him, but she doesn't dare to.

Finally, Tara reaches out and grabs the lollipop.

The man sighs. "There you go. Now, that wasn't so hard, was it?"

"Say thank you," Maria says.

"Thank you," Tara sniffles.

The man reaches out and touches Tara's hair. Everything is turning inside of Maria. The man stares at Tara's hair. "You're welcome."

"Now can we go home?" Tara asks.

The man burst into a sudden laughter that makes Maria jump. "Ha!" He leans over them and says: "No, you can't. But we can play a game. Now, what would be fun to play? I know it! How about hide and go seek?

Yes, that is my favorite game of all time."

"I love hide and go seek," Tara says.

The man clasps his hands. "How wonderful!" He grabs Tara by the chin. "I have a feeling you and I are going to be GREAT friends." He leans over and whispers. "Now, go…hide."

PART ONE

GENTLEMEN PREFER BLONDES

1

APRIL 2016

"WELCOME TO CHEATER'S."

The half-naked woman greeting Danny Schmidt in the doorway smiles. Danny nods and walks to the back of the place and finds somewhere to sit. Two girls are dancing on the podium, slithering up and down the poles. Another girl approaches him and asks him what he would like to drink. He orders a beer and hands her a tip that she puts in her bra. She winks and leaves him. Danny watches the dancers. One of them is young, barely eighteen, he thinks. Her eyes are blurry. She is very pretty and the men seem to like her. Especially one guy smoking a cigar, he claps at her every move and rains money on her. She barely notices it.

The waitress comes back. She places his beer in front

of him. He gives her another tip that disappears into her bra. As she is about to leave, he grabs her wrist.

"Say, don't you have anyone younger than these two?" he asks.

She stares at him for a few seconds, scrutinizing him. "Sure." She rubs her fingertips against one another to tell him it'll cost him.

Danny smiles. "Naturally."

He hands her a hundred-dollar bill. She smiles even wider now, then leans over and whispers.

"How do you prefer them?"

The way she is standing, Danny can look down her cleavage. "Blonde and young."

"How young?"

"Fourteen-fifteen?"

She doesn't react. She is used to this kind of request. "Sure. We can get them even younger if you're willing to pay. But it's very expensive."

Danny nods. "The younger the better. He opens his jacket and shows her a bundle of money."

"All right, cowboy. Come out the back. To the VIP-section."

Danny throws a bill on the table, throws one last glance at the dancing girls, then follows the woman out behind a curtain. She tells him to sit on a couch while someone brings him a bottle of champagne. The girl opening it rubs herself against him. When it has popped she pours him a glass, then sits on his lap and rubs herself against his crotch.

"Enjoy the show, tiger," she whispers in his ear, and bites his lip before she leaves.

Danny sips the champagne while he waits. A few minutes later, the woman returns followed by three young blonde girls all dressed in sexy lingerie. By looking at their faces, he guesses them to be no more than twelve or thirteen. They're all wearing heavy make-up. The woman tells them to stand on the podium in front of Danny. They're posing for him. He rubs his chin while observing them. Music is put on and they are told to dance. They show him what they can do. He is very impressed and smiles. The woman approaches him.

"You like what you see, huh?"

"Yes."

"You want to touch? Touching costs more."

He hands her more money. She signals the girls to come closer. They swarm Danny now and he leans back on the couch. Their hands are on him, everywhere…on his chest, in his crotch. He looks into their eyes. They're all drugged, blurry. One of the girls is younger than the others, he realizes when looking into her eyes. He grabs her by the chin and looks at her face.

"You like her, huh?" the woman asks. "This is August."

"I like her," he says.

"Very good," the woman says. "She is a beauty."

"I'd like to spend the night with her."

Before the woman can say anything, Danny pulls out more money from his jacket and places it on the table. The woman doesn't say anything else.

"The back entrance is over there," she says, and grabs the two other girls and disappears.

2

APRIL 2016

"YOU FORGOT TO PACK HIM A LUNCH?"

I stare at Joey. We're standing in his townhouse. There is a mess everywhere. Clothes on the floor, cereal boxes left out on the kitchen table, dirty dishes in the sink. He looks like crap. Hasn't shaved in a week, or even showered, from what it looks like. I only stopped by to grab Salter's stuff. He's been with his dad for a few days.

I've brought Snowflake so he can say hi to his old friends. Clyde is barking at him while Snowflake sniffs Bonnie's behind. It doesn't seem like the animals have been out much, with the way they're acting up when they see us.

"Well, I didn't forget; I gave him some money to

buy something."

"You know I hate it when he has to eat that food they serve in the cafeteria at the school. What is going on, Joe? You never used to be this sloppy."

He shrugs with a sigh. On the floor, I see a bra that, for obvious reasons, isn't mine. I look at it. "Is that... hers?"

Joey chuckles. "Yeah. Probably."

"So, that's it. You're partying with her and not taking anything seriously anymore?" I ask.

"What's it to you?"

"We have a kid, Joe, that's what it is to me. I don't want him to come here if you don't take care of him and if there is underwear lying all over the place." I pick up the bra, holding it between two fingers and hand it to him. "Please, tell your girlfriend to stop throwing her undergarments everywhere. At least keep it where my son won't find it."

"You tell her yourself."

"She's here?"

"Yeah. She kind of...lives here now."

My eyes widen. "What? She moved in? Just like that?"

He shrugs again. "It was easier."

I can't believe him. I don't know what to say. I don't want to say any more. I am exhausted with this entire situation. I feel so hurt that he would move in with the woman he cheated on me with. Of course, to him it wasn't cheating, since we were separated at the time. I can't just move on. My son needs his dad and I need Joey to be a good role model for him. He isn't with the way things are right now. Joey is hardly working, he hangs out with Jackie, his girlfriend, who now apparently has moved in; they drink beers and party while I am left picking up the pieces of my son's broken heart. Salter is ten now. He is beginning to figure out what is going on and asking questions I have a hard time answering.

"So, that's it now? She is definitely a part of our lives?" I ask. "Because I sure hope you're planning on staying with her, since you chose to bring her into your son's life."

"Don't be so uptight. It's annoying," he says with a groan.

I want to shake him. I want to yell at him and tell him I need him to snap out of this, whatever it is that's going on with him. I owe the guy so much. I owe him my life. We have known each other since we were in preschool and we were married for what felt like an eternity. But now, as I am standing in front of him, I don't recognize him anymore. All my life I have known and loved this guy, but…now I feel like I don't know him at all. Why would he choose this life?

"Don't you have to work today?" I ask.

"Nope. Nothing out there for me."

"You're telling me no one needs a carpenter today or even later this week?"

He rolls his eyes at me. It makes me angry. I can't

believe him. Joey has barely worked in two months. I can't help wondering if he isn't doing enough to get something, to get the jobs. Is he even out there, or does he just stay at home with her? She works at Juice 'N Java downtown, but only a few times a week. She can't be making much. I have no idea how they're getting by, how they're paying the rent.

"You know what, Mary? It really is none of your damn business," Joey growls. Clyde is barking and Snowflake runs after him. Bonnie trots after them, not really engaged in their little fight.

Joey picks up Salter's sports bag, pulls a few clothing items from the floor and throws them in, then hands it to me.

"Here. This is what you came for, right? Now you can go."

3

APRIL 2016

SHE IS ALMOST BURSTING with excitement. Paige Stover can't hide it in the car when she sees the rec center. Paige just started taking basketball lessons and loves hanging out with Coach Joe. Once a week, he gives her a private lesson, since she is very new to the game, and then the team meets every Saturday. It's expensive for her mother, Nicky, but since her parents died, Nicky inherited a good sum of money.

It feels good to finally be able to give Paige what she wants in life. After twelve years of being a poor, single mother, Nicky is finally able to give her daughter what she deserves. What all the other kids have. Paige is such a good girl, does well in school, and wants to do a lot of sports, even though she isn't among the most athletic around.

"There she is. There's my Paige-girl," Coach Joe yells when they enter the center.

Paige grabs the ball from between her mother's hands and runs towards him. They hug.

"Have you been practicing flipping your wrist like I told you to?" he asks, and shows her how to do it.

Paige repeats the gesture and he laughs putting his hands on both her arms. He hugs her again. "You sure have."

Nicky sits down and pulls out her phone, while Coach Joe starts instructing Paige. He asks her to run first to warm up, then dribble while running with the ball. Then he asks her to shoot hoops. Twenty-five shots. She misses most of them. Coach Joe laughs heartily and makes her run again, then do push-ups to build up the strength in her arms. Paige is skinny. She hasn't played many sports until recently, since they can now afford to pay for it. But she has barely any muscles.

Nicky looks at the display of her phone and goes through her emails. Her decorating business is doing well and there are several requests from new costumers. She looks at Paige and the Coach, then walks outside to make a few calls.

Nicky is very pleased to finally be able to make a living for herself. It has taken her years to get to this point, where the costumers come to her and not the other way around. It all travels by word of mouth, but it takes years to get people talking. It used to be that she had to work another job on the side. She has held many jobs as a secretary for years, but her dream has always been to have her own business. Like her father always used to say, there are two ways to live your life. Either you are busy making someone else's dream come true or you're busy making your own come true. Nicky has always known she would one day make her own dream come true. But being a single mother, after Mike left when Paige was just a baby, was hard and required that she have a steady income for many years. She couldn't just quit her job and devote herself to her business. Not until she had enough clients.

Nicky makes a couple of new appointments and plots them down in the calendar of her phone. She looks at the clock. The time is almost up. She hurries back inside, but finds the rec center empty.

"Hello?"

Nicky looks around the empty basketball court. Where can they be?

"Paige? Coach Joe?"

Nicky's heart is in her throat as she walks to the office, only to find that empty as well. "Coach Joe? Paige?" she yells again, this time slightly panicking.

They can't have left, can they? I was right outside all the time. I would have seen them. Could they have used the back entrance?

"Mom! We're right here!"

Nicky turns and sees Paige. She is standing in a doorway leading to a room Nicky hadn't noticed before. Behind her is Coach Joe, both his hands placed on Paige's shoulders. He is smiling.

"I just showed Paige a small clip from a game last weekend. We have a TV in here."

Nicky swallows hard while the worry and anxiety are pushed back. She curses her own paranoia. Of course, everything is fine.

4

SAIGON, VIETNAM, 1975

DANH NGUYEN LOOKS at his sister. She smiles and unwraps his present. He feels the excitement in every bone of his body. He has been looking forward to giving her this doll. His sister is his everything. His beautiful—three years younger—sister, Long, who makes every room brighter when she enters.

Today, she is turning eight years old. All her siblings, five brothers and four sisters, and her parents and grandparents are gathered in the house on their father's estate. Their father is a wealthy businessman, and they're fortunate enough to belong to the upper class.

"Thank you! Thank you!" Long exclaims when she sees the doll. She throws her arms around his neck. Danh holds her tight and closes his eyes.

"You're welcome," he whispers lovingly. "Only the best for *your majesty*."

Long giggles. She loves it when Danh calls her that, when they pretend she is a princess.

"Let's eat," their mother says and claps her hands.

Her face is growing new wrinkles every day, it seems to Danh. He knows she is concerned by what is happening to their country these days. Everyone is afraid of the Communist Government and what they might do next. Danh understands some of it and sees it on his parents' faces, but he feels certain they are very safe. Their dad is a respected person in the area. He has always kept all of them safe.

Danh looks at the table with all the food and smiles again. Unlike many others, they have money enough to live well, even though they can't get the supplies they usually do, they manage to get by anyway.

"Did you hear what happened to Uong?" his grandmother suddenly says when everyone has started eating.

Danh looks up and sees his parents' reaction. Uong is the man who lives only two houses down the street. Danh hasn't heard what happened to him.

"Not now, *mẹ*," his mother says.

"I would like to hear it, *bà ngoại*," Danh says, adressing his grandmother. He has known Lan Uoung since he was born and likes to hang out around his store. "What happened to him?"

Danh's mother shakes her head. "Not now, Danh.

Today we're celebrating."

"But…"

"*Không! No!* I said not today, Danh."

Danh can tell by the look on her face he has to let it go. He sinks into his chair and goes quiet. Still, he can't stop wondering what it is they won't talk about. Sometimes he hates being one of the young ones. His older siblings all know when to stay quiet and when to speak. Danh never does. At least he isn't the youngest anymore.

They eat in silence. Long doesn't look as happy any more and Danh makes a few funny faces at her to cheer her up. It is, after all, her birthday.

Long giggles and clasps her mouth. Danh feels better when he sees her happy. As long as she is happy, there is nothing wrong with the world.

Not until the door is kicked in.

They all hear it, but it goes so fast, Danh hardly realizes it before they have them surrounded. Ten police officers storm inside, guns pointed at them. Danh's mother starts to scream when they throw themselves at Danh's father and hold him down while putting him in handcuffs.

All Danh can think about is Long. He grabs her in his arms and covers her eyes.

"It's all part of a game, your majesty," he whispers in her ear. "They're here to celebrate your birthday and they'll just get upset if we don't play along."

The policemen order all of them to sit on the floor in the living room, while they drag their father away. Danh's mother tries to stop them, but is knocked down and beat up by an officer. The grandparents and siblings scream and cry for them to stop. Finally, they do. Bruised and beaten, their mother crawls back to her family.

Danh closes his eyes too and tries to imagine being in his favorite spot, in a canoe on the river, fishing with Long by his side. While the policemen trash the place and steal all their belongings, Danh whispers stories in Long's ears of the many times they have been fishing together, trying to get her to stop crying.

"Remember the time you fell in the water? Do you?"

"*Vâng. Yes*," she whimpers.

"We couldn't stop laughing, remember?"

"I remember," she whispers, and he feels how she calms down in his arms, while the sound of glass shattering becomes nothing but a distant noise.

Hours later, when the sounds slowly disappear, Danh dares to open his eyes again and look around.

Everything is gone. All their belongings are either gone or destroyed. Nothing is left. A note on the wall tells them the house now belongs to the government, along with the family's other houses.

They have one day to leave.

5

APRIL 2016

MY DAD'S HOUSE IS SO QUIET. Salter is still in school, my dad is sleeping, and so is Snowflake. I am sitting in front of the computer wondering if I can shake this morning's fight with Joey. I don't understand why he gets to me the way he does. Well, if I am being perfectly honest, then maybe I can. I am so angry with him for moving on and for acting like a teenager in love all of a sudden, not living up to his responsibilities.

After leaving him with Salter's sports bag in my hand, I had to drive to Subway and buy a sandwich for Salter and take it to the school. Call me controlling…I don't want him eating that food in the cafeteria.

The blank page is staring at me from the computer. I am trying to write an article about a democratic senator that has been travelling to spots around the globe on trips sponsored by private people, people that were known for conservative views. I am sitting on the story, since no one else has discovered this. Chloe is actually the one who gave me the information. Apparently, the guy is also known to be active in the websites and chat rooms she observes for use of child porn. She tracked him down, then broke into his computer and found all the material we needed to take him down publicly.

I, for one, can't wait.

I make myself another cup of coffee, push Joey out of my head, then start writing. Seconds later, the keyboard is glowing, and I can't stop. The material is so good and I can't wait to publish it and see this guy taken down. I know this will be a big story, one that the newspapers will have to quote us on in the morning.

Snowflake wakes up as I press publish, and someone is at the door. I get up and open it. It's Marcia. I smile happily.

"You have time for coffee?" she asks.

"Always. Come on in."

I make a new cup for myself and one for Marcia, then find some cookies in the cabinet that I bring out with it. We sit in the living room overlooking the glittering ocean. The waves aren't very good today. There is too much wind for it to be fun. Suits me well enough. I needed the time to write.

"So, how's it going?" I ask, with a cookie half eaten in my mouth.

Marcia smiles. "I'm getting the kids for the weekend," she says.

"Really? That's amazing!"

She nods. It's been a long time since I have seen that kind of light in her eyes. It makes me happy. She is doing really well on her medicine and with the help from her sister.

"Carl finally agreed to let me have them for three days in a row after my doctor called him and told him I was ready."

"I am so happy to hear that," I say, and put a hand on her shoulder. "And you're sure you can handle it, right? It's not too much? Four kids for three days can be a lot with all you're going through."

"My sister will help me," she says. "I just want to be with my babies again. I have seen them only a few hours here and there since they moved back with their dad. I miss them so much. I miss being a part of their lives, you know? I miss noticing the little differences every day as they grow older."

"I understand. I have to get used to being without Salter for several days in a row. I'm not sure I'm doing so well on that part," I say with a light laugh. "I'm not doing well with any of this, having to give up Joey and see him with that…that girl. Knowing they're together as a family with Salter when it should be me. It ain't easy, I tell you that."

"I hear you met someone?" she asks.

I grab another cookie. "You mean Tom? Yeah. We've

been on a few dates. I met him through Tinder. I can't believe I tried that, but Chloe persuaded me to. He seems like a nice guy. Not a local, which is good, since we know all of them from back then. Moved here four years back from South Florida, works at the Space Center. Something with the weather stations, I am not quite sure I get it. He's tried to explain it to me several times, but I just pretend like I understand. Basically, he's the guy who tells them if the weather is good enough for a launch or not. That's how far I am." I laugh again and eat yet another cookie. Marcia follows me, which pleases me immensely, since I hate eating alone.

"Have you heard from Sandra lately?" Marcia asks.

I shake my head. "No. Not in a really long time. I have a feeling she's avoiding me. She's probably fooling around with Alex still."

Marcia stares at me and I clasp my mouth. "Whoops."

"She and Alex are fooling around?"

I make a grimace. "Yeah, well, I wasn't supposed to say anything. Me and my big mouth."

"That totally explains everything," Marcia exclaims. "I've noticed how they look at each other, but always thought it was all about them longing for each other, since they can't be together. But they're both married?"

"You're telling me. I've tried to explain that to them. I even threatened to tell their spouses, but they still continue this charade behind their backs. I can't get myself to meddle in it, though. They're grown-ups; they'll have to deal with it themselves."

"Wow," Marcia says, and leans back on the couch with her coffee between her hands.

"I know, right? To be frank, it's actually nice to have told you, because now I'm not the only one who knows."

"Speaking of betrayal, are we getting any closer to catching that brother of yours?" she asks.

I grunt. I hate talking about my brother, Blake. He is the one who poured acid on Sandra's face, making her lose her modeling career and destroying her marriage. He is a killer on the run, and I want to get him so badly.

"There's nothing new since Naples, where they found the body of Olivia Hartman," I say. "Detective Fisher has tried to work with the local police over there, but so far they haven't found any traces of him. He was long gone when they found the body inside the mattress at the motel. They're looking for him in the area, but there is no way he'd stay there after he killed her. He's not that stupid."

"Where do you think he is now?" Marcia asks.

I shrug. "Chloe is trying to track him, but he is being very clever. Doesn't use any credit cards, not any in his own name. His picture has been shown in the news over there, but they have no idea where he is. He is gone, again."

I grab another cookie, deciding if I make this my lunch, then I am allowed to have a couple more. Talking about Blake always makes me want to eat.

"So, what's the plan?" Marcia asks.

"There is no plan," I say. "We wait. We wait for him

to make a mistake. Which he will sooner or later. I know that much about my dear baby brother."

END OF EXCERPT

Get YOU CAN'T HIDE here:
http://www.amazon.com/gp/product/B01FN57QEE

ABOUT THE AUTHOR

THE QUEEN OF SCREAM, Willow Rose is an Amazon ALL-STAR, best-selling author. She writes Mystery/Suspense/ Horror, Paranormal Romance, and Fantasy. She is inspired by authors like James Patterson, Agatha Christie, Stephen King, Anne Rice, and Isabel Allende. She lives on Florida's Space Coast with her husband and two daughters. When she is not writing or reading, you'll find her surfing and watching the dolphins play in the waves of the Atlantic Ocean. She has sold more than a million books.

CONNECT WITH WILLOW ONLINE:

http://willow-rose.net

http://www.facebook.com/willowredrose

https://twitter.com/madamwillowrose